WE WERE RESTLESS THINGS

PAPL
DISCARDED

WE WERE
RESTLESS
THINGS

COLE NAGAMATSU

sourcebooks
fire

Copyright © 2020 by Cole Nagamatsu
Cover and internal design © 2020 by Sourcebooks
Cover art by Sasha Vinogradova
Internal design and illustrations by Jillian Rahn/Sourcebooks
Internal images © Dr D Sietsema - V-SQUARE Photography/Getty Images; Nikaya Lewis/EyeEm/
Getty Images; Victor Cabrera Borja/EyeEm/Getty Images; larisa_zorina/Getty Images; malerapaso/
Getty Images; Tomekbudujedomek/Getty Images; jayk7/Getty Images; spxChrome/Getty Images;
SCIEPRO/SCIENCE PHOTO LIBRARY/Getty Images; fotograzia/Getty Images; R.Tsubin/Getty
Images; ioanmasay/Getty Images; robert reader/Getty Images; agalma/Getty Images; CSA Images/
Getty Images; Ailbhe O'Donnell/Getty Images; gaffera/Getty Images; loops7/Getty Images; MAJA
TOPCAGIC/Stocksy United, Zoltan Tasi/Unsplash; Hisu lee/Unsplash

Sourcebooks and the colophon are registered trademarks of Sourcebooks.

All rights reserved. No part of this book may be reproduced in any form or by any electronic or
mechanical means including information storage and retrieval systems—except in the case of brief
quotations embodied in critical articles or reviews—without permission in writing from its publisher,
Sourcebooks.

The characters and events portrayed in this book are fictitious or are used fictitiously. Any similarity to
real persons, living or dead, is purely coincidental and not intended by the author.

All brand names and product names used in this book are trademarks, registered trademarks, or trade
names of their respective holders. Sourcebooks is not associated with any product or vendor in this
book.

Published by Sourcebooks Fire, an imprint of Sourcebooks
P.O. Box 4410, Naperville, Illinois 60567-4410
(630) 961-3900
sourcebooks.com

Library of Congress Cataloging-in-Publication Data is on file with the publisher.

Printed and bound in the United States of America.
LSC 10 9 8 7 6 5 4 3 2 1

for my mother

JONAS

On his way to the place that would be his new home, a nervous, mothy feeling beat its wings against the inside of Jonas Lake's throat. His father had informed him that he could choose his own bedroom in the Lamplight Inn from three options, all suites with private bathrooms, and had texted him photos of the rooms in an attempt to elicit enthusiasm.

His mother said, "He's trying. Just try back."

Jonas replied with brief niceties like *Cool* and *Looks nice* and *Will think it over.*

Jonas's mother drove them in her Jetta. The suitcase in the trunk held his clothes, and his laptop waited in his backpack. He'd left everything else he owned in his room at his mother's house—"For when you come home," she'd said. "It's still your room"—though there wasn't much to part with beyond the TV and video game posters he had taped and torn and re-taped to the walls, and Jonas didn't know when he'd go back except to visit.

He would now be a guest in every house he stepped into.

The closer they drove to Lamplight, the farther they got from the Twin Cities. Cornfields replaced retail, and traffic thinned until not a single car was visible for miles. Static punctuated each line of music on the radio, and Jonas wondered what *home* really was: a place you loved or a place you lived, and what it meant when the two weren't the same.

"Well, the houses down here sure have a lot of character," his mother said.

To their credit, the houses *were* less uniform and dull than the subdivisions they'd passed earlier. "Yeah," Jonas said. "I guess."

When they pulled into the Lamplight Inn's circular driveway, it too proved to have character. It was a large, squarish mansion with a nearby stone carriage house cloaked in vines. The building's gray, green, and cream paint was caked with a darker green mildew, and the gables' decorative embellishments had intermittently cracked or gone missing.

It looked odd and in need of some love, and Jonas appreciated that about the place. His father had explained that the building had been a home before being converted into an inn, before being abandoned, before being made a home again. Though it retained its business sign—a hanging wooden oval with a simple oil lantern carved into its surface—it now served only as a private residence.

More or less. There were some boarders there who helped with cleaning and other household chores.

Matt Lake exited the house and stepped onto the front porch. His girlfriend, Cesca, followed. Less than a year ago, his father had informed Jonas that the two were moving in together. Matt had never offered to introduce her to Jonas, and Jonas had never asked. He was young when his parents had divorced, and he hadn't expected he'd ever live with his father again, so there had been no reason that Cesca should matter. Now that Jonas saw her, he saw that his father had a full life that stood on its own without him.

Matt introduced everyone in an anxious, caffeine-enhanced rush of names. He even awkwardly shook Jonas's hand, as though it were their first meeting. Cesca greeted Jonas and his mother cheerfully.

Both women were willowy, olive-skinned brunettes—glamorous, though Cesca's glamour was of a different kind. Where Sara Lake wore sleek pumps, Francesca Amato bared her feet. Sara donned a pencil skirt and jewel-toned blouse, while Cesca had on a flower-patterned T-shirt dress so short that Jonas averted his eyes, trying not to stare too long at her legs. She had styled her hair into a messy bouffant and painted her eyes with winged, black liner. His father looked incongruously like an L.L.Bean ad in comparison.

Jonas let his mind smooth over, turning the small talk into a murmur of background noise he could tune out. Then, somewhat unceremoniously, his mother returned to her Volkswagen and backed out of the driveway and out of his new life.

Matt and Cesca gave Jonas a tour of the house, which smelled of rain-soaked wood and old wallpaper, and Jonas leaned through each doorway just far enough to feign attention. Cesca worked at an antique mall, so the building didn't hurt for unusual decorations. The plants by the main stairwell grew from bald, ceramic doll heads, and a chipped, white rocking horse stood sentinel by the door to the sitting room.

For his room, Jonas chose the suite he thought other people would find the least desirable, which seemed the place best suited to a boy no one wanted. Dingy green wallpaper peeled away from the corners of the room, and a cage filled with colorful taxidermic birds hung from the ceiling. Cesca had decorated the walls with framed prints of insects pulled from old textbooks.

Matt and Cesca left Jonas alone in the room to unpack, shutting the door behind them, and it stayed closed in its warped frame without latching. Leaving his suitcase in the middle of the floor, he flopped onto the bed. From below, the taxidermic birds were just round, colorful bellies, a system of very small planets.

It was difficult to imagine his father living in this house. Matt Lake was quiet. Jonas liked loud music, rap and rock that he could feel lighting up his rib cage. Matt listened to white-noise sound files with names like "babbling brook" and "summer storm." He assembled very large puzzles that, when he'd still lived at home with Sara and Jonas, had usually taken over the surface of half the dining room table. He flossed daily. Matt knew how to use a sextant, but Jonas doubted his father could adequately roll a cigarette. Cesca could probably roll a cigarette.

In the nightstand, where many functioning inns might have stored a copy of the Christian Bible, Cesca had *The Complete Works of Hieronymus Bosch*. Jonas passed hours reading the illustrations' accompanying descriptions, and he absorbed exactly no information, the words wilting from his brain like a garden planted on a hill made of glass.

Lamplight had exactly seven bedrooms. There was Jonas's, as well as the two he had not chosen, which remained uninhabited. Cesca and Matt shared the largest, and Jonas was not interested in seeing it.

There were two tenants, who helped with the cleaning and upkeep, utilities and property taxes—the extent of their rent—and each had a suite of her own. One was Audrey, a tattoo-covered hairstylist in her twenties who hugged Jonas when she met him, much to his dismay, for he was as friendly and pliant as a stray cat. The other was a tall dancer with frizzy hair named Diana, clearly older than Sara and Matt, though not quite old enough to strike Jonas as grandmotherly.

That left one more room for one more inhabitant. Jonas knew

that Cesca had a daughter his age, or so Matt had said. Cesca appeared several years younger than his father, unlikely to have a daughter preparing for eleventh grade. Matt had assured Jonas that Noemi Amato would "show him the ropes," as though he were unaccustomed to the concept of high school.

Noemi's room was across the hall from his, and while the door had been closed when he'd first arrived, it was now open. Jonas folded his immense self-consciousness into as small an animal as he could and let it burrow into the back of his mind. Eager to establish an ally close to his own age, he knocked on the door, which was not ajar enough for him to assume entry. He noticed the doorknob, a white metal swan, and thought the person inside might be gentle, like a feather or a ballet.

Jonas had never met a swan, and so he did not know about their surly dispositions.

"Yes?" called a voice from within.

He pushed into the room.

You could tell a lot about a person based on the things with which they surrounded themselves—Matt's puzzles and star charts, Sara's carefully sculpted topiaries, Cesca's resuscitated old toys. Noemi's room was half-painted: deep purple from the hardwood floor until partway up the walls, where it tapered off in haphazard streaks left behind by a roller, as though some-one had soured on the color before finishing. Photos hung from clotheslines everywhere—portraits of girls wearing plain dresses outdoors, strange photos in which girls' limbs faded from sight like ghosts' appendages, where their hair floated above them as though they were drifting underwater when they were not. In one corner of the room a featureless mannequin wore a deer skull where the top half of its head should have been.

Jonas had never entered a girl's bedroom before, and he did not know whether this one was usual or unusual, or if there were such a thing as usual.

In seventh grade, he had "dated" Melanie Nelson for two weeks, during which time neither of them spoke to each other or even made eye contact, until she dumped him for being too invisible. He had not seen her outside of school and certainly had never seen her room.

In ninth grade he dated Abby Pierce for one and a half months, and he *had* seen her outside of school, but only at the movies or other public places and always with other people around. She texted him photos of herself in a new bathing suit once, and he could see part of her bedroom in those: a cork board covered with birthday cards her friends had made for her, inscribed with messages he couldn't make out. It was not where he'd devoted most of his attention.

He dated Katie Simms for four months (his record) last year, and he'd gone to her house when he picked her up for homecoming, but he didn't make it past the living room before she came downstairs in a sequined dress. They skipped homecoming and went to a party at Emma Little's house, but that was in the basement, not a bedroom. They got tipsy on Keystone Light and kissed on the love seat until their mouths felt the way raw chicken looked, but even then he couldn't have guessed what Katie would keep inside her room.

At the center of Naomi's room was a canopy bed, and she had drawn the nearly sheer, white curtains so that Jonas could see only her shadow like a slim imperfection in milky quartz. He wondered if it would be strange to approach the bed, if she meant for him to. He knew nothing about this person with whom he would now live, eat, and attend school. She liked purple, presumably, though not whole-heartedly, and she maybe took photographs and was at ease with strangeness. She did not seem as eager or friendly as her mother.

"I'm Matt's son," he said to the bed. "Jonas. My room's across the hall."

The canopy parted to reveal the half-moon of a small, angular face that looked little like Cesca's. The face was olive and covered with as many freckles as a sidewalk at the start of a storm. Its owner did not smile or rise to meet him. She shook her long hair from her eyes and surveyed him as though just spotting a halo of mildew that had sneakily formed on the wall beside her door. Her gaze was heavy and her posture defensive.

Jonas felt like a trespasser. She said "Hi" and then nothing more, and somehow it gave him the sense there might be no place in her life where he would not be trespassing.

"You have a cool house," he said.

"My mom would like to hear that." She pulled her lips into an asymmetrical smile, a dimple forming on only one cheek. She had full lips, barely a hint of a cupid's bow. They looked soft. They probably would not feel like raw chicken. Her hair was dark brown and very curly.

Jonas stood by the doorway, unsure of what to do with his arms. He folded them, but it didn't feel right. Had he always folded his arms in this way? One over the other. Where did his hands belong? His body had become unfamiliar, almost hostile, a desert that would not let him get comfortable, and he second-guessed the work of every muscle.

"Do you need something?" Noemi asked. Her voice was low and husky. Jonas didn't know what she normally sounded like or if she had a cold. She didn't look ill, but he had no basis for comparison. Regardless, he liked the timbre of her voice.

"No," he said. "Just thought I'd say 'hi.'"

"Well, have a good night." She released the canopy and disappeared from sight. He had been formally and unmistakably dismissed.

Matt treated Jonas to dinner, just the two of them, at a diner called Hilda's where the staff greeted Matt by name, knew his order in advance, and asked after Cesca. His father snagged a tourism brochure from a display near the register, and once they were settled in their booth, he slid it across the table to Jonas.

Shivery, Minnesota, was a small town in the southern part of the state. It was technically an "unincorporated community," which meant the students—Jonas soon to be included among them—attended high school in the neighboring town of Galaxie. Jonas, while thumbing through the pamphlet between bites of his breakfast-for-dinner, felt vicariously embarrassed that the place might ever hope for tourists. It was home to a popcorn factory, which kept the local cinema well stocked with more flavors than it had theaters: one theater, precisely, boasting only seventy-five seats, courtesy of adjacent, mismatched couches. Also calling Shivery home was an artists' and craftsmen's supply store where Matt Lake—who put his philosophy degree to use building custom doors and furniture—bought some of his supplies, and a hardware store where he bought the rest of them.

Shivery was, according to its own tourism bureau, most famous for its lupine flowers in varying shades of pink and purple that had apparently chased most other wildflowers out of town. An entire field of them was featured on postcards sold at the diner's register.

Finally, there was a river that bisected town and flooded "roughly all the time." Matt's words, not the brochure's. The riverside storefronts were slick, window-high, with stubborn algae during bouts of rain. Matt had heard that once, the postal workers had to deliver mail from canoes. Jonas would have thought he was spinning a tall tale, but Matt wasn't the type, unless Cesca had instilled his practical father with a sense of romanticism.

"Sounds unlikely," Jonas said. "I don't believe you believe it."

"Well, here's an odd thing I *do* believe," Matt said. "A few months ago—and this is after I moved here, so it's not exactly hearsay—some local kid was found drowned in the middle of the forest out by Lamplight."

Jonas frowned. "Does the river go down that way?"

"No. Which is what was weird." Matt cut his bun-less hamburger into neat, bite-sized pieces. "Ten thousand lakes, and someone managed to drown where there wasn't so much as a puddle."

Jonas fiddled with his lip ring. "Isn't that a riddle? Or one of those lateral-thinking puzzles, like, 'There's a plane crash. Where do they bury the survivors?' I know it's one of those, but I can't remember how it goes."

"Maybe, but it's a thing that happened too."

Jonas shrugged. "I give up. I can't think of it. How did the drowned man get in the forest?"

Matt rubbed his fingers through his ashy hair. "What was his name? It was definitely Miller. Forget his first name. Logan, or something like that."

His father wasn't kidding. Jonas had the urge to pull out his phone and search *Miller Shivery, MN, drowning*, but he thought Matt might feel the same way about phones during dinner or conversation as Sara did, which was, "Don't use them." Because this was the longest conversation he could remember having with his father, Jonas erred on the side of caution and politeness. What little good that did. The conversation switched to Jonas's interest in extracurriculars (he had none), and by the time they returned to Lamplight, Jonas had forgotten about the riddle that wasn't a riddle.

NOEMI

Noemi hadn't known anyone who'd been kicked out of high school before, and when Matt had told her that was why his son would be coming to live with them, she'd privately concocted an image of Jonas Lake as a bully and a troublemaker. She didn't need a reason to dislike him—she assumed the worst of most strangers anyway—but this colorful bit of backstory had helped.

She imagined he would be something like Gaetan Kelly. It was nothing short of miraculous that Gaetan hadn't been expelled, so Jonas must have been truly nightmarish to have been ejected from his school. This portrait of her new housemate might have made other people apprehensive, but not Noemi. She wasn't afraid of a sixteen-year-old boy, no matter how many teeth he'd knocked out of other people's mouths. Instead, she resolved to make him feel as unwelcome as possible, lest he get the idea that Lamplight was his home too.

It turned out that Jonas was tall and lanky and didn't look like he could beat anyone up. He little resembled his pale, bespectacled father but had a similar unassuming air as he stood fidgeting in Noemi's bedroom when they first met, flushed and quiet. That he failed to be immediately unpleasant or hateable made her dislike him more. He had a lip ring that didn't make him look tough, which she assumed was its intended purpose.

After some growing pains, Noemi had made room for Matt in her life: he was there because he made her mother happy. Jonas had been inflicted upon them because of his own childish misbehavior, and she could not forgive him for changing the shape of their lives.

"I still wanna meet him," Lyle said.

Noemi's best friend, Lyla Anderson, sat beside her on one of the stone benches at a riverside smoothie shop named Blended. The girls ordered the same thing every time—strawberries and banana with yogurt for Lyle, strawberries and kiwi, no yogurt for Noemi—and talked about things that weren't the Miller drowning...usually people they disliked.

In the last weekend of summer before school began, this meant Noemi's new housemate.

Lyle plugged her straw with her finger and lifted a pillar of pink smoothie out of her cup. "I can't believe someone as nice as Matt would raise a crappy kid. Who knows why he bashed some guy's head in? Need I remind you of the black eye you gave Gaetan Kelly in first grade? Maybe he's a Gaetan-punching kind of expellee."

"Need I remind *you* that Gaetan Kelly is a creep who deserved to be punched for putting his hands on you?" He had jabbed Lyle in the forehead during recess, teasing that her fair eyebrows were "invisible," until Noemi nestled a fist under one of his dark ones. She had seen him pull other boys' chairs out from beneath them or put gum in girls' ponytails, and she wouldn't let him go that far with Lyle.

"I'm not criticizing. You cold-clocking Gaetan is one of my most treasured memories."

"Matt is a loud chewer," Noemi said.

"So you've said."

"You know how I feel about mouth sounds." Noemi squeezed her cup a little too tightly, and the lid popped off. "As much as I like Matt, I still have trouble being around him when he eats. Which is a problem when you live with someone. Even if Jonas is a decent person, he's bound to have some habits that become grating when sharing a roof with him."

"You're looking for reasons to dislike the kid." Lyle noisily slurped her smoothie through a wide grin.

"Very mature."

"Ack!" Lyle clamped a hand over her mouth. "Cold," she complained, voice muffled through fingers. "My teeth."

"Serves you right."

"You afraid he'll forget to refill a Brita pitcher or something?" Lyle folded her legs on the bench. Bony knees poked through large tears in her jeans. "And you accuse me of 'vigorous chewing' all the time. Does that mean you hate *me*?"

Noemi tsked. "Didn't say I hated anyone. I'm just not interested in being Jonas's friend."

"Well, that's nothing new." Lyle pulled her cell phone from the shaft of her boot and began flicking through photos. "In lighter news, I was thinking about dying my hair this color." She brandished her screen to show Noemi a picture of a girl with grass-stained hair.

"Your hair's light enough. Shouldn't be too hard."

"That I know." Lyle fluffed her platinum bangs and rolled her eyes upward. "It's just that I didn't know if you had any photos planned soon, and I wasn't sure if a color change would be a problem."

During her sophomore year, Noemi had discovered the thrill of photography. She'd apparently shown enough promise that one of the school's art teachers had let her borrow a camera far more expensive and professional than anything Noemi or Cesca could have afforded.

Noemi took mostly outdoor photos, self-portraits, pictures of Lyle or Amberlyn Miller. Even a few of Cesca. The girls would raid Cesca's closet or page through the racks at a local consignment shop for the right wardrobe. Noemi styled her friends' hair and makeup, but it had always been collaborative, at least to some degree.

When Noemi had brought the camera back to the AP art

teacher at the end of the school year, the woman told her she could sign it out over the summer.

"You don't need my permission to dye your own hair, Lyle."

"Right. No, I know. Thought maybe it wouldn't pop enough in outdoor photos. Just wanted to check."

"It'll look fine. You going to do it yourself?"

"I was thinking of asking a very crafty and stylish friend of mine to do it for me."

"Amberlyn?"

"Guess again."

Noemi's smoothie was mostly juice now, speckled with a few strawberry seeds.

"Really, though, can you help me dye it?"

"Sure. But definitely at your house. I'm sick of Lamplight."

"To-mor-row," Lyle sang.

A sudden onslaught of rain chased Lyle into her Chevy, but before Noemi could follow, an orange cat darted past her legs to seek shelter under the bench where she had been sitting. Lamplight had two cats, Rosencrantz the calico and Guildenstern the stripy gray tabby, and Noemi considered them to be the only potential rivals Lyle had for the role of her "best friend." Ignoring the rain—which would probably stop soon anyway, as the sun was still shining—she bent to peer at the visitor below.

"What are you doing?" Lyle called. She held her plastic smoothie cup above her head as she leaned out the car door, though it wouldn't be enough to keep her hair dry.

The cat's wide eyes fixated on Noemi's dangling curls. Its pupils unspooled. Rosencrantz and Guildenstern played with her hair often at home, and she'd grown used to having her scalp tugged each time one of them pounced on a curl. She shook her head and made the ringlets dance for the new cat.

She wanted to bury her nose in its wet, golden-orange fur and breathe in the animal's smell. There was something familiar about its coat: it reminded her of Link's hair. If Link had had dark brown hair like Noemi's, she'd have thought nothing of seeing that color in an animal's fur. That color was everywhere: the soil in the terra-cotta pots on Lamplight's porch, the branches of the dogwood in the lawn damp with dew, the Jacobean wood stain stored in the carriage house and how it looked when Matt used it on white oak. Link's hair color, on the other hand, was not everywhere, and that's why it was so hard not to notice when she did see it in a fox crossing the road in the early morning or in the white blush of dehydrated carrots.

Although he had died, Link had not stopped texting Noemi. The texts did not come from the phone number he'd had when he was alive. The messages arrived from *Unknown*.

It first happened in June, not long after Link's funeral, which she had not gone to. Gaetan Kelly had come into school with an expletive shaved into the side of his head. If that was Gaetan's way of grieving his friend's death, Noemi didn't understand it. She stood amid a crowd of other students and watched as two teachers dragged him to the principal's office, while he shouted drunkenly about how the dress code made no mention of what words students' hair could or could not say. Gaetan had friends besides Link, but Link was the most important and the only one who'd been a sobering influence. Noemi wondered if, without Link around, Gaetan had finally snapped.

That was when Unknown first contacted her, as though he too had been watching this scene unfold.

UNKNOWN

Keep an eye on Gaetan.

Noemi looked around her, searching to see who nearby was on their phone.

Who is this?

I would ask him to keep an eye on
you too, but he already does.

Your number is blocked. Who is this?

I miss you.

She should not have thought of Link because, of course, it was impossible. But she did.

Stop screwing around.

Noemi was disappointed when no one answered.

In art class, she was reprimanded for being on her phone. She could not help but take surreptitious glances at it, which turned into not-so-surreptitious moments spent reading and rereading the few texts exchanged that morning. Then, as the school bus carried her home, and though Unknown had not contacted her since 8:00 a.m., she asked again:

Who are you?

Link.

She pressed her thumb beside his name and stared at the letters until they didn't look like anything. Someone wanted her to think Link was texting her, but it was probably not anyone who had access to his cell. After all, if this person wanted to impersonate Link, texting from his number would have made better sense. That ruled out his sister, Amberlyn. This kind of nonsense had Gaetan written all over it, but he'd been detained by the teachers when she'd gotten the first text.

Who are you really?

Sorry.

Whoever was texting her was an asshole, and she told them so.

This is messed up. What do you want?

Someone killed me.

You going to tell me it's my fault Link's dead?

I would never say that.

The police had interviewed her, even though Noemi had been in Minneapolis for an art festival with her mother during the weekend Link had died. When the cops had told her what happened, she actually fell to her knees like someone in a movie. Noemi hadn't believed emotions could be powerful enough to overwhelm her legs until it happened.

The bus arrived at her stop, and she disembarked. Instead of walking home, Noemi cut across the field and headed for the woods. She hadn't stopped going even though Link had died there, though the visits were shallower and less frequent.

Then whose fault is it?

Hard to explain.

Noemi googled "texts from unknown numbers," but her cell data slowed, then dropped off entirely as she got farther from the road.

You should stay out of that forest.

She stopped.

Where are you?

Here and not. I don't know.

Noemi turned from the woods and ran back to the road, relieved her choice of shoes was more practical than usual that day. Once home, she knelt in the rose garden and set the phone in the soil. A green caterpillar explored the edge of it, then turned slowly away when the cell buzzed once more.

I'm sorry.

I wanted you to know I'm near. I
feel like you're mad at me.

I don't even know who you are!

Her heart thrashed against her chest, and her skin prickled.

I drowned in the lake.

Noemi ran into the house. Matt washed paintbrushes in the sink, and Audrey sat in the living room with the television on. Noemi ignored greetings from both of them and ran up the stairs and into her room. The door slammed behind her. Though it was daytime, she flicked on the lights, then drew the sheer curtains across her windows. Finally, she looked again at the screen once she was tucked behind the gauzy drapes of her bed. A message was waiting.

The lake in the woods.

There is no lake in the woods.

Don't pretend.

She wondered if Link had told anybody about the impossible lake. It had just appeared one day, fully formed, lighthouse and all. Some days it stretched so far it looked more like an ocean, and she couldn't even see the trees on the opposite side. He'd promised to keep it a secret, but she could imagine him absentmindedly telling

Amberlyn or Gaetan. Yet Gaetan couldn't have texted—not this morning.

Is this Amberlyn Miller?

No.

Gaetan Kelly?

It's Link.

Link is dead.

Yeah.

Can you call me?

No.

Link was never so difficult.

I'm sorry.

And I was a little difficult.

The morning before the new school year started, after a weekend of avoiding Jonas as best she could, Noemi had entered the kitchen only to discover Matt Lake's son drinking milk directly from the carton. Jonas stood in front of the fridge in sweatpants and a white crewneck T-shirt. He looked surprised when he saw her, though not as embarrassed as he should have been to be caught defiling a shared food item with his saliva.

He wished her a good morning and she responded by saying, "That milk is for everyone in this house to share."

Jonas wiped his mouth on his wrist and gave the carton a look of earnest curiosity, as though searching for the words *DO NOT DRINK WITHOUT GLASS* on its surface. "You're right. I'm sorry. I'm used to living with my mom. She doesn't drink milk."

Noemi had been considering inviting him to ride to school the next day with her and Lyle, and though she had not yet mentioned the option, she now considered him *un*invited. She huffed and made a great show of loudly slamming cabinets and thrusting the faucet on at full blast as she made her oatmeal with water.

As Noemi dressed for school the following day, she relished knowing that Jonas, having been sentenced to taking the bus, would have had to wake and leave much earlier. On her way downstairs to wait for Lyle, she stuck her head into his room. Rosencrantz lay in a pile of T-shirts on his bed, the traitor. She woke the sleeping cat and called her as much, then plucked her from the quilt and carried her out to the hallway on principle.

Only Matt was awake at this hour, even though he worked from home and had the most flexible schedule of anyone in the house.

"Hey, kiddo. Didn't you miss the bus?" His brows arced over the rim of a Louvre coffee mug that Cesca had purchased during a semester abroad in college.

"Juniors can drive, so Lyle is taking me."

"That's right." He set his coffee back on its coaster and spun the two of them together along the woodgrain in the table he had made. "I guess Jonas didn't know that," Matt mused. "He left to catch the bus a little while ago. Could have hitched a ride with you two."

Noemi avoided his eyes. She bent to unearth the toaster from one of the lower kitchen cabinets. "Well, he'll meet more people this way."

"True. By the way—do you know why our milk is sorry?"

"What?" Noemi stood, still empty-handed. On the table in front of Matt, alongside a near-empty cereal bowl, sat a carton of milk and a box of Shredded Wheat.

"Not this one." He nodded toward the table. "There's an unopened one apologizing in the fridge."

Noemi tugged at the stainless-steel door. Sure enough, there was a fresh container of 2 percent milk on the top shelf, identical to the soiled one Matt had used in his cereal but for its expiration date, presumably. It proclaimed in black Sharpie, *I Promise I'm New Sorry!* with every word capitalized as though it were a title. A very round smiley face hovered beside the exclamation point. Noemi didn't need to recognize Jonas's handwriting to know who had written it.

"No idea. Probably Diana. You know she anthropomorphizes everything." Noemi would not be drinking from this milk. Rightfully, Jonas should have replaced the old one, but something about the fact that he had actually done so didn't sit well with her. She'd ended up being the brat.

Because the school year had just started, even the seniors and juniors who had driven were at school early enough to join the bus riders in the gymnasium. That's where everyone waited until all buses were present and accounted for, at which point they were dismissed to homeroom. Most students who drove timed their arrivals so that they wouldn't have to wait with the underclassmen, and by this time next week, that's exactly what Lyle and Noemi would do. But today they had arrived earlier than necessary and fended off compliments on Lyle's dip-dyed hair and Noemi's handmade jewelry (which had been assembled out of parts from old Barbies).

She led Lyle to a stretch of bench that was just two rows

behind where Jonas sat. They filed in next to Tyler Olsen, who, during sophomore year, had begun wearing a shirt and tie every day. He brightened when he saw them and shifted his guitar out of their way.

"Hey, Tyler," Lyle greeted him.

"Hey. Hi, Noemi. I like your skirt."

"Why thanks." She wore a patterned skirt and a black crop top, the latter in victory after her outspoken criticism (or "rabble-rousing," to the administrators) of the school dress code a year prior.

Gaetan Kelly's broad-shouldered form cast its shadow in Noemi's peripheral vision, between their row and Jonas's. Gaetan turned at the sound of her voice and gave her an exaggeratedly lascivious once-over. His hair had grown in since he'd shaved it last spring. Now it was dark and lush again, loose waves pushed aside in a way that could have been very lazy—or could just as easily have taken a good deal of time.

Next to Gaetan, a shorter senior with acne, Steve Warton, mimicked his expression, and Noemi couldn't help but groan in disapproval. "Nice" was Gaetan's eventual evaluation.

"It's somehow creepier when you say it," Noemi said.

For a second she thought, *He wouldn't have said that if Link were here.* But before she could feel Link's absence, she realized that wasn't true. Link's disapproval had never really stopped his friend from being rude. People considered Gaetan *devastatingly handsome,* but Noemi mainly found him devastatingly difficult to tolerate. She sometimes searched for his attractive qualities by pretending she was looking at him for the first time, letting his face fall into its separate parts until it was no longer familiar. Never much success.

"By the way," she said to Lyle, "that's Jonas sitting in front of Gaetan."

"Milk-defiler," Lyle told Tyler, though he would have no idea what she meant. "Dark hair, navy tee?"

Noemi nodded.

Word had spread of the newest addition to the town of Shivery, to Lamplight, and to Galaxie Regional High School. Having heard Noemi point out her famed new housemate, Gaetan blurted, "This kid?" with no attempt at subtlety, just beside Jonas's right ear. Jonas turned to regard Gaetan over his shoulder.

"Wasn't talking *to* you, man."

"Oh." Jonas diverted his attention back to whatever game he was playing on his phone.

If anyone could inspire Noemi to immediately ally herself with Jonas, it was Gaetan. While Lyle and Tyler chatted about their respective summers, Noemi kept her eyes on Gaetan and his friend, now in the process of lighting matches and shaking the flames out right behind Jonas's hair. Gaetan held a lit match beside Jonas's ear, and the freshmen sitting on the bench nearest him inched away from the fire.

Tyler Olsen was in the middle of telling a story about a family trip to Yellowstone, but Noemi stepped right across his sentence.

"Lyle, I need your water bottle." Her friend surrendered her plastic, refillable bottle, no questions asked.

Climbing carefully one row down on the bleachers, Noemi sipped from the water, then sat directly beside Gaetan. A sloppy grin spread across his face. He had very white teeth. The thought of Gaetan wearing a bib in a dentist's chair, having his teeth cleaned, amused her.

"To what do we owe the pleasure?" he asked.

"Can I have a match?"

"What for?" Gaetan asked.

Steve handed her one without waiting for her answer.

She frowned at the single matchstick in her palm. "Well, I need the box to strike it."

He reached to pass a sleeve of matches to her, but Gaetan intercepted it before it crossed his lap. Noemi squeezed Lyle's water bottle, and a forceful stream splashed across Gaetan's hands, the matches, the knees of his jeans. She had planned to unscrew the lid and drop the whole matchbook in, but this worked just as well.

"What the fuck?" Gaetan shook his hands dry and dropped the soggy matches on the floor. "You are such a fucking buzzkill."

"It's water," she said. "You'll survive. Try not lighting fires an inch from people's heads."

Tyler chuckled behind them, and Gaetan turned his glacial eyes on him. "You're awfully cheery for someone dressed like an Allstate agent."

Tyler shrugged.

"Too bad this wasn't coffee." Noemi nodded toward the bottle.

"Piss off."

She stood and mouthed an apology to Lyle. Jonas didn't say anything or even turn around, but he did give her a sideways glance.

Though she had not felt it vibrate in her bag, Noemi checked her phone anyway, to see if her mysterious texter had chosen to weigh in on the encounter. Nothing new since their last exchange, before Jonas had even arrived.

She returned it to the inner pocket of her bag before Lyle, Tyler, or anyone else could see, just as the gym teachers summoned them all to homeroom. Jonas waited for her at the foot of the bleachers, and she allowed him to walk beside her.

THE FLOOD

Water could not be held in a fist.

I dreamt that water seeped up from the ground and crept across the front yard of our house until it became a lake. ~~My mother walked outside carrying a bucket. She filled it~~

My mother walked outside carrying a bucket. She filled it with water, but there was no place to pour its contents but back into the waves lapping at her legs. She redistributed the lake around her as though spilling the flood into itself would bail out the lawn. Finally, she released the bucket, lifted the water instead with bare hands, and splashed it into her pockets.

Even in dreams, water could not be held in a fist. It fell between her fingers and rained down onto the cotton folds of her skirt. I watched from the window of one of the bedrooms. In the nearby bathroom, something slapped against the dry inside of the claw-foot tub. I left the window and walked toward the sound.

The bathroom should have been white, but instead it was blue, as it had been when I was much younger. A sea lion spun out of the drain, whiskers first, into the basin of the tub. It was small and gray, and it undulated like a slug through a garden. I remember thinking how strange it was, not that our pipes had birthed it, but that they had done so very far from any ocean.

JONAS

Jonas and Noemi had been placed in the same homeroom, but he was seated a few rows away in the Ls. She held a copy of a book open on her desk, though rather than read it, she spent the entirety of homeroom talking to a girl in a plaid jacket with a bob haircut the color of pesto-drenched pasta. Jonas wasn't sure he had ever seen anyone wear heels as high as Noemi's in high school before, but somehow they didn't look out of place on her. Each of the heels was impaling a little toy skunk, which made it look like she was walking perched atop two mini carousel seats.

Because Noemi turned out to be in advanced classes, Jonas didn't see her for the rest of the morning. He spent his day among other average students who didn't seem interested in the new kid. Each of his teachers loaded him down with another textbook until he had no choice but to return the mountainous stack of them to his locker.

On his way back from the locker to English, he saw the sneering boy who'd been lighting matches by his hair that morning, and Jonas ducked into the lavatory to avoid another unwanted encounter. The water from the sink smelled sulfuric, but he rinsed his face in it anyway, raked his fingers through his hair so it only just covered his ears.

Despite the violent circumstances under which his previous school year had concluded, Jonas did not go searching for trouble. Typically, he tried to escape notice altogether, and trouble with it, but sometimes people like the boy with the matches didn't let that happen. When trouble sought him out, Jonas kept his frustrations tightly coiled; unfortunately, those frustrations were then prone to building up pressure.

Last spring he'd erupted into a classmate like a cold-water geyser. Now, he was depressurized, a near-empty, placid pool, but a shove in the hallway or a match behind his hair could change that. Someone might stir memories Jonas had worked to push down: in first grade, his classmate gluing his shoes to the floor during math, or a "friend" sneaking a dead grasshopper into his tuna sandwich at lunch. He wondered if everyone at his new house or in his new classes could somehow sense the small, pathetic truth of him: that he was still a sensitive, sheltered little boy who did not know how to exist in a room with other people.

The English teacher reprimanded him for walking in as the bell sounded, and Jonas didn't bother to offer any excuse.

They had to form small groups and talk about the summer

reading Jonas hadn't known about, but which he had read at his old school by coincidence. He watched as the people around him paired off, leaving him an island in a sea of awkwardness. Someone tapped him on the shoulder, and Jonas turned to see a boy with light brown skin and black-framed glasses he recognized from the gymnasium that morning.

"Jonas, yeah?" the boy asked.

"Yeah."

"Tyler Olsen. You live with Noemi Amato, right?" He pronounced her name with only two syllables: *No-mi*.

"Noemi? Yeah. Our parents live together."

"Nice. Noemi's really cool." Tyler pointed toward a plump, bearded boy in a yellow T-shirt who had slid into the desk next to him. "This is Brian Kowalski."

"Yo."

"Nice to meet you." Jonas nodded once toward Brian, then turned back to Tyler. "You're friends with Noemi?"

"Friend*ly*. I mean, she doesn't hate me, I think?" He gave two thumbs up. "What are we supposed to be talking about?"

"The dissolution of the 'American dream,'" Brian suggested. "That one book of required reading people seem to really like for some reason."

"This guy," Tyler said, rolling his eyes at Brian. Jonas felt like he had missed something. "Did you do the reading?"

"No, but I had to read the book for English last year at my old school."

"Cool, cool. I thought it was okay."

"Yeah."

"Yeah," Brian agreed.

"Well, now that that's settled, how're you liking Shivery?"

There wasn't anything to like, but Jonas didn't want to say that to someone who, for all he knew, had grown up there and bled the place. "It's fine. Um, the inn where Noemi lives is pretty cool, so that's good. I haven't seen much. The town smells like popcorn. That's different. My dad took me to a diner called Hildi's."

"Hilda's."

"Right."

"Great pancakes," Tyler said. Jonas had thought their pancakes were pretty regular. "Brian lives here."

"In Galaxie," Brian clarified. "Not inside the school."

"Right. But a good chunk of the people who go here live in Shivery."

"My dad said one of the kids who went here drowned in Shivery last year? Or something. In the woods?" It was a clumsy effort at small talk, but Jonas knew little else about Shivery outside of what was in a single brochure.

"Oh. Yeah." Tyler picked at one of his cuticles. "Did Noemi not give you the details?"

"We haven't crossed paths much. She's not at home that often."

"Oh." Tyler nodded, satisfied with the extent to which they'd discussed the subject. Jonas turned to Brian.

"Um, some guy who would have been a senior this year,"

Brian offered. He looked at Tyler, whose eyes widened as though to show how devoid they were of answers. "His sister is in our grade," Brian continued. "I mean, I'm from Galaxie, but Tyler would know better."

"Not really," Tyler said.

"So all I know are the same rumors everyone else in school knows," said Brian. Though the class had barely started, Brian glanced at the clock. "It looked sketchy, but I think they eventually decided he must have drowned in a puddle accidentally? It had been raining. It rains here a lot."

"That seems weird. Was he drunk or something?"

"Don't think so," Brian said at the same time Tyler said, "No." When Tyler fell silent again, Brian continued. "They didn't rule it a suicide, but some people think that. I guess his girlfriend just broke up with him."

"What girlfriend? People talk a lot of nonsense," Tyler said. "How about that Gatsby, though? Great or not? Discuss."

And they did discuss—or Brian monologued, really. Tyler took notes in horrendous handwriting, and Jonas contributed very occasionally when his memory aligned against something Brian said. Mainly, he spent the class discretely perusing the internet on his phone.

SHIVERY, MN, TEEN'S DEATH RULED "ACCIDENTAL"

The death of local high school student, 17-year-old Lincoln Miller, was ruled accidental. Miller's body was discovered in a wooded area by 69-year-old Garret Browning who was walking his dog on the morning of May 20. When autopsy results revealed the cause of death was asphyxiation by drowning, investigators considered foul play, believing that Miller's body would have had to be relocated from the place of death due to the absence of any water source, natural or man-made, near the site of the body's discovery. However, the coroner's report showed no signs of struggle or external injury, and pine needles in the deceased's stomach and lungs were consistent specifically with the area where he was found. Toxicology reports came back negative.

When asked for comment, police chief Mark Gallagher said, "It's possible to drown in less than two inches of water. What we suspect is that the deceased may have drowned in a puddle of rainwater after fainting or deliberately lying down to rest due to exhaustion." Miller's family confirmed their son, a junior at Galaxie Regional High School, was planning to apply to colleges this coming fall.

"The stress and exhaustion that some teenagers face when they start thinking about graduation and after is really unbearable," said Katherine Miller, 42, mother of the deceased. "It might not seem like a big deal to be a little tired, but if your child faints in an isolated place with no one around to help them, it suddenly becomes a very big deal." The Miller family says they hope their loss will encourage other parents to be mindful that children are taking care of their health, regardless of the academic pressures many teens face.

For the first time in their shared existence, Matt Lake had made Jonas lunch to take to school with him. It consisted of a red delicious apple and a sandwich of unknown specifics (American cheese and some kind of lunch meat) in a brown paper bag. Matt had forgotten to add a drink, so Jonas purchased a bottle of orange soda from a well-stocked vending machine. Fortunately, the cafeteria seating far exceeded the number of students having lunch that period, and Jonas wasn't forced to ask strangers if he could sit with them. He sat at the very end of a long row of tables that stretched the entire width of the room. This was *almost* like eating with someone else, but he was far enough away from the nearest group of people that he didn't infringe on their territory. Jonas was not someone who minded eating alone in a room of near-strangers.

But Noemi seemed to mind seeing a person eating alone in a room of near-strangers. She appeared at the end of Jonas's table, holding a metal *Sleeping Beauty* lunch box that somehow didn't appear childish in her arms. He suddenly became self-conscious, feeling for remnants of sandwich around his mouth.

"Jonas, did you want to eat with us?" She pointed a few tables away where, amid a swath of empty seats, two girls turned and waved.

"Um." He looked back and forth, Noemi to friends, friends to Noemi.

"You can say *no*. But I'll probably never invite you to do anything again." Though she was smiling, it did not sound like a joke.

"Okay."

He followed Noemi to a seat beside her, putting him directly across from a girl he hadn't met yet. The other person was the green-haired girl from homeroom.

"This is Jonas. He seems shy, so please be nice to him."

Jonas wasn't sure he would describe himself as shy. The word was gentler than he felt. But what she had said was that he *seemed* shy, and that at least was true.

"Jonas, this is my friend Lyle—short for Lyla. You'll probably see her a lot at home. She comes over all the time."

"Well, hello, Jonas," the green-haired girl said. Except for her jacket, she was dressed all in black. Her lipstick left bold, red rings on the straw of her milk. "I wasn't invited over for Labor Day because apparently you were a big mystery."

Noemi ignored her and gestured to the other girl. "This is Amberlyn. All one name."

"Nice to meet you. Are you taking bio?" Amberlyn asked. "If you are, then my dad is probably your teacher." She was dressed in a plain T-shirt and jeans, like so many others in the cafeteria, yet it made her seem out of place at this table. Her hair was very red, and the way it was braided loosely atop her head reminded Jonas of a milkmaid's.

To his left, Noemi set to work unlatching her lunch box with strawberry-colored fingernails, then prying open the lid of the Tupperware inside. Lyle slapped her hand on the lid. "Wait! We didn't guess."

"Fine."

Lyle looked at Amberlyn, who held her chin in an exaggeratedly thoughtful way. "A deer," Amberlyn said. She placed her index fingers along her temples and wiggled them, smiling. "Cute little antlers. No?"

"I'm going to guess a tiger. No! Wait. We've had that. A squirrel," Lyle said. "Have you never done a peanut butter squirrel? That seems like an oversight."

"Pick an animal, Jonas." Noemi regarded him coolly. Her eyes were green bursting through brown. He had no idea what she was talking about. His mind filled with trees and moss.

"A pine marten?" he asked. More than asking whether "a pine marten" was the correct answer, he was asking, *To what question?*

"Pine marten? Wow. It's a good guess," Noemi told the others. "Never made a pine marten before. Very unique answer."

The lid popped off, and Noemi's lunch was revealed. A crustless sandwich had been cut into a raccoon-shaped face and given little red eyes, a snout, and ears with slices of strawberry. Beside it were thin cuts of kiwi ordered into a stack of hearts.

"It's supposed to be a badger," she lamented. "Pine marten might actually be the closest guess, come to think of it. They're both mustelids."

"That must take time," Jonas said.

Noemi shrugged, then flicked Lyle on the hand as she stole a piece of kiwi and popped it into her mouth.

All three girls worked to invite Jonas into the conversation: Lyle asking questions, Amberlyn providing explanations for people and practices he wouldn't have encountered yet, and Noemi shading everything with her opinions.

The match-lighting kid from that morning squatted on the chair beside Jonas and leaned against the table, his whole body tilting in Jonas's direction. Jonas's temporary optimism deflated. Everyone turned to look at the intruder, and Jonas silently assessed the potential danger. It was hard to tell half sitting down if the boy was taller than Jonas, who was admittedly tall. But where Jonas was lanky, this person was lean and athletic, and he looked like he could have detached Jonas's head from his neck using only one arm. A Misfits T-shirt had parted with its sleeves to emphasize this fact.

"Are you lost?" Noemi spoke through Jonas without casting the newcomer a glance.

"You're in my seat," the boy said to Jonas. He perched with one foot bent onto the chair, knee crammed between the table and his own body.

"Your name's not on it," Lyle said. Her eyebrows disappeared behind her bangs.

"I sat in it last year." His eyes were so blue they would be better suited to a robot, two bright LEDs. "And I farted in it. Like a lot."

Noemi set her sandwich delicately within her lunch box and swiveled toward him. Jonas straightened and leaned back so she could see the other boy. "Oh, grow up. First of all, Gaetan, you sat there." She pointed to the empty seat next to Amberlyn. "And second, no one now at this table has ever *invited* you to sit here, so why you would want to is beyond me."

"Someone's in a mood. I'd guess you were on the rag, but who could tell?" Gaetan stood, and Noemi prickled at Jonas's elbow.

"Asshole. Shouldn't you be selling drugs in a bathroom or something?" Noemi's voice sharpened.

Gaetan offered no retort, just a lazy salute before sauntering off to a crowded table on the opposite side of the cafeteria.

"I hate that guy."

Lyle nodded in agreement.

"Staying out of it," Amberlyn said.

"Did you guys used to date or something?" Jonas asked, oblivious.

Noemi laughed, fierce and humorless. "Don't be so grotesque. People are eating."

"I'm not squeamish," Lyle interjected, jabbing her potato-burdened fork in Noemi's direction.

Noemi lifted a strip of strawberry with a wooden fork. "A friend of Gaetan's sat here last year, so we tolerated that pain in the ass on his behalf."

"I'm surprised you have friends in common."

She glanced to the girls across the table. While Lyle stared back, round-eyed, Amberlyn's gaze was narrowed on the apple wedges atop the insulated lunch bag in front of her.

"We don't." Noemi shifted in her seat. The gravity around her changed.

Jonas thought of the ornery calico at Lamplight, who could look so restful but for a thrashing tail. Noemi had no overt tells, yet her calm voice and light demeanor still smacked of mechanical affectation.

"There was a student who used to sit here, despite his horrible taste in friends. Last year." She kept her voice low and her chin inclined toward Jonas as though to prevent the others from hearing; it made it difficult for him to make out her words even sitting right beside her. "Amberlyn, when does hockey start?"

Amberlyn blinked and murmured a confused *uh*, processing the sudden change in subject. Jonas used the beat to probe further.

"Your friend...graduated?" Staggering mid-sentence, he softened his voice.

He'd never been great at reading a room, always tended to assume the worst-case scenario: that he'd said something wrong or everyone disapproved of him. Here the worst-case scenario would be that their friend had *not* graduated, that something else had happened, and Jonas looked from their faces to the crumpled paper bag in front of him, remembered the story about the boy in the woods, and dropped the subject.

By then it was too late, and, unfortunately, this was a rare case in which Jonas had indeed brought up the worst possible subject.

Noemi bristled, but she did not answer.

"He passed away last year," Lyle said, cautious.

"Oh. I'm really sorry." Jonas's nerves jittered. He sensed the unwelcomeness of the topic, but he wasn't sure how now to steer the conversation away from it, and no one else was throwing him a lifeline.

Finally, Amberlyn spoke, and the moment of interminable stillness ended. "You might have heard about the boy who drowned in the woods near the inn."

She bit her lip. Her words didn't seem like a question, but the thought felt incomplete, like she was waiting for him to confirm he knew this story. *Stop me if you've heard the one about a dead scuba diver found in a tree.*

"An accident," he said. Another question that wasn't.

"That is what people seem to believe," Noemi said.

"You don't?" Jonas asked. This felt like an opening, some uncertainty they had been carrying, waiting to uncork. "Some people were talking like it might have been a suicide?"

Lyle shoved almost an entire roll of bread into her mouth, eliminating herself from the conversation entirely. Amberlyn had naturally flushed cheeks, but now her fair face drained of even that color.

If only his life were a video game. Jonas could have reloaded, repeated this conversation, choosing different dialogue options.

"Are people saying that?" Noemi asked.

"Well, some people in my English class thought..." He shrugged, hoping that would be enough of a conclusion to the thought. *People said things, etc.*

The girls leaned in, listening—not because he might have stumbled upon some new kernel of knowledge, but because they wanted to know what lies had been spread about their friend. Jonas remembered Brian and Tyler, their hesitancy, the way they too seemed suspicious of rumor, and he wished he could explain that it hadn't been conjecture for drama's sake, that they'd been trying to explain things to the new kid without claiming anything they didn't know for certain.

"Don't worry," Noemi said. "You can't help what other people tell you. Especially being new here."

She watched him, waiting for him to elaborate, but it felt too much like a dare.

"What did they say?" Amberlyn asked, direct but somehow less intimidating than Noemi's attempted encouragement.

"Just that there are some rumors his girlfriend broke up with him, and, you know..."

"What?" The mask of calm fell from Noemi's face. "Who said that?" She set down her fork and curled her fists in her lap, her fine jaw set and rigid. "That isn't true."

Before Amberlyn or Lyle could confirm or deny the rumor, he said, "Tyler Olsen was talking about it earlier, but only in the sense that—"

"Tyler?" Noemi nearly shouted, her voice gravel in his ear. If the general din of students eating and chatting hadn't been so noisy, they would have drawn looks. Jonas was almost surprised Tyler hadn't manifested at the mention of his name. "I find it very hard to believe Tyler Olsen was gossiping about anybody." Her words were hard, accusing.

"No," Jonas corrected. "Tyler kind of denied it, actually. Another kid said it. Brian Something? But they weren't saying that's what happened. Just that some people had been wondering."

"Brian *who*?"

"I dunno. Big guy. Beard." Jonas got the sense he'd just exposed Brian as an enemy. "I'm sorry. I didn't know you guys were friends with, uh, him." He couldn't remember the name of the dead kid, and he'd nearly slipped and called him *the dead kid*. "I shouldn't have asked."

"It's fine," Noemi said. She nearly sounded convincing. "You didn't bring it up, exactly. And you couldn't have known. Link was Amberlyn's brother."

Jonas's insides twisted, and his whole body grew hot. "Shit, I'm sorry."

"Noemi, it's okay. Really," Amberlyn said. She turned to Jonas. "Don't worry about it."

"Anyhow." Noemi closed her lunch box, though half of its contents remained uneaten. "I work decorating desserts at a cupcake shop, so I guess I've gotten into the habit of making cute lunches. I'll make you lunch someday."

It took him a moment to realize this was her way of dropping the subject. She stood. Though Jonas had only just met her a few days ago and had barely spoken with her since, he got the distinct impression Noemi did not make a habit out of dispensing nurturing kindnesses.

"Thanks. I'd love to help." After he'd said it, he realized it was true.

"I'm going to art early to show Ms. Greene I didn't drop her camera off a bridge." She lifted her schoolbag onto her shoulder. "See you in history, Lyle. And we can give you two kids a ride home after school if you want. Later." Without once looking back, Noemi trotted for the exit.

"I'm so sorry," Jonas said again once the door swung shut behind her. "I had no idea. Amberlyn, I never would have—"

"Really, Jonas, it's fine," Amberlyn said. She forced a little laugh. "Honestly, I'm more worried about you. What an awkward corner to talk yourself into the first day at a new school. You couldn't have known. We all realize that. Don't let it ruin your day."

"Did Noemi think I brought it up on purpose?"

"Noooo!" Amberlyn shook her head. "I think the fact she left was more my fault."

"Nothing was your fault," Lyle corrected.

"Bad choice of words. I don't think you offended Noemi or anything, if you're worried about that. I think she just didn't know what to say with me here. And you didn't offend me either."

"Noemi and Link didn't date," Lyle added.

"Oh." That she'd needed to clarify this, that it was at all a question that hung before them, made Jonas's stomach tighten. He wondered how badly he had transgressed, then decided, based on what little he knew of her, if he had really said something to upset Noemi, she would have told him off.

"I think some people thought they were a couple because he obviously liked her." Lyle looked at Amberlyn, who nodded in encouragement. "But they weren't, and now she feels weird about it."

"Especially with us still being friends," Amberlyn added. "It's not a topic we bring up."

Jonas's father had told him about the Miller drowning like it had been an amusing ghost story. How could Matt not have known the dead kid was a personal friend of someone under his own roof? That Noemi was still friends with his sister, whom Jonas would likely run into?

All in all, the first lunch at his new school could not have been much less successful if he'd eaten alone in a bathroom stall.

AMBERLYN

The first lunch of junior year could have been worse. At least
Amberlyn hadn't been alone. Seven years ago, when Gaetan had
returned to school after his brother's death, the other fifth-grade
boys who usually ate lunch with him avoided him because they
didn't know what to say. He ate alone with only Link for company.

Amberlyn and Link were still in grade school when Gaetan's
older brother shot himself in the Kellys' backyard. Their parents
went to Elijah Kelly's funeral; Link and Amberlyn did not. Kate
and Ben Miller did not believe their children were old enough to
attend, so while they went to the service, the siblings spent the
afternoon at a neighbor's house. When their mother and father
returned to pick them up, they found the children playing horse-
shoes in the backyard. Amberlyn's parents resembled two dark

gravestones in the center of the lush lawn, and it reminded her of what she had allowed herself to forget that morning: that someone she knew had died.

At the reception, where Link and Amberlyn *were* allowed, Amberlyn trailed after her brother while he tried to find Gaetan. They searched his room, but he wasn't there. It was technically the den, and someone had tidied it for company: people in black suits and skirts eating tiny, defrosted pizza bites.

Elijah's room, on the other hand, was empty of guests. His things were still in it, of course; Amberlyn didn't know then that Gaetan's mother would never change his brother's room, even if it meant Gaetan had to sleep in the den forever. Elijah was several years older than Link, and his bedroom seemed sophisticated to Amberlyn, who had no other knowledge of teenage territory. Elijah kept his room clean, his shelves lined with books. He had a desk of his own for doing homework.

Link slid the closet door aside and found where Gaetan had hidden himself. His head rested against his knees, and his fingers laced across the back of his head. He looked up at the Millers with eyes as blue as a pilot light, but he didn't say a word. Link sat beside him.

"Can you give us a sec?" Link asked Amberlyn. Then he closed the door.

She bent to look at them through the slats, but the boys just sat together silently, saying and doing nothing, so she left them.

The other kids at the reception were Elijah's classmates, who seemed as old and huge as adults. Even their grief was somehow very adult and opaque, and they surrounded her like towering trees in an ancient forest. She stood beside her parents while they spoke to the others in hushed tones, skirting the topic of *how* Elijah had died and focusing mainly on his youth and all the things he'd never get to do. She was old enough to understand death, and she knew what suicide was, but the profound despair that had led Elijah there was inscrutable to her, and she felt strangely guilty for the distance between herself and the boy they were all there to mourn.

The first real funeral Amberlyn went to was Link's years later. Since she had never been to a funeral—just the one reception—the word conjured very specific images. In movies, people dressed in black and gathered in a very green graveyard while a coffin was lowered into the ground, and maybe they tossed fistfuls of dirt or flowers onto the lid while it drew away from them. The weather was either very sunny, or it was raining and everyone huddled under black umbrellas.

In reality, Link's funeral was held indoors because his body had been cremated and placed into a little urn with a yellow-and-orange sunburst mosaic on its surface. Classmates who had never even spoken to Amberlyn or her brother made an appearance, but not Noemi. Cesca Amato arrived without her daughter, accompanying Lyle and her parents.

Everyone at the funeral asked where Noemi was—asked Lyle more than Cesca. Amberlyn said nothing about it, but her friends did: Brianna called her absence "suspicious," while Carly dubbed it "insulting." This was the first thing either of them had said to her at the service. At best they were trying to maintain some semblance of normalcy by focusing on something frivolous; at worst, their priority, even at Link's funeral, was mean-spirited gossip. Amberlyn shrugged and slipped away from them while they were too busy whispering to each other to notice.

Despite sharing a bus and a school and Link with Noemi for years, Amberlyn found her distant and unknowable, but she had always thought snap judgments an ugly quality in others, so she tried to keep an open mind. Perhaps Noemi was too sad to come. Amberlyn could understand that. There was a part of herself that didn't want to be there.

Gaetan stood next to Mr. Miller like he was one of their children—which he might as well have been—glaring at Lyle through the entire, interminable service. He was so still and serious he could have been carved to hurl rainwater off the side of a cathedral. The Millers both cried, Lyle cried, several random nobodies cried, but Amberlyn did not. Her nose was warm and twitchy, but she did not weep.

Immediately after the service had concluded, Gaetan asked Lyle, "Where the hell is Noemi?"

"She couldn't come."

"Why not?"

"I—I mean, I don't know. Maybe she wasn't feeling well?"

"I didn't want to be here either," he said. He looked around to make sure no one had heard him admit it. Amberlyn stepped back, out of his line of sight. "It's just as well. Link would have hated this anyway. He'd probably rather be flushed down a toilet. But still, it would have been nice." Gaetan sniffed, and for a second he looked like he might cry, which was by far the most troubling thing Amberlyn had seen all day. Then he stalked off and out of the funeral home altogether.

"He's probably right," Amberlyn said, her voice barely a puff of air.

Lyle startled at the sound of her words. She wore a simple black shift dress, and Amberlyn tried to remember if she had ever even seen her wear a skirt before.

"My parents and I talked about doing that thing where you launch someone's ashes into space. That seems like a Link thing to do. But it's pretty expensive, so..." Amberlyn looked up at one of the canned ceiling lights until the muscles in her face stopped aching.

"Do you want to go for a walk or something?" Lyle asked.

"Yes!"

So they walked to the edge of the block and sat together on one of the concrete bumpers in a pet groomer's parking lot, watching people bring their dogs in and out. The strip of landscaping between the building and the lot was filled with crushed white stones, and the girls each selected one for writing on the asphalt: their names and pictures of hearts and spirals and other simple things because neither was as gifted at drawing as Link had been. Then Amberlyn wrote Link's name and drew a thick-lined rectangle around it until her stone was just a nub.

Just a week before he'd died, Link had taken Noemi to prom. Technically, Noemi had declined his invitation to the event, but she'd agreed to a private anti-prom with him in the woods instead. Amberlyn detected something invisible crackling between them. She had asked him whether he and Noemi were in a relationship, but he couldn't say.

She had seen how hard he had worked. Link bought a new necktie—new for him, at least, since it was purchased second-hand like most of his clothes. He couldn't afford a jacket, but he did find some suspenders he liked. Locating suitable slacks was a challenge, as barely anything he tried on fit his very tall frame. He bought the closest fit he could find, and Amberlyn folded the cuffs up in a way she hoped looked deliberate. Any luck and Noemi wouldn't look at his feet. Amberlyn helped him make a picnic dinner, and her brother had smiled and laughed when he flicked a piece of avocado into her copper hair.

He'd purchased a small bouquet of bright pink tulips from the grocery store because he had seen Noemi wear the color, and it was all he could afford, especially after breaking his budget on dinner supplies. Carnations were cheaper, but Amberlyn had forbidden them.

He had been determined not to smoke that day, but he came home before the sun had fully set, smelling of cigarettes with his tie undone, and when Amberlyn asked him how it had gone, he shook his head and went upstairs to his room.

Amberlyn was sure Noemi had rejected him. Maybe she

should have been angry with the girl who'd broken her brother's heart, but she could only imagine what it must be like to hurt someone you care about, then never get a chance to speak to them again because they'd died.

When she thought of it like that, she could understand why Noemi might not want to be at the funeral. Besides, Link's death had been an accident. There was no point in being angry at anyone, nothing to blame for her sorrow but unlucky circumstance. So Amberlyn kept her sorrow inside, and it pooled in every hollow of her body.

5

NOEMI

After school, Lyle drove Noemi and Jonas back to Shivery. Noemi rode shotgun, which she didn't even need to call, and Jonas sat quietly in the back looking out the window. Lyle always took her cues from Noemi, and Noemi was content letting their extra passenger space out, so the three of them remained silent. Lyle could not occupy silences with much comfort and punched The Clash onto the stereo.

They passed the lupine field, which meant they would soon approach Lamplight's narrow drive. Just as Lyle turned onto the old inn's road, Noemi spoke for the first time since leaving Galaxie.

"Do you think we could drop Jonas off and then go back out? There's something I want to show you." She stared straight ahead, even though she wasn't the one driving.

"Sure. What is it?"

"It's more of a *where*." Noemi tinkered with the school-issued camera, which had never found its way back to the art room.

"Interesting. And a little ominous."

"I'm being vague because Jonas is here." Noemi didn't allow little things like social niceties to prevent her from speaking exactly what was on her mind.

She caught a brief glimpse of Jonas in the rearview mirror. His attention was on her, unfazed by her eye contact.

"I wouldn't snitch on you," he said. He managed to sound gentle where some might have been defensive.

"I'm not worried about that," Noemi said. "I'm not *worried* about anything, really. It's something personal, and I think Lyle would understand its significance. You'd be bored."

"I'd be bored at home. You don't have to worry about that with me. And if you don't want people to be curious, don't be so mysterious about wherever it is you're going."

Noemi spun to face him now. "Testy. We're going into the woods. It's not a big deal. It's where I take photos. We're just going a little farther in this time."

"I'd like to watch you take photos."

"No photo shoot today."

"We just need a little girl time," Lyle said. This sounded ridiculous, though Noemi was sure she'd meant it to be consoling.

"Okay." When Jonas climbed out of the back seat, he told them to *have fun*, and he sounded sincere. He thanked them for the ride.

Lyle waited until he got into the house before backing out of the driveway. Though Noemi barely knew a thing about him, she couldn't help feeling guilty at the sight of him walking off alone. Being the new kid couldn't have been easy. Being a kid, period, was trying enough.

"He seems nice," Lyle told her. "It's hard to believe he got kicked out of his old school for fighting."

"Knocked out some kid's teeth," Noemi said. "I'm just going to assume he had a reason. He does seem nice. In an aggressively mild way. He's like lukewarm tea."

Lyle snorted, then pulled back onto the road. "Even when you're complimenting someone it comes off kind of harsh."

"Well." Just that one word, insistent, a defense on its own. Noemi rolled up her window so she didn't have to shout against the wind. "I feel bad hating someone so *nice.*"

"Don't feel bad. How dare he be nice?" They parked in a patch of bare grass at the edge of the lupine field. "Why didn't we walk?" Lyle asked the question more of herself. "You should have said something. Where is my brain right now?"

"Well, it might actually be good to have the security of the car on the way back."

Lyle's hand froze on the latch for her seat belt.

"You're being really weird," she said. "It's just us. Tell me what's going on. If it's not to take photos, why are we here?"

Noemi looked away, wrapped the strap around her camera, then tucked it beneath the passenger's seat. She never made direct eye contact with Lyle—or anyone—for very long. "If I just tell you, it *will* sound really weird. It'll make more sense if I show you."

Over the summer, whenever Unknown texted, Noemi could pretend Link was still alive. Logically, she knew this wasn't the case, but she let the corners of her mind that struggled with his absence believe that he was still there. He could have been somewhere in the world, holding a cell phone and typing with fingers of flesh and bone, nerves tingling, blood flowing through his veins.

She had not told anyone about Unknown or his texts. They might think she was grieving and, in her grief, imagining things. Then, if she showed them—Lyle, her mother—the texts, they would tell her someone was harassing her, and she could no longer reply to Unknown without feeling it was naive to do so.

He seemed to understand her need for secrecy. She'd asked him about it once.

Who else have you texted?

No one. Why?

Just wondering if anyone
else can commiserate.

And why not?

I don't know who else could handle it.

Or keep an open mind.

Both Noemi and Unknown believed no one else would understand their correspondence. She didn't know what it meant for him—Link was a cryptic sort of person, even in life. But for her the secret made him real, and telling Lyle or anyone else would have meant confronting the impossibility of it. Subjecting Unknown to scrutiny would render him an imaginary thing, the way a shadow cannot survive a beam of light.

Being back at school for the fall meant confronting the fact that Link was not there. Someone else had his locker and his desk in French class and his seat at lunch. She could not push the fact of his death from her mind because it continually greeted her at each new point in her day. The texts from "Link" were at odds with his absence. Someone else would now have to witness an impossible thing and confirm its existence, independent of her imagination.

She would show the lake to Lyle.

Noemi made Lyle close her eyes, and Lyle let herself be led by one hand, the other spread across her eyelids to show she wasn't peeking.

Lyle knew the woods better than anyone but Noemi. They'd played there together as children. Noemi would wear a black dress that was far too long for her, and it dragged on the earth, collecting pine needles and robins' feathers. Sometimes she harvested owl pellets from underneath the trees, took the mouse bones with her when she left. She'd clean the bones at home, and when she returned, hang them from branches with string. Lyle, head crowned in a wreath of golden paper, pretended to be a prince on a quest to chase the Sorceress Noemi from the woods at the edge of the kingdom. She attacked the canopy of mouse bones with a rubber sword.

Lyle had seen firsthand there was no body of water in the woods where Link could have drowned. And so she would understand the significance of the sudden appearance of a very large lake.

"Open your eyes."

It stretched before them, so huge they could not see the trees that should have been on the other side. Just a few steps from where they stood, a rowboat bumped rhythmically against a stone dock that sprouted from the grass. The boat had flat, geometric planes assembled from time-worn wood.

"What the hell? How long has this been here? How did we miss this?"

They hadn't walked long today. They could be standing in any place they'd been before, taking photos, playing Vanquish the Witch.

"I think this is where Link drowned."

The town had marveled at the impossibility of Link's death. Had the police fished him out of a lake as big as an ocean, the mystery of where he'd drowned would have never been a mystery. Yet here it was.

"So you think someone moved him out of the water?"

"Or the lake moved, or I don't know. It's hard to find sometimes. Link could never find this place unless we came together. Until, I guess, he did." Noemi bit down on her lip and looked out onto the water. "So you really shouldn't ever try to come here without me."

"In case the vanishing lake comes after me? I feel like I'm missing something. When did you become superstitious?" Lyle stepped to the edge of the water and peered into it. Her reflection was dark, her face full of rocks. A small fish swam through the silhouette of her head.

Noemi had refused to make wishes on birthday candles for as long as she could remember. She'd ruined Santa Claus for the entire first grade. She photographed fairy tales, but she didn't believe in them.

Her hand fluttered, dismissive. "I believe in things for which there is concrete evidence. I can *see* this lake. Hear it. I don't know why the police couldn't find it, but here it is."

She waited for Lyle to argue, but there was nothing to say.

"Link was the first person I brought here. It was a private place just for us, and now I'm showing it to you."

"Why?"

"Being back in school now," Noemi said, "I guess it's a reminder." She tiptoed down to the water and nudged the side of the boat with her toe. "Summer was nice. His absence wasn't everywhere. In school—I don't know. There are empty places he should be. It wasn't as bad in the spring because Gaetan was either suspended or cutting classes. Amberlyn missed school a lot too. Mr. Miller had a sub for the last few weeks, and the year was almost over. But now everyone who cared about him is back, and I feel like I'm keeping something from them. I had to tell somebody. The only person it makes sense to tell is you."

"So you haven't said anything to Amberlyn?"

"Of course not. What could I say? 'Would you like to hear my unfounded theory on how your brother was murdered in a magic lake?'"

"Well, not that exactly."

Amberlyn had a far greater reason to investigate claims of an undiscovered lake than Lyle, and Noemi did not want anyone else to drown because she had shared the place with them. Better to understand it more before dangling it in front of Link's sister. The woods—Noemi had once thought she'd gotten to know them well. The ocean had crept through the trees and made them strange, like a thing in a dream that tells you you're sleeping.

THE PAPER BOAT

I knelt on the shore of the lake. It was night, and the ghost of the moon lit the clouds from behind: great blue lanterns that helped me see like a cat through the dark. A sheet of paper lay in the grass, large enough that I could have rested on it, arms outstretched, and still my fingers would not have reached the edges. I folded it into a boat, pressing my bare shins along its creases. My boat was sturdy. I pushed it out onto the water and leapt inside.

The lake soaked my boat's bottom until the paper was transparent, and the white beneath where I sat was dyed black. Somehow, the water did not leak through the paper, stopped short of dampening my legs. The boat did not soften.

I drifted far from the shore on the clear-bottomed boat, so far that I could no longer see the trees. The water mirrored the clouds above. Glass water, glass sky. I dipped my finger over the edge and created a series of ripples. The sky cracked above, replicating the pattern, buckled and spidered like ice in early spring. My boat stopped, and the water all around me had stilled. My paper boat was frozen in the middle of a lake with no edges.

Something began to take form beneath me, on the other side of the soaked-clear bottom: a mass of algae and goose barnacles, covering a face or arranged like a face, I couldn't tell. I pressed my hand against the bottom of the boat, fingers splayed. Between my thumb and index finger an eye opened—a seal's eye, a horse's eye, black as the eye of Equuleus.

6

JONAS

Matt Lake spent most days at home, woodworking in the old carriage house. This meant Jonas was alone in the house except for the cats, Rosencrantz and Guildenstern, while Noemi and Lyle went off gallivanting through the woods. He preferred it this way. Six people lived in this house, and though it had seven bedrooms, six still seemed to Jonas like a few people too many. He understood the practicality of so many people in one house, but regretted sacrificing his solitude, no matter how much he liked the boarders.

Diana insisted unwelcome spiders be carried from the house and set outside in the grass instead of killed. Audrey, though she worked on her feet at a salon all day, made dinner every night that she was home (a celebrated alternative to Matt's cereal-for-dinners). While Jonas couldn't fault friendly or generous people, he did find them exhausting, as he was far more conservative in sharing his own time and energy.

The only person he didn't really mind sharing a home with was Noemi, even though she was by far the thorniest of the lot—or perhaps *because* she was the thorniest. When she returned from whatever she and Lyle did all day, whoever crossed her path before she retired to her room was lucky to be greeted with a "hey." If Jonas was the only person present, she didn't greet him at all.

With the house to himself, Jonas wandered through the open doorway and into the room of the girl who never expected him to be pleasant when all he felt like doing was being invisible. He didn't know why Noemi had finally acknowledged him at lunch that day. He had a few theories: one, that he'd looked thoroughly pathetic eating alone; two, that he'd looked thoroughly pathetic with Gaetan Kelly mock lighting his hair on fire; three, that he'd served as a distraction by filling her dead boyfriend's empty chair. This last possibility he could understand intellectually if not emotionally. In the same position, would he have wanted someone to fill the seat or leave it empty forever? He knew the seat was a question, but he had trouble imagining what his own answer would be.

Jonas didn't snoop through anything that wasn't in plain (enough) sight, but he was curious about the photographs hanging on the walls. Lifting them up now, he found titles and dates and models' names written in Sharpie on the back. Most of the photos prior to this summer had been taken in wooded areas. More than one photo featured Lyle, though there was one in which Jonas would not have recognized her had it not been for the handwritten description on the back.

Sheer, white fabric cocooned most of Lyle's form, which floated, weightless, against the bark of a lichen-crusted tree. She was either nude underneath the fabric or wearing something flesh-matching and skintight, which made his presence in Noemi's room feel even more transgressive than it had just a moment before. From what he could make out from the few wisps of Lyle's hair visible through the fabric by her face, it was platinum, not yet tinged green. Every one of her features except her red lips had been washed out, barely evident through the chiffon.

The effect on her body was one of a floating streamer that had been snared by the tree, captured in the midst of taking human form—just the strip of her face around her mouth had fully materialized. The title was "Dream: Chrysalis."

A less surreal portrait was a close-up of Noemi's face. A bare tree branch spread its fingers over her head, thin strands of her curls reaching upward to twirl each around a single twig. She had done something to her freckles, either with makeup or Photoshop, blocking most of them out except a swirl on one side of her face, sweeping down from the inner corner of her eye and along her cheek like the tail of a comet. The blurred background and the branch tangled in her hair gave him the impression that this was taken sometime in winter, though her shoulders were bare, dark freckles streaming down only one.

It dawned on him. These girls took near-nude photos in the

woods by Lamplight, and it made sense to Jonas why he had been uninvited from their company this afternoon.

Jonas only found one photo of a boy, more candid than most of the others. It was not on a wall; it slept forgotten on the desk, one blue-gray eye peeking out from behind a simple photo of Guildenstern watching rain through a window.

He slid it carefully from beneath the image of the cat, half-fearful Noemi would sense the disturbance in the organized chaos. The person in this photo was not naked. He wore a charcoal zip sweatshirt, the frayed hood around his head like a halo in negative. The boy had fair, strawberry-blond hair, longer than Jonas's, and it swept against the angles of his face down to his jaw. His eyebrows crinkled upward as though they weren't anticipating the whirring click of a camera's shutter. On the back of the photo, the same handwriting had written—this time in green Sharpie rather than black—the word *Link* and nothing else.

It surprised Jonas that Link wasn't particularly handsome. Petty insecurity sowed thistle in his lungs.

The more he considered it, the more he'd have preferred that the dead boy looked something closer to Gaetan, with obvious features for which he might be admired. Whatever made Link special was something invisible, perhaps a thing that could be felt or understood without being seen. And yet the only information Jonas had about him was that he'd drowned, and that everyone who'd known him seemed to think it was strange.

Saliva caught in the back of Jonas's throat. He didn't know why he felt threatened by the shadow this boy cast across his new life. It was not as though Link Miller had lived at Lamplight. Jonas was in no way stepping into Link's footprints, and what anyone thought of the dead boy should not have mattered.

It didn't matter.

It *didn't* matter.

One boy leaves a town and another arrives; it doesn't mean that the new boy has to fit into the old one's place. Matt hadn't even known Link's name. This wasn't a new brother with whom he had to vie for attention.

Besides, Jonas had never fit in before—he didn't need to fit into Shivery just because it was new to him. If it were a puzzle, Jonas would be a piece from an entirely different image, a frozen planet in the midst of a field of lupines, but that was how it had always been. He replaced the photo on the desk, blanketed it again with the picture of Guildenstern, returned to the bedroom that was his but not quite.

AMBERLYN

Lyle drove Amberlyn to the playground of the Galaxie public park. Rather than wood or rubber mulch, its ground was paved with cement. All the equipment was ocean themed. A pirate ship with slides in place of planks. Seahorse spring-rockers. A wooden whale large enough to climb inside, a scratched-up periscope poking out of its blowhole. In the warmer summer days, children ran through small water fountains in their bathing suits. It was too chilly for that today, and though the water sprayed gently against the pavement, the place was quiet. The children who might normally come to play after school were nowhere to be seen.

Amberlyn had brought two skateboards, Christmas gifts their parents had given her and Link back in middle school. It was the first time she and Lyle had hung out one-on-one since her brother's funeral. Amberlyn hadn't seen much of anyone this past summer. She'd been invited—never by her old friends, but by Lyle and sometimes even Noemi—but she'd rarely accepted. In the months following Link's death, Amberlyn had been a compressed nerve, and even if no one commented on it, they saw her, weak and pulsing. Then, eventually, the ache dulled, and she was able to accept it as a new part of her shifting self. This time, when Lyle had asked her to hang out, Amberlyn could agree without worrying she wouldn't be fun enough, that Lyle might regret asking. It helped that Lyle would be alone. She could dissolve in the middle of the playground, and Lyle wouldn't hold it against her.

"Do I have to wear knee pads?" Lyle asked, eyeing the gear Amberlyn held out to her.

"And wrist pads. You don't have to, but you should."

They each took one of the skateboards, and Lyle mirrored Amberlyn's movements, shaky but determined. Amberlyn held on to Lyle's arms to guide her, the dip between her thumb and forefinger cupping the inner crevice of her friend's elbow. Despite the weather, Lyle's bare skin was warm. Amberlyn pushed her own skateboard aside and led Lyle down the soft hill that curved from the outer lip of the playground to one of the fountain drains.

"We should get you some skate shoes," Amberlyn mused.

"What's wrong with these?" Lyle had brought the only sneakers she owned: a pair of black-and-white All Stars. Outside of gym class, Amberlyn had never seen Lyle in anything but combat boots.

"They're flimsy. I mean, they work okay, but you're going to tear them to shreds if you start skating regularly. Converse makes skate shoes, but I've never worn them. Try these on."

Amberlyn kicked off her own dirty, lilac Vans. She stood on the pavement in just a pair of socks, the tip of the big toe on her left foot poking through a hole.

"Your feet are going to get cold. Switch with me." Lyle began working her own shoes off.

They'd be uncomfortably snug, but Amberlyn put them on anyway. Her feet found the shapes of Lyle's memorized by the insoles. The shoes were even warmer than her arms had been, and Amberlyn lost herself in marking out the indentations made by Lyle's toes with her own.

In Lyle's too-small sneakers, Amberlyn demonstrated how to do an ollie. She used part of an octopus climbing frame, launching herself over a tentacle. Her movements were fluid and graceful, like they were on the hockey rink. Lyle watched from her perch on top of the octopus's bulbous, orange head.

"I think it's going to rain," she called down. "Is it bad to skate in the rain?"

"It's not a great idea."

They gathered up the skateboards and set off for Lyle's car while droplets began to plink on the colorful metal of the playground equipment. By the time Amberlyn was in the passenger's seat, the rain was falling steadily. The two girls kicked off each other's shoes, but rather than trade back, they stayed in their socks. Lyle set the keys in the ignition but left the car off, slid her seat back, and folded her legs against the steering wheel. Amberlyn gave the lever by her seat a tug, and after some effort, it shot all the way back with a loud groan.

She selected a single water droplet from the windshield and kept her eyes on it, rooting for it to get to the bottom without encountering any others, but it only got about halfway down before its path merged with a second drop, and they formed one thick, jagged line down the center of her vision.

The region was not excessively rainy, but it rained enough. It had rained enough to drown her brother. Amberlyn couldn't even remember the May storm that had killed Link. There were a few memorable storms in Shivery, very few that felled trees into houses, littered the streets with branches, and stained the sky green. Storms in Shivery usually left little impression. Except for when it came to Link.

They had found him lying on the ground against a tree, half-clothed with his shoes, pants, and jacket beside him. He had nothing with him but his wallet, his lighter, a pack of cigarettes, and a small cylinder of cat treats he liked to set out for the raccoon family in their backyard. No note. No marks on his body indicating the involvement of a person or animal. He'd been at the wrong place at the wrong time. When a place—when nature—kills a person, it doesn't leave signs that spell *foul play* on the body. A place doesn't have hands.

"Did Link skate?" Lyle asked, breaking the silence and Amberlyn's reverie.

People tended not to ask about him. People liked talking about her brother when she wasn't around, but it was more the strangeness of his death that interested them—not the strangeness of Link—so he was an awkward subject for them to bring up to her face. Some days, she was grateful for this. Surviving hours at a time without involuntary thoughts of him seemed a major accomplishment.

Other days, though, she wanted to talk about him to anyone who would listen, until her voice ran out. But they wanted to hear about the mystery, the drowning. They didn't care that he checked out a book about cows from the library in sixth grade, or that he counted robots instead of sheep, short-circuiting one by one as they jumped into a river. No one wanted to hear that even though he liked to draw, his favorite art to look at was sculpture. He liked being able to walk around a statue and see it from all sides.

"No," Amberlyn said. "He didn't skate."

"Hmm." Lyle rolled her bottom lip between her fingers, and her red lipstick pilled in little loaves. "Of the two of you, I'd have thought Link would be the skater."

"That's just because he dressed like a kid who'd get yelled at by a store owner for goofing off in a parking lot." Amberlyn angled her legs onto the dashboard. She felt the cool glass from the window through her socks. "But I don't really consider myself much of a skater either, honestly. Not the way some people are serious about it. I prefer ice-skating."

"Is that why you play hockey?"

"I guess. I mean, that's part of it. There's a leap from just ice-skating to actually playing ice hockey, but it's a really fast-paced sport. That's head-clearing in a way."

"Maybe I can go to one of your games sometime." Lyle gave a tight, shy smile and lay her head on the wheel as though it were a pillow, her face still turned to Amberlyn. "For moral support."

"I'd love that," Amberlyn said. "Though if you're offering moral support, there is a small favor I could use help with."

After Lyle drove her home, Amberlyn led her into the garage. It was only large enough to fit one car, though it was currently being used for storage. Her parents' cars were parked in the driveway instead, just in front of Lyle's.

They lifted the rolling garage door together, and it hung up by the ceiling, rivers of rainwater running from its edge to the ground.

Even without a car inside of it, it still had that heady garage smell of rubber from the snow tires and the fuel in the lawnmower. The floor was filthy, covered in grease spots and dead spiders, but when she caught the garage's scent, Amberlyn got a strange urge to press her tongue to the cement and soak up its pleasant repulsiveness.

The garage was filled with boxes of seasonal ornaments, pantry overflow, assorted tools, backyard toys Amberlyn hadn't touched since she was twelve, recycling, and other various knick-knacks. There was a bike of Link's propped up against the wall; its tires had gone flat years ago. A deflated swimming pool was crumpled into a messy pile and crammed on top of a metal shelf.

"Should we leave the door open?" Lyle asked.

"It'll be less stuffy," Amberlyn said.

Link had kept the garage stocked with a collection of street-art supplies his parents had learned to conveniently ignore. They were mostly confined to a blue, plastic milk crate, though they overflowed into the immediate surrounding area. Amberlyn could detect no organizing principle to it. The pile was mainly made up of spray cans but also included markers and refills, brushes, pens, graffiti remover, gloves, face masks, metal paint, various caps, and several items of ambiguous purpose.

Normally her father would be bothering Link by now, urging him to clean his garage space before the winter so at least one of their cars could hide under cover, away from the snow. This year, though October loomed, Amberlyn's parents let the dust collect on the piles of old paint supplies. If they avoided the garage they wouldn't have to make decisions about which of Link's toxic chemicals to keep or trash, and no other parts of him would be discarded. The cans would decay under rust and salt while the paints dried up, waiting to become something more.

No one had tasked Amberlyn with cleaning the supplies in her brother's stead, but someone had to do it before the nights froze over and rendered it all useless. His comics, his T-shirts, his mecha built with off-brand interlocking plastic bricks, and everything else imbued with memory slumbered in the museum of his room. But unlike Link's bedroom, his corner of the garage didn't necessitate preserving. The leftover spray paint was just leftover spray paint. Link wouldn't be coming back to add it to the wall by the convenience store dumpster, and no one left alive in the Miller house knew how to put it to use without him.

Lyle pulled a new, disposable respirator mask from its packaging, while Amberlyn donned the cheap plastic one that always had Link looking like a bipedal ant. It weighed down the front of her head, trapped her breath warm against her face, and made her feel apocalyptic. Together, they tore a swath of cardboard from a broken-down box stacked against the recycling bin and dragged it to the rainy entry of the garage.

Amberlyn didn't know much about spray paint, but the cans had been sitting in the garage through the summer, and she couldn't imagine they would be of much use. The girls shook the cans, clattering the pea inside, and tested them against the box. Some were empty, others congealed. They sprayed the nearly empty ones until they were cleared out, leaving a mess of colorful circles soaking the cardboard. A few cans had paint dripping down the sides, and on one, the curve of Link's thumbprint had been pressed into a thick blue splatter.

While Lyle continued to separate the supplies into rows of items to discard and rows to donate to the school art room, Amberlyn's thumb settled into the little wedge her brother had left smeared in the paint. Lyle paused to inspect her nails, which—like the tips and edges of her fingers—had been dusted with specks of bright pink paint. She leaned forward and extended her arm past the threshold of the garage and into the driveway. Her hand unfolded like a crocus into the rain. She turned it over and over, but the paint didn't wash away.

Amberlyn remembered Link's graffiti at the gas station and the custard stand and under the bridge and in an alley downtown, and she wondered how many rains it could weather, if the world could end and it would still be standing in whatever rubble of humanity remained.

JONAS

Noemi worked at Hummingbird Cupcakes after school, crafting buttercream flowers that could fool even a honeybee until it flitted close enough. Jonas first visited a week after school started under the pretense of wanting a cupcake, though in truth he believed them to be a birthday-only food. Teenagers whose names he hadn't yet learned sipped coffee at wooden high-top tables and talked over mostly ignored textbooks. From behind the counter, his housemate's eyes flickered briefly in his direction at the sound of the door chiming—once, twice—then back down to whatever she was working on.

Taking a stool by the side counter, Jonas fished through his backpack for his trigonometry homework.

"You generally order at the register," Noemi said.

"Right. Just wanted to see what you recommend."

"I don't really know. I just decorate them." She adjusted her grip on a plastic bag stuffed with coral-colored frosting.

"You must like to cook."

Noemi shot him a confused look. She wore a heather-gray T-shirt with the shop's logo on the back, and her usually voluminous hair was knotted at the base of her ear, which somehow made it look more unfettered than usual. None of the employees in view wore hats or hairnets. Jonas wondered if Minnesota health laws were really that lax.

"Because of the cute lunches," Jonas mumbled by way of explanation. "And even if you don't like the cupcakes, you still chose to work here of all places."

"The cupcakes are good." She swept a sidelong glance to the woman working the register. "I'd guess any food gets old when you're elbow deep in it four hours a day. But I don't like cooking. For me it's about aesthetics. Check that out." She tilted the tray of cakes she was working on so Jonas could see them: intricate flowers constructed from colorful frosting. They were very dainty, even though her hands moved quickly, and she seemed to give the work less than half of her attention. "I wanted to work someplace that required a little creativity, but I have no real patience for food preparation—just decoration."

"I'm sure lots of bakers would be offended. Making something taste good takes creativity."

"I don't disagree. It's just not where my strengths lie. Do you cook?"

"I defrost," Jonas admitted.

"Same."

As the weeks went by, Jonas kept visiting. Noemi snuck him samples of everything that wasn't strawberry flavored (her favorite, but he had an intolerance). At first, he relished the free samples, though before long he worried the sugar would make him ill. But he'd completed more homework recently than he had ever done in his life. It embarrassed him that he needed Noemi to explain his physics homework, that she had to correct his English assignments. But he didn't mind so much the way she leaned across the counter when she wasn't busy, so close that he could see the freckles on her cheek peeking through a stray smear of violet buttercream. She smelled like sugar and berries.

In the evenings, they walked home from the bakery, the backs of their hands brushing together like wind chimes. Neither of them apologized for the accidental invasion of space. She spoke sternly to him about direct and indirect objects, teased him for his ham-and-rice lunch tigers that looked more liked dissolving cows. Noemi was the type of person who took to things with skill the first time she tried them, and she held most others to lower standards, but Jonas didn't seem to be among them. He learned to map the galaxies of her freckles. He invited her to stream shows with him, and when she grew tired of sitting, she stretched out on the sofa with her legs bent over his.

He'd started walking to work with her. She'd never invited him, and he'd never offered. It just happened. He just fell into step behind her. When Lyle dropped them off at home after school, Noemi would change into her Hummingbird T-shirt, paired with a miniskirt and heels or some other impractical articles of clothing. Then Jonas walked with her to downtown Shivery, and when they got to the shop, her coworkers would greet them: "Hi, Noemi. Hi, Noemi's shadow." She would shoot him a conspiratorial eye roll, and he wouldn't mind the teasing.

One afternoon, as he sat drinking his water from a to-go coffee cup and suffering through his math homework, a customer bypassed the line at the register and directly approached Noemi.

"Uh, yeah, excuse me, miss—"

Noemi glanced up from her work with a look of pure loathing. "I don't work customer service."

"I literally just saw you talking to the new kid when I walked through the door. Or was that just because he's *so* sad?"

Jonas was good at ignoring people who gave him shit—to a point—but Gaetan Kelly was already well on his way to reaching that point. The older boy sneered at him, then reached across the counter and dipped his thumb into a flower Noemi had just finished forming.

"Seriously?" Noemi said, jaw clenched.

"Does that mean I can just take the cupcake now?" Gaetan pointed to it, his finger threatening. "Yes? No?" When Noemi stared in boiling silence, he plucked the ruined cake off the tray and shoved it into his mouth. "Uck. Banana," he complained, words muffled.

"You need to pay for that."

"Thought you weren't customer service. What do you care?" To Jonas's dismay, Gaetan settled onto the stool beside him. He rested his chin on his fist and said something Jonas missed, though it set Noemi off.

Noemi swore at Gaetan, and her manager, Vera—a middle-aged woman, and the only employee in the shop who was older than twenty—picked this moment to start paying attention. She plucked a barista from an espresso machine and shifted her into place before the register, then marched Noemi into the kitchen for a talking-to.

"Guess that was my bad," Gaetan said without a hint of remorse.

"Yeah, I guess it was," Jonas mumbled. He roughly flipped to a new page in his textbook, even though he hadn't finished with the last.

"You know, if you're angling for that you're out of luck."

Jonas didn't know what Gaetan was talking about. He scrutinized his math homework, expecting it would have the explanation he needed.

"You're not her type," Gaetan added.

Whatever that meant. What wasn't Noemi's type? Skinny? Pierced? An underwhelming student? Whichever case Gaetan was implying didn't bother him. What bothered him was the implication that Jonas was angling for anything.

"Noemi doesn't like guys." Gaetan shrugged.

Jonas hated how much this disappointed him. Her preferences were none of his business. Still, the thought that he would be sexually and romantically invisible to her gave him a nauseated feeling like a bellyful of wasps. Like a chestful of wasps. His entire bloodstream surged with every agitated insect imaginable.

Then he remembered that she had dated Gaetan's friend. Or something. He knew nothing about Noemi's private life, and he shouldn't unless she wanted to tell him.

But even though he didn't want to be *that guy*—the guy who got territorial with another over a girl whose feelings were none of his business—he resented Gaetan just as much for being *that guy* along with him. So, Jonas chose to be petty.

"She doesn't like you, so she must not like men?" Jonas asked. All of the mirth drained from Gaetan's expression, and Jonas was sure that he was about to have his nose broken for the second time that year.

"You don't know shit. I'm giving you advice."

"Yeah, you're real generous." Jonas tried to pivot back to his homework, but before he could Gaetan's hand came crashing into the side of his head. It was a tap, really, but he happened to catch the cartilage of his ear so it folded painfully.

Before Gaetan could hit Jonas again (or before Jonas gave in to the urge to choke the life out of him), Noemi stormed out of the kitchen, past the counter, and toward the door. She pulled her Hummingbird T-shirt over her head, loosening her bun and sending a hair tie skidding across the floor in the process. Without her uniform, she was clothed in what looked to Jonas like a black bra with a lot of extraneous, crisscrossing straps, the purpose of which he couldn't begin to guess. He gathered his things and pushed past Gaetan, stooped to grab her hair tie off the floor, and nearly fell over when his backpack tipped off his shoulder to the ground.

Regaining his composure, he jogged out the glass door and after her. Though Noemi was clearly angry, Jonas had to chuckle at the sight of a mother hustling her child out of the way of the one-woman stampede, leveling a disapproving look at the half-clothed sixteen-year-old.

"Were you fired?" he asked once he finally caught up with her.

"I was sent home for the day." She stopped and gave him a once-over, incredulous as to how he had ended up on the sidewalk beside her.

Jonas passed his backpack from one arm to the next as he slipped out of his hoodie. When he handed it to her, Noemi wrinkled her nose, disapproving, but she took the sweatshirt anyway and shrugged it on. Then she resumed clomping toward home.

"This is a top, you know," she said some minutes later, once they were away from the storefronts and on the grass-lined sidewalks closer to Lamplight.

It took Jonas a moment to realize she was talking about the bra-like crop top. His eyes wandered the length of her slim figure. He caught himself before he could linger too long.

"Sorry if I embarrassed you," she said.

"I'm not embarrassed."

"*I'm* a little embarrassed." Noemi finally slowed, and the muscles in her shoulders slackened. "Not for storming out. Mainly for getting kicked out in front of everyone. I'm not embarrassed for being angry. Maybe I'm a little embarrassed for showing it. He was being a shit to *you*, and I made it about me. Are *you* okay?"

"I'm fine," Jonas said. "Honestly, I don't care that much what Gaetan Kelly says about me. I wasn't even paying attention. Seems like he gives a lot of people crap. Let it be his issue."

She stopped, receded into the navy cocoon of his hoodie. It was big on her, and her fingers just barely peeked out from the edges of his sleeves. Pink polish chipped away from her short nails. Those fingers were uncertain—they reminded him of subterranean animals, sniffing cautiously at the edges of their dens. Jonas became aware of how ragged the cuffs of the hoodie were, how he sometimes absently caught himself chewing at them when his mind wandered in class, and he hoped she wouldn't notice.

"I wish I could think like that. Sometimes I get lost in the moment," she said, "and I just want everyone to know exactly what I think. It's like starting a fire, but then I take stock of everything that's going to burn down around me and wish I'd reacted differently."

"You got in trouble for telling off some asshole. I like that you don't take shit." She was forceful and surly, and she seemed so confident. Jonas had thought these were things that drew him to her, but the gaps in her armor—he liked those better. Those he could understand.

"Most people call that being a bitch."

"Well, I don't think you need to pretend to be okay with someone that you're not okay with. You're not a robot."

She pulled her lips inward, biting a smile. "You're a considerate person, Jonas."

He didn't know if this was true, if he was particularly considerate, but he must have said something right, so he could live with her assessment.

"I'm much more judgmental than you," she continued. "And you're very laid back. I admire that."

"I try." He knew he was quiet, that he sat on the outskirts of conversations, working hard to listen while giving the appearance of being off in his own world. If he weren't laid back, his life would be a lot angrier. Bullies tended to pick their victims based on who was most reactive. Maybe that was why Gaetan singled out Noemi, but that was his fault, not hers. Jonas lost his cool once, beat the lights out of a classmate he barely knew. What Noemi had described, the fire she couldn't put out—it was not so unfamiliar a feeling.

Noemi skipped dinner that night, and she didn't emerge from her room until after everyone else in the house had retired to their respective beds. Jonas lay awake in his, reading *Macbeth* for English. Only the small bedside lamp lit his room, its warm, dull glow casting a haze of taxidermy bird shadows against the ceiling.

Through the wedge of hallway darkness created by his half-open door, he saw Noemi emerge from her own bedroom, though he didn't hear her—the foam earplugs he wore each night were already in. She seemed younger without her heels and manicured outfits, barefoot and clad in a loose-fitting T-shirt and cotton shorts. A pair of work boots dangled off the tips of her fingers. In any other house, she may have been heading to the bathroom, but all the bedrooms in Lamplight were suites.

She stood, head tilted to one side, and swayed gently like a tulip bowing to a breeze. She seemed to be listening for something—signs that any adults were awake, perhaps—and when she turned toward his bedroom door, Jonas diverted his attention back to his book and hoped she hadn't caught him watching.

He read to the bottom of the page, but his brain absorbed nothing, the words never making it past his pupils. When he hazarded a look back at the hallway, Noemi had gone.

Jonas crept to the bottom of the stairs, expecting to see the headlights of Lyle's car retreating into the night, but all he saw through the window was Noemi stepping out of the house and onto the lawn alone.

The choice to follow or not confronted him. He knew well what it was like to have a bad day and want to be alone. But earlier that afternoon, when she'd run out of work and he'd followed her, he'd managed to be of use, to smooth over whatever rough thing had been gnawing at her, even if just a little.

Jonas murmured a curse and searched the closet by the door for shoes. He found a pair of sandals—worn and practical and property of Diana if he had to guess—and he put them on his too-large feet so that his heels hung over the edges. Though the days were still late-summer-tinged, the night was chilly, and his skin soon grew numb to the whipping of the cold, wet grass.

Jonas slow-jogged behind her. He whisper-yelled her name.

Even when he'd removed the earplugs and transferred them to pocket of his pajama bottoms, it was difficult to judge the volume of his own voice, whether she would hear him. He worried she was sleepwalking, but he didn't know whether sleepwalking people had the wherewithal to don practical footwear before wandering outside.

He hadn't brought his phone; he wore only a T-shirt and a pair of flannel pants now soaked to the ankles. Noemi's clothes were dark, her hair was dark, and he nearly lost sight of her when she turned into a field of lupines that he recognized from the brochure at Hilda's diner.

Somehow a frog found its way between the curve of Jonas's foot and the dirty, dented sandal, and he squirmed when its slick, strange back shivered against him. The boy and the frog leapt away from each other.

Jonas's eyes searched the field.

Noemi was gone.

He ran to the place where he had last seen her, taking awkward, jumpy steps to avoid squishing any other wildlife. The moon was eyelash thin and shed little light, but finally he found her silhouette, a dark stroke of black against the blue-green tree line of a forest edge. Far enough from the house now, he yelled her name, but it came back high and hoarse, and he choked on the final syllable.

Keeping Noemi in view was harder under the canopy of leaves. They scratched out even the flimsy aid of starlight. Listening for Noemi, he heard not just her steps but those of every nocturnal animal until he was surrounded by sighing grass and creaking wood. Crickets screamed from every direction, and his head ached. Jonas replaced his earplugs, pushed the sound out. He stopped trying to hear her and focused instead on running to where Noemi had last been, on closing the stretch of space between them before she could disappear completely.

Then the trees parted.

Jonas stood on the shore of a lake as huge as memory.

He felt Noemi's hand on his wrist.

She pulled him back through the trees by his arm, reprimanding him all the way. With her back turned to him, he only got a vague impression of what she was saying, though he decided this was probably for the best.

They finally stopped when they reached the lupines. Noemi released his hand and whirled on him, shook her head in disapproval, then grabbed him once more and resumed her enraged march back to Lamplight.

She didn't lead him into the inn but instead to an empty, narrow, two-story stable that sat in the back of the property. Noemi slammed the barn door behind them, then directed Jonas up a ladder to the lofted second floor with the jab of one finger. He climbed first, then waited for her to follow.

The walls had been decorated with papier-mâché horses. They didn't appear mounted but instead seemed to be passing through the walls, heads and front legs of unicorns and mares emerging from the wood as though they galloped across dimensions. Fairy lights tented the room, strung from the ceiling and cupped painstakingly in tissue paper flowers. He envisioned Noemi folding each of them by hand. At the center, a swinging daybed heaped with white linen hung suspended on thick, rough ropes. *That* Noemi could not have hung herself. Jonas wondered how long it had been there. Had his father, the furniture maker, helped give someone else's kid a second bedroom? A wisp of jealousy swirled within him.

"Pay attention."

He turned to face her, and as he rotated she pushed him gently toward the bed. He let himself stagger backward onto it. It swung beneath him, and he tipped forward, nearly pitching onto the floor. Noemi stopped the motion of the swinging bed with her knees, one between Jonas's legs and the other alongside his left calf.

"You need to listen to me, Jonas."

"I'm listening." He removed the earplugs.

"What you did tonight was really dangerous. You cannot go into those woods alone."

"I wasn't alone. You were there." *She* had been the one to go on her own.

She sighed, then sat down next to him. He held the swing steady with his sandaled feet flat on the wooden floor.

"Just because we live together doesn't mean that you can sneak around sticking your nose in my business."

"What were you doing?"

"It doesn't matter." Noemi set her jaw and glared straight ahead with a look that might have cast him to stone had she turned it on him.

"I wasn't trying to spy on you." It hadn't felt like that at the time, but now it did. Now it felt like he had watched something more private than if he had seen whatever she did when she took photos with Lyle. "I thought you were asleep. Or—" *That you were upset. That I could help. That we could be friends.* All the possibilities he'd entertained when he left Lamplight now felt silly pressing into the back of his throat. That he'd assumed anything about the way she felt embarrassed him. They were still near-strangers, after all. Finally, he finished: "Or something."

Noemi's top lip curved upward in a smooth hill. He tucked his own bottom lip sideways under his front teeth, scraped the hole his lip ring would fill again come morning. When he was in middle school, other boys teased him for having "girly lips," a red, snake-bitten mouth they blamed on lipstick, when that was just the way it had always been. They chapped in the winter, and in the summer gave him the appearance of a child who was constantly devouring cherry Popsicles.

"My friend, Lincoln—Amberlyn's brother—they found his body in that woods. You remember."

"Yeah." How could he forget?

"I go there sometimes still. I didn't for a while, but I'm fine with it now. Well, not fine, exactly, but close enough. I grew up here, and I know my way around. But I guess I'd feel better if my friends didn't go there alone anymore. I don't mean to be controlling. I just don't want anyone else to get hurt." She tilted her head, searching for the right things to say. "When I saw you, it just felt like a really close call."

Jonas nodded. Were Noemi and Lyle counting him as a friend? He'd grown up surrounded by the same people for so long that he'd doubted he still had the ability to make new friends. His friends from his old school...they had been strangers at first, and there must have been some transitional acquaintanceship somewhere in between, but Jonas could barely recall how it had happened. It was much easier recognizing he was now in the midst of those friendships waning. Distance and circumstance chipped away at something that had never seemed ephemeral until he'd moved to Shivery.

"You live here too now, and you can go where you want. I guess I just want you to know why it bothered me. I can take you out to the woods sometime if you're curious. During the day. If you want to walk back there, just let me know, and we can go together."

"I get it." He sort of got it. He wasn't sure if he bought that she was worried about his safety, but he could understand how her going there might be like visiting a grave. Jonas didn't want to become a tourist of something so intimate to someone else.

"I cleaned up the stables to have somewhere to go that wasn't always full of other people." She gestured around the loft with only her head. "I hate never being alone at home."

He'd wanted to ask her about the water, about the newspaper articles he had read describing the body found on the forest floor, miles from the nearest lake or river. As usual, he'd been too slow to gather the courage, and now she had changed the subject.

"Don't come in here without me either. Not because it's dangerous. But this is my room, and you aren't allowed."

Jonas leaned, playfully knocked his shoulder into hers. She mirrored the movement, then rose and approached the ladder.

When he returned to his room, he showered. He washed the dirt and grass from his legs and the leaves from his hair. Pieces of the forest gathered in the shower base where they became insignificant. The lake, too, drained away as Jonas began to doubt what he had seen. The moon may have bathed a forest clearing in light so it only looked like an ocean stretched between the trees. Otherwise, Noemi would have told the police or Amberlyn. What was the purpose of keeping a lake a secret, if that was where Link had drowned?

Jonas wrote the names of everyone he had recently met on the shower wall, invisible, with the edge of the peppermint soap someone had left for him. He surrounded them with stick-figure trees.

NOEMI

When Noemi returned to her room that night, there was a text waiting on her phone.

> Who is the guy with the crooked nose?

Who? Noemi texted back, though she knew what Unknown meant. Jonas had facial features that were delicate and sharp. His jaw, cheekbones, the bridge of his nose—somehow all both fine and pronounced. But his nose in particular, when viewed from straight on, had a slight curve to one side, as though it had been broken and healed divergent. Noemi didn't mind this little imperfection. Jonas had a good face. He had dark, thoughtful eyes. She found his lips pretty, even if his piercing was out of place.

He lives with you now?

If you knew who he was, why ask?

Link hadn't been the jealous type, which made Noemi that much more suspicious of Unknown. Though what would he have to be jealous of? For Noemi to admit just how cute, how sweet Jonas was would have been cruel. Regardless, Unknown seemed to see everything. Maybe he could see right through to the little corner of her that liked her job more now that Jonas accompanied her to Hummingbird after school.

Link had always been far away, his head in outer space. He was good at drawing, but teachers discouraged it because he had a habit of doodling during classes. His legs were so long that there was no space for them under his desk, so they bent into the aisles like batwings. Even the art teacher had thrown him out of class, though in that case it was for using a found rat carcass in a project. For someone like Gaetan, that may have been an attempt at mockery or rebellion, but Link had had genuine intentions. Before she'd started spending time with him, Noemi had occasionally run into him spray painting something on the wall of an abandoned gas station. He converted derelict buildings into canvasses for artwork, but never canvasses that displayed beautiful things. Link painted toilets running across brick walls on chicken legs or bruised, taffy-stretched people vomiting colorful streams of bile.

The first time Link asked her out had been while they waited for their bus to pull away from school at the end of the day. She was about to finish ninth grade, Link tenth. Lyle took a different bus to one of the nicer developments in Shivery, and Noemi rode with Link and Gaetan—Gaetan brainstorming cruel nicknames for freshmen, Link quietly distracting him with lewd drawings in his notebook. Usually, after school, the bus wasn't crowded, and she could sit with her back to the window in a seat of her own and read. One day Link and Gaetan got on the bus and settled in behind her so Gaetan could knee the back of her seat. Link had barely sat before jumping to his feet again and sliding up one row to shuffle into the edge of her bench, his skinny, mile-long legs splayed seemingly everywhere.

Noemi drew herself upward, the edge of the window digging into her shoulder blades. She created room for him and folded her own legs neatly so that Link had at least half the space to himself. He wore the same canvas jacket over the same black hoodie every day, faded from wear, not washing. He pulled his hood down so his fox-red hair spilled out around his face. His eyes were lighter than his sister's: Amberlyn's were brown, but his had always been blue-gray, like water in a drain.

"What are you reading?" he'd asked.

"A book."

Gaetan snorted.

"A century-old book of fairy tales from the store where my mom works," she clarified. "It's interesting, but I hate the way the pages feel. I found a dead beetle between two of them."

"Have you ever smelled cat pee?"

"I—what?"

"It's worse than the mildewy smell books can get. I mean, maybe not after one hundred years."

"This is painful," grumbled a voice from the back seat.

"I saw some photos online," Link continued, "of these old manuscripts written by monks that had cat pee or paw prints or dead mice in them. And the monk had written, like, 'This fucking cat!' Except in Old French or whatever."

"*Le* fucking *chat.*"

"Incorrect. Obviously," Noemi informed Gaetan through the space between her seat-back and window.

"I've started collecting found notes." Link opened the front pouch of his backpack. The zipper must have broken because he'd fastened it instead with safety pins. Inside was an uneven stack of paper—some sheets lined and yellow, and some small, white, and torn. "Like this one. It's my favorite so far." A handwritten scrap in nearly rubbed-away pencil said, *Your life is beautiful.* "I found it in a library desk drawer. It was the only thing in there. I think it would be cool to find a book with a bug in it, or cat prints or something. It sort of adds to the story of whatever the words say."

"I'll piss on your papers for you," Gaetan volunteered.

"Gee, thanks."

Link asked her to walk home with him, and when Noemi said that walking from the school back to their neighborhood in Shivery would take an hour, he'd simply agreed, oblivious to the fact that she'd meant this to be an indirect way of declining. But when he'd seemed undeterred, she'd followed him off the bus. Link didn't look back, but Noemi did. Amberlyn gesticulated wildly, and Gaetan gaped. Noemi grinned and flipped him off, then descended the steps.

She doubted sometimes how much Link really paid attention when other people spoke. It was different from the half-listening adults had done when she was a child. Link's mind made strange connections, drew what seemed to Noemi like non sequiturs into conversation. Asked something as simple as "Are you hungry?" and he might answer with a story of how he saw footage of a python swallowing a goat.

For all his idiosyncrasies, because he was kind, easygoing, patient, and good-natured, Lincoln Miller was the only person with whom Noemi had never found herself exasperated. She never snapped at him and then wished she hadn't. When she wanted to be alone, she could do it with Link there. He befriended a family of orphaned raccoons that lived in his yard, made them mac and cheese. Sometimes Link smoked, and for whatever reason, Noemi didn't mind the scent of tobacco when it was on him, braided with his own shower-aversive scent of sweat and winter air. Even in summer he was always cool.

In the July between ninth and tenth grade, she went to see

Blue Velvet at the theater in Shivery with Gaetan and Link. Being around Link usually meant being around Gaetan, and no one in the trio but Noemi really seemed to mind the third wheel. This time Gaetan had brought a girl—one who'd already graduated—and when they piled into the cab of Gaetan's Jeep, Noemi had to sit between Link's legs. They were late to the show, stuck at the end of the row closest to the screen with Gaetan and his date behind them. The two kicked Noemi's chair, giggled, kissed, and generally annoyed everyone around them so much that Noemi was embarrassed she'd even walked in with them. She and Link left midway through. As he walked her back home, he took slow steps so he didn't outpace her with his stride. When he hustled a turtle out of the center of the road, she halted traffic and scolded drivers through the glass of their windshields.

The only time Noemi had ever seen Link angry, it had been directed at Gaetan. Someone had left a vase of coral-pink peonies on the front porch of Lamplight on the morning of Valentine's Day her sophomore year. They arrived without a card, but he'd asked her unsubtly about her favorite flowers via a messenger app a few nights before. When she asked Link about them—in Gaetan's truck on the way to school—he seemed surprised, and said, "I can't afford flowers." Then his face flushed, cheeks pink as his sister's, when they were usually so pallid.

"You're supposed to say yes, man," Gaetan said.

The flush bled from Link's face. His expression grew cold and white. A shadow twitched across his mouth like a vein through polished marble. Gaetan kept his eyes on the road, uncharacteristically quiet. Neither boy said anything, and the air buzzed jagged between them. At the school parking lot, Link poured out the passenger door. Not many people could have stood beside a truck that rode as high as Gaetan's and still been tall enough to fill the door, but Link could.

Link took a ragged breath, seemed about to say something. Then he turned and stalked toward the school, not waiting for either of his friends to follow. In his place, Noemi would have unleashed her full fury on whichever friend had sent a gift of courtship on her behalf and shouted her disapproval in no uncertain terms. Gaetan would express his disgust with fists. Link's quiet disapproval was almost more frightening. Unbuckling her seatbelt and shuffling across the bench to the door, Noemi looked back at Gaetan. He turned away from her, toward his knuckles tight and translucent on the steering wheel, even though the car was parked, the engine off, silent.

"Sorry," he said. "I thought it would help."

"You don't need to say sorry to me. You should have at least warned him."

"I did!" He nearly shouted, but then corrected, quieter. "I did. I mean, I offered, and he said *no*. I sent them anyway and figured it would be fine."

"I know you wanted to help," she said. It had been a while since she'd felt anything but annoyance for Gaetan. "I'm sure he knows too. But Valentine's flowers aren't really his way."

"Did you like them, at least?"

"Yeah, the flowers were fine. That's not the point. Where did you even get peonies in Minnesota in February?"

"I bought them. With drug money!" He said it a little too enthusiastically, and Noemi couldn't tell if he'd meant it as a joke.

"Forget I asked."

Noemi jogged across the parking lot to catch up with Link. A passing school bus momentarily erased him from view, but she finally reached him once she entered the doors that opened into the hall by the gymnasium. She called out to him, and he greeted her like it was the first time he'd seen her all morning, like nothing had happened.

Link and Noemi sat with Lyle and Amberlyn while Gaetan kept the company of a more criminal element. Then Link walked her to her locker outside of homeroom.

How he'd gotten the lock open she didn't know. It wouldn't have surprised her if he knew how to pick a combination padlock. The gift Link had intended was inside all along, and she knew immediately without needing to ask that it was from him. The material was simple: colored paper he could have easily acquired from the art room. Her books had become a forest floor for a paper diorama of trees, every leaf cut by hand, tiny rabbits and squirrels delicately folded with narrow ears and curling tails. A single hedgehog wore bristles made of paper cones that Link's long fingers had somehow avoided crushing.

"You can store your other books in my locker if you need to," he said over her shoulder. He held up a hand wrapped in Spider-Man Band-Aids and paper cuts, and wiggled his fingers.

Noemi hugged her chemistry book to her chest, pressing it against her as she'd never do with him. In all the time she'd known Link, they'd barely ever touched. The only time she could remember touching him was prom, though neither of them went. He'd asked and seemed relieved when she said she had no interest. Instead, they dressed up and went into the woods.

There, they danced. Her heels sunk into the dirt, so she took them off. She still had to stand on tiptoe or she'd get lost in his chest. Noemi was no shorter than average, but Link was still more than a foot taller, and her arms didn't rest comfortably on his shoulders. She pressed the heels of her hands against his thrift-store shirt, below his clavicles. The wind over the water played a soft song for them, like a distant violin coming from where the lighthouse sometimes stood. Dusk settled in, and fireflies blinked between trees like stars born and dying over and over until the rain chased them away. Link and Noemi hid under the leaves and waited for the rain to pass, and it did—as quickly as it had come. It was gone before the sun had fallen behind the horizon.

A week later, Link was dead.

THE LIGHTHOUSE

I dreamt there was a lake in the woods behind Lamplight. Rising from the water was a white lighthouse made of concrete and shaped like a human torso. Long appendages sprouted from its center, two insinuations of wings or fins. Where the head should have been, a blue, mercury-glass roof domed a lantern room. The lake had no shore, so I stood at the seam between it and the grass. Mud rose between my toes. I could not discern the time of day. The leaves and the grass and the water were graying. Beeches and maples eclipsed the structure at the water's edge, so tall now that I could have nestled in the crevices of their bark like a boxelder bug. The eye of the lighthouse blinked onto the water, swung its gaze in an arc toward the forest. The diffuse light at the edges of the beam illuminated dark figures looming between tree trunks, human-sized and featureless, detached shadows. They vanished under the light, reappeared in its wake. Everywhere was watching.

10

AMBERLYN

On Halloween, Amberlyn arrived at the Anderson house with
her dress in a garment bag slung over her arm, and she waved
from the porch as her father's Subaru Outback backed out of the
driveway. Lyle, who planned to go as David Bowie (as Jareth the
Goblin King), had enlisted Amberlyn's help with her makeup.
Normally that sort of thing was Noemi's job, but for some reason
Lyle had asked Amberlyn. The request delighted her—sent pinpricks up and down her legs—and Amberlyn watched more
makeup tutorials than she'd ever thought possible in preparation
for getting it right.

Amberlyn might not have been much for costumes on her
own, but as Lyle discussed her plans for the holiday, she had
eventually come around. She'd phoned it in last year, showing

up to Lamplight wearing a pointed witch's hat from Five Below. Now, Amberlyn unzipped her bag, and the shiny taffeta skirt of her gown rustled free, alternating from blue to purple in the light of Lyle's bedroom. The two of them had brainstormed Amberlyn's costume together and searched Halloween supply and thrift stores for parts. Amberlyn would wear a vintage prom dress with parts of a werewolf costume and go as Beauty *and* the Beast this year.

Lyle sat at the edge of her bed as Amberlyn deepened the hollows of her cheeks.

"I know it never looks great," Lyle said, "but I got a can of temporary spray paint for my hair. Hopefully it covers the green."

"We'll get it to look right. Now if you don't mind holding still."

The only makeup Lyle ever wore was her red lipstick—a signature part of her daily look—but she couldn't have done a worse job at the face paint herself. Amberlyn's strokes were gentle and attentive, but her lines were wobbly in trembling hands. As she applied mascara, Lyle kept her eyes open despite the big black wand diving straight for her pupils. As she penciled in Lyle's eyebrows, Amberlyn rested the edge of her hand against her hairline.

"How old were you when you stopped trick-or-treating?" Lyle asked.

"I think middle school was the last time." She combed Lyle's eyebrow with her fingernails. "I wore the same costume the last three years in a row, from sixth to eight grade: a generic pink princess dress. It was huge the first year but fit the way it was meant to by the end. Though by then the hem was all holey from being dragged around the sidewalk."

"I used to have to take Parker once we got old enough that our parents were okay with us going out without them. I think that's what put me off trick-or-treating." Lyle crinkled her nose with the luxury of a person who still had a brother to annoy her. "Otherwise I'd probably be going now. Parker still goes with his friends, actually."

Amberlyn released Lyle's face. She applied some eye shadow to a brush, then absently swiped it onto the back of her wrist in a fat, gray strip.

"I never went trick-or-treating with Link," she said. "Gaetan's older brother took the two of them, and by the time he died, they were old enough to go on their own. I just went with my mom when I was little."

"I always forget Gaetan had a brother."

"Well, Elijah was a lot older than Gaetan, so it's not like you'd have seen him around. Even Link doesn't remember him much. *Didn't* remember him." Amberlyn rolled her eyes, like Link existing in past tense was just a silly little detail. Though, of course, it wasn't.

"Do you see Gaetan much these days?"

"Only at school." Amberlyn shook her head. "He doesn't come over much without Link around, though sometimes he helps with stuff around the house. Mulching leaves and stuff like that."

"Do you ever go back to the woods anymore? We haven't

taken pictures there in a while, so I wasn't sure..." Lyle trailed off, left the thought open. Amberlyn got the sense she was supposed to finish it, but she couldn't guess where Lyle might be leading.

"I haven't been back, no," Amberlyn said. "I pass it on the way to Lamplight, obviously, but I have no reason to go back if it's not to be in photos. Not that I've been actively avoiding it. But then... it doesn't give me such a great feeling when I see it." She placed the brush on Lyle's dresser and ran a lock of red hair through loose fists, one over the other again and again, ready to climb out of the room on a ladder of her own hair. "It makes me think of what happened there, of course. Or what might have happened."

They had posed for several photographs in those woods, before Link had died there. Amberlyn kept one on her phone: Lyle and herself, taken at sunrise. They almost disappeared against the forest, dressed in black veils draped across antlers Noemi had made from branches and plaster. Looking at it afterward, Amberlyn could only guess at which figure was her: with their faces obscured, the two silhouettes in the photo could have been anyone, and the antlers made it hard to tell that Amberlyn was nearly half a foot taller. At the time, she and Lyle had made ghost sounds...*oohs* and *boos* back and forth from under their headdresses, not permitted by their photographer to move or look at each other, but giggling quietly. Now there was no one Amberlyn recognized in the photo— strange that one of the eerie people in it was herself staring back.

"It's a shame," Amberlyn continued. "We used to have a lot of fun there."

"If you ever want to go back," Lyle said, "make new memories there, I would go with you. It doesn't have to be for photos. We could go, just the two of us, and take all the time you need to figure out how you feel about it."

"It might not be such a bad idea." Her eyes met Lyle's. "Would it be weird of us to go without Noemi?"

"No," Lyle said. She sounded uncertain.

Lyle had a habit of drawing on her skin with pen during class. It reminded Amberlyn a little of Link, who'd often colored his fingernails in with Sharpie throughout the day. For Link it had seemed a fidgety habit. Lyle was more patient. She took mainly honors classes, so Amberlyn's only chance to watch her do it was during the Spanish class they had together. On Friday, Lyle had spelled out L♥VE on the fingers of her left hand with black ink.

These letters were still on Lyle's hand come Halloween, though they had faded to gray and blurred, the heart on her middle finger looking more now like an inverted tear. Amberlyn walked beside her into the forest, a blanket of sunset-colored leaves rustling underfoot. Though Amberlyn knew her friend preferred the bulkier headphones she usually wore around her neck, Lyle had switched to a pair of earbuds they could share. Most of the music Lyle listened to had been made decades before her birth.

"Love → Building on Fire" played into Lyle's right ear and Amberlyn's left. They kept pace easily, the cords connecting their heads never tightening. The slipping sunlight reflected off the blue satin of Amberlyn's cheap, vintage dress as it would the surface of water, the color calm, quiet, but arresting against the warm shades of autumn and day's end.

"That color suits you," Lyle said.

When Amberlyn looked to see Lyle's eyes on the bodice of the dress, she became very aware of the body she inhabited, folding her arm across her torso so her fingers came to rest along her ribs. As she did, her bare elbow touched the soft curve of Lyle's arm, and the rest of Amberlyn's body may well have ceased to exist.

She didn't know what to expect from this return to the woods. The same puddle from five months ago, strands of Link's red-gold hair floating on its surface... An outline of flame-orange leaves demarcating the face-down position in which he had died...

Amberlyn used to love spending time in these trees with Lyle and Noemi. She had never been there with Lyle alone before. What was wrong with her that she was so excited to revisit it now, with Lyle, when she was supposed to be thinking about Link? Her mind wandered to the possibility of her fingers threaded through Lyle's. She reminded herself of Link's cracked, blue lips. Letters spelled out *L♥VE* on Lyle's skin. Link was a pile of ash on a mantle. The world was ablaze with fall-flowering colors. The world was drowning in an ocean inch-deep.

Lyle stopped, plucked the earbud from her ear. "I'm not sure

where to go," she said, looking around for signs Am[...]
weren't there.

Of course there would be no markers showing them [...]
place where Link had died. Maybe it was better that t[...]
seemed untouched, the same version of itself that Amberly[...]
find when she looked at Noemi's photos. What had the[...]
looking for anyway? A headstone, sprung up out of nothing?
had made no mark on the forest. It had swallowed the men[...]
of him.

"No worries," Amberlyn said. "I didn't expect us to find t[...]
exact spot where—Link's spot. I'm glad we came. It's probabl[...]
better that we don't know exactly which tree they found him under
or anything. It's easier to think of this as more than just a place
where he died."

"Really?" Her expression uncertain, Lyle nodded, reassuring herself. "That's good then. I thought—I thought we might find
water...or something that would give you answers. When I was
here before, I saw something that might make sense to you. But
I don't know my way around this place as well as Noemi does,
apparently. If just walking in circles helped, I'm glad. I wish I could
do more."

Had Lyle hoped to solve a mystery the police couldn't?
Identify a dip in the ground once filled with rainwater two seasons ago? As naive as that plan may have been, it made Amberlyn
smile that Lyle would take on that impossible task in an attempt
to provide her with closure. Lyle's eyes searching for something

…at would console Amberlyn, trying now to retrace those steps… …or some reason, the image of Lyle standing in this place, thinking …f her when she wasn't around, worrying for her, wanting to do something—

It was all too much, and Amberlyn wanted to throw her arms around the smaller girl and hold her closer than anything else could ever get. Within her fist the song had changed, and the earbud now sang Please, please, please through muscle and bone.

And then, above it, Noemi asked, "What are you doing here?"

While her presence surprised Amberlyn, it didn't worry her until she saw Lyle stiffen, like she'd been caught picking at a dessert before dinner. Noemi and Jonas were both also already dressed in their costumes: hers was some kind of nightmarish tooth fairy, as many parts glitter as it was fake blood and enamel extending the corners of her frown. Jonas wore plain clothes and a black, cat-ear headband likely lent to him. He rested with his head slightly tilted, his hands in his jeans' pockets, far less perturbed than his companion.

"I wanted to show Amberlyn what you showed me," Lyle said. She steepled her hands and bounced her fingers off one another. "Why's Jonas here?"

What you showed me. That sounded more specific than the "water…or something" explanation Lyle had given moments ago. It seemed she had been hoping to lead Amberlyn to something specific after all; it was unlike Lyle to be so elusive.

"All right, then," Noemi said. "Let's go together, I guess." She

wore a pastel dress like a ballerina's. The gauzy, bloodstained skirt looked like it had been artfully shredded, and Noemi rolled one of the dangling bits between fingertips painted mold-blue. She wasn't annoyed; she was nervous.

Noemi marched through the woods, outpacing everyone even in her platform shoes. She grasped Jonas's wrist and pulled him along behind her, and he parlayed that into holding her hand.

Noemi tended to treat people like stray animals: appreciation was measured like treats, and nothing was up for discussion because if they didn't like something, they could just go beg for someone else's attention. Every decision she made was a directive, and *that* behavior was with the people she liked. Most others she just ignored until they did something to annoy her. With Amberlyn, who was especially forgiving, her spikes didn't matter so much, but Jonas had to live with her.

"I'm less surprised Jonas seems to have a crush on her," Lyle whispered, "than I am about the fact she doesn't give him hell for it."

"What are we looking for?" Amberlyn asked. She wasn't completely above gossip, but Noemi's love life didn't sit foremost on her mind at the moment. "I thought we were here for Link."

"I'm sorry. We are. You'll have to see it to believe it. I didn't want to say in case I couldn't find it. I thought bringing it up without being able to show you would do more harm than good. But I hope seeing it—"

They both bumped gently into Jonas's back, not realizing he and Noemi had stopped.

Lyle had not, as it turned out, been searching for a dip or puddle.

Amberlyn didn't know these woods as well as her friends did. They'd taken many pictures there without her, and long before Noemi's photography hobby had taken its hold, they'd played there as children. But Amberlyn thought she'd at least learned the trees well enough that she understood what had happened to her brother. No one would have killed Link. Everyone agreed it had not been a murder or suicide, but an accident. Based on the contents of his lungs and stomach, he had not been swimming elsewhere only to dry-drown here later. That he had asphyxiated in shallow rainwater, as unlikely as it seemed, was the story that Amberlyn—that everyone—had accepted.

Or perhaps "everyone" hadn't.

How long had Lyle known about this lake? It spread out in front of them, so large Amberlyn couldn't see the trees on the other side. Link had been found in the dirt, not dredged from water. There should not even have been water here today. *When was the last time it had rained? Hadn't it rained this week?* After everything, even Link had known these woods better than Amberlyn.

This place belonged to everyone but her.

Jonas bent for a closer look at a boat tethered to a stone dock at the water's edge. It *bump-bumped* against the structure as though in greeting, as though to say to Amberlyn, *I too have a secret history with Link.*

"Was the boat here when we came by the other night?" Jonas asked. "I didn't notice."

Amberlyn was happy to see Lyle's face register the offense she herself felt, though neither questioned aloud why Noemi would take Jonas here before Link's own sister. Then Lyle shaded her eyes with her palm and peered into the impossible distance.

"Probably. It was dark," Noemi said. Then, "Lyle." Without confirming she had Lyle's attention, Noemi pointed across the water. "That wasn't there when you were here either."

There, in the middle of the unmapped lake larger than the forest that hid it, was a lighthouse. Little more than a gray sliver in the distance, but Amberlyn saw it. The trees ringing the lake—oak trees taller that the redwoods in California, the ones cars famously passed through—overshadowed the structure, scraping the sky in every direction. Their branches spread at odd angles, casting the four visitors under shade.

"The leaves are still green here," Lyle murmured.

"That's your takeaway?" Noemi had begun fanning herself with a wand shaped like a cracked molar. Though the day hadn't exactly been cold to begin with, the weather had warmed considerably since they'd arrived at the lake.

"Have you taken the boat to the lighthouse?" Jonas asked.

"No."

"Why not?"

"Going alone seems unwise." Noemi pitched a stone into the water, but instead of skipping it plunked once and vanished.

Link would probably have gone without a thought. What she'd said was that she hadn't gone *alone,* and Amberlyn could see her brother and Noemi rowing out to the lighthouse together. He would have told his sister about something like this, if they'd even made it across without tiring.

But then again, he was Link. He could have found a volcano filled with rubber ducks in his own backyard and not thought to share the knowledge unless someone asked.

"Did you want us to go with you?" Lyle asked. She too had an adventurous streak that might draw her toward the boat if someone else didn't talk her out of it.

"Certainly not." Noemi pushed past Jonas and knelt beside the boat, where she began tugging at the ropes.

"I don't understand," Amberlyn finally said. She could say nothing more.

"I was afraid if I tried to bring you here, I wouldn't find it," Noemi said. "I tried to take the police here, but it was like it had disappeared. The lake is fickle, and I didn't want to taunt you, coming out here and finding nothing." She pushed the boat away from the shore. It slid through the water, curling it into tiny, translucent waves.

"So Link drowned here?" Amberlyn asked. "What do you mean it disappeared? Did it dry up?" As soon as she asked it, she wished she hadn't.

This wasn't just some flooded, sunken part of the forest floor. The boat, the lighthouse...the size of the clearing. She felt like a child, struggling to make sense of an adult's riddle; she used to feel that way with Link sometimes. When they were little, he'd had a tendency to frame things so they seemed like jokes. He'd say, "We're foraging for dinner" when he meant they'd be eating leftovers. Amberlyn would call his bluffs before learning he had never been trying to trick her at all. Today she'd believed Lyle's hope to find the place he'd drowned was mere fantasy, and now here she was, the only one without a clue how attainable this quest had really been.

Noemi watched the boat, now drifting several yards from the dock. "I don't know. The police accused me of lying. I tried to show them, but I couldn't find it either. Not until after they left. I told them it had been a long time since I was back here, and that maybe an old pond had looked a lot bigger when I was a kid, that I was misremembering."

Though no one spoke, Amberlyn could sense without looking at her friends that they were waiting for her to do something. Explode. Disintegrate. But she wasn't angry. She didn't even feel betrayed. She felt more like a ravine that had dried up, a pattern of cracks in parched earth.

"Did you come here with Link?" Amberlyn hadn't meant it to be an accusation, and she hoped it didn't seem that way. The question came out small, frightened, the way it had tasted inside.

"Yeah." Noemi nodded. "A few times. It was obviously a strange place, but it didn't seem dangerous. It didn't feel ominous until after Link died. I'm sorry, Amber. I never would have brought him in these woods if I'd thought for a second—"

She'd used the name only Link sometimes called her—so intimate, Noemi never would have done it on purpose. Link must have talked about her to Noemi sometimes. Amberlyn didn't mind so much, hearing Noemi call her *Amber*. In this word, Link lingered.

"It's not your fault." Amberlyn approached her, set her hand on Noemi's shoulder. Noemi looked at it like it was a leaf that had landed there—something that didn't belong. "Link could take care of himself. He knew how to swim. I don't know why the police couldn't find a giant lake."

"I couldn't either," Lyle said.

"But there was no reason to think it wouldn't be perfectly safe for Link to know it existed. You don't need to worry so much about us, either. What happened to Link was a fluke, but if you're still anxious about it, none of us will come here alone." Amberlyn looked at Lyle and Jonas, waiting for confirmation.

"You shouldn't be the one comforting me," Noemi murmured, so quiet no one else could have heard.

"If it's so dangerous, *you* shouldn't have come out here on your own," Jonas said. He wasn't scolding Noemi. Just concerned. Amberlyn wondered what he was like when it was just the two of them, whether Noemi thought less about Link with Jonas around.

"Jonas followed me out here a few weeks ago," Noemi explained. "That's the only reason we even came out here today. He's been asking about it, pretending to be all casual, like he wasn't super curious."

Jonas shoved his hands into the front pockets of his hoodie, and his cheeks flushed. Like Noemi, he was olive-skinned with delicate features. They looked like one of those couples who could be cousins.

"Rules don't apply to Noemi," Lyle said.

"It's not dangerous if you know how to swim," she retorted.

"But Amberlyn said Link did."

"Yeah, but—I don't know. You guys don't get a weird feeling? I feel like someone's watching us." Noemi glanced quickly toward the trees as she said this, as though expecting someone to be standing at the edge of the clearing. Amberlyn followed her gaze but saw nothing, not even a squirrel.

The lake did unsettle her, but not in the sense that it made her feel watched. It was more than just the fact that Link had died there. They were trespassing. They just didn't know in whose home they trespassed. Someone had engineered the lighthouse. The outer walls of the tower had already half-crumbled. Yet apparently it had not been here when Noemi first showed Lyle the lake. It wasted away on an island, perhaps only reachable by the boat Noemi had just cast away. Amberlyn wondered what lay inside. At the same time, she didn't ever want to go near it.

"Do you know when the lighthouse went up?" she asked.

"Some point within the last year. Not sure. It's only here sometimes too. I could never tell whether it would be there until seeing for myself."

Lyle raised her eyebrows until they vanished beneath her poofy, goblin fringe. She looked the way Amberlyn felt. "If Link was on his own," she said, "we can't know what happened, but it can't help that you have all kinds of bad dreams about the forest. That's probably why it creeps you out. It's hard for Amberlyn too." Lyle flashed her a weak half smile. "Maybe we could all look at it with fresh eyes. Come here in a group. Make sure everyone can swim. Isn't Gaetan a lifeguard at the community center?"

"Let's not involve anyone else. Especially not Gaetan. He'd let us drown. And I like my dreams," Noemi said. "That's why I photograph them."

"Have you photographed any here?" Amberlyn asked.

"No. Not at the lake. I never took those kinds of photos with Link, and no one else was here. Plus, I think it's camera shy. It's never around unless I leave my camera outside the woods. But I try every once in a while anyhow."

"Maybe we can all make better memories here," Amberlyn suggested. "Start helping you with your photos again, by the water this time."

"You'd be okay with that?" Lyle asked.

Amberlyn nodded.

"I can swim." Jonas's fingers traced his bottom lip. His thumb tugged at the unpierced corner of his mouth, and his words warped around the gesture.

Just then, Noemi's phone vibrated. Amberlyn had never been able to get a signal even in the shallower part of the forest. Lyle and Jonas joined in watching as she checked it. Noemi's phone case was pink with bunny ears. She scowled at it, and the serious expression she directed at the cute case might have been funny if Amberlyn weren't so preoccupied.

"It wouldn't cooperate," Noemi said. "The lake." She slipped the phone back into her bag. "We shouldn't even be here anyway. Let's just stick with the *nobody-comes-here-without-the-group* idea, if that's okay with you."

She looked around at everyone, but her eyes settled on Amberlyn, who nodded. Together they walked back to Lamplight, and by the time they reached the lupine field, the talk had turned to everyone's favorite candy. Noemi liked York Peppermint Patties, Lyle, Twizzlers. Jonas, apparently, would eat anything and was already in trouble for, over the course of the week, surreptitiously devouring half the fun-sized Snickers that had been designated for trick-or-treaters.

Amberlyn said her favorites were Goetze's Caramel Creams and contributed nothing else to the conversation until they reached the inn and it was time to choose a movie. She didn't even particularly like caramel. Her favorites were Kit Kats: she liked their tidiness, their layers, the way they could be broken so cleanly and pieced out into even bites.

Link liked Caramel Creams, and that was what first popped into her head. Link had dreadful taste in candy: Cherry Mash, Red Hot Dollars, Mary Janes. Amberlyn wanted to go from house to house and collect all the Strawberry Bon Bons and Bit-O-Honeys other kids would toss. She might even eat them, let them melt on her tongue and wonder how they had tasted to him, why he had liked them.

She wanted to, but she wouldn't.

Instead, she would sit on the sofa in the living room of Lamplight, stiff beside Lyle in her ball gown, and think about water. She would think about a lake that the police and Lyle couldn't find, but which Noemi could—which Link had found.

Link was the sort of person who would dismiss perceived "magic" and instead work out the mechanics of it. Amberlyn had never believed in magic either, but she didn't need to dismantle it. After all, a fire would burn her whether or not she knew about the chemical reaction that produced it. If she and her brother both saw a stage magician perform a mind reading trick, neither of them would believe anyone's mind had really been read.

But where Link would roll the trick's logic through his head for the rest of the day, Amberlyn could simply trust there was an explanation without needing to know what it was. It was no wonder Link would go back to the lake alone, while Amberlyn could file it away as a thing that could never make any sense. It was as nonsensical as the fact that Link was dead, or that the Millers were expected to go on without him, to adjust their lives around the loss like some bizarre elastic family. Whether the lake was rainwater or just difficult to find—whether it was a cursed ocean that only existed when certain people were around to perceive it, like the crack of the proverbial tree falling in a forest—the truth of it wouldn't bring him back.

NOEMI

You brought them? Unknown asked. She didn't know how it worked. He had no phone, no voice, no body. He asked her, and his words formed in LED-illuminated text, no name or number attached. Unknown. He was still Unknown. He'd told her his name, but she less than half believed.

She looked at her phone, but she didn't text back.

Is that safe?

Answer me.

He may have meant it as a plea, but on her phone it was a demand, and she rolled her eyes.

Where does the lake come from?

She typed it. She sent it. He received it. He haunted the air she breathed and every electrical signal she transmitted through it. He knew her words without seeing or hearing them, with no eyes or ears to see or hear.

It's part of the forest.

That much is obvious. So helpful.

She'd always found him cryptic, but now that Link was dead, she also found him frustrating.

I don't know.

Link—or whoever this was—didn't want her to go to the woods. He didn't want Gaetan to go there, but he couldn't warn Gaetan, or even talk to him because he would absolutely go, would chop down every tree, burn it all down even if it landed him in jail. He didn't want Amberlyn going into the woods either, but he couldn't warn or talk to her any more easily than he could Gaetan. He told Noemi all of this.

My sister compartmentalizes, doesn't dwell
on things unless you remind her of them.

Or she dwells really hard and tucks
the dwelling down deep.

I could never tell.

It's safer if you don't go back.

Any of you.

But Noemi dreamed. Her dreams weren't safe. She made art from her dreams. She did what she wanted, and as usual, what she wanted was not the same as what Link wanted.

The first time Noemi brought Link to the woods behind her house, it was before the photographs and the dream journal and the endless ocean that was there sometimes and gone others. The woods were simply a collection of trees, a habitat for certain animals. Noemi was in ninth grade.

Everyone who rode on her bus to school had figured out that Gaetan lived with the Millers through much of the week. He boarded the bus with Link and Amberlyn most mornings, and he disembarked at their house most afternoons. On the days the bus picked him up at his own house, he didn't bring his lunch with him and instead stole food off of other people's trays, acting as though it were something he did out of fun rather than necessity. No one had the guts to interrogate him about the reason the Millers took care of him, but his classmates had been able to piece things together from fragmented whispers.

Gaetan and Elijah had different fathers, and it was Elijah's who had been Mrs. Kelly's true love. After Elijah had died, her second husband left. Left her, left Gaetan. Gaetan joked that even his own father had preferred his brother, despite Elijah's being another man's son. He joked in a way that wasn't really joking. It wasn't funny at all, and when Gaetan smiled, Noemi could see in his face the crack that had formed across him.

Elijah Kelly's funeral had been expensive. Without Gaetan's father, Mrs. Kelly had been the sole provider until her boyfriend entered the picture. Noemi knew more about him than most: she'd learned from Link that he was the younger brother of Elijah's father, who had also died. The boys called the boyfriend Uncle Stepdad, even though he hadn't married Mrs. Kelly. Link admitted he was afraid of Uncle Stepdad, and Gaetan, who admitted nothing, was too.

Noemi hated Gaetan because she hated bullies, but Uncle Stepdad was a bigger bully, and when Link told her about the cigarette burns on Gaetan's arms, she was furious. "I'm going to tell my mother, and she'll call the cops," she said.

"You can't. Please."

Noemi knew telling an adult was "right" on paper. It was right in every TV show or movie about abused children. It was right, albeit vaguely addressed back in her sixth-grade health classes. But in real life the consequences felt more complicated. Where would Gaetan go if the state got involved, pulled him out of his house? Link asked Noemi this, but she didn't have an answer. Could he move in with the Millers?

"Maybe," Link said. "I don't know what would happen. I know my parents would do the same thing your mom would do. And I get it." He yanked on the drawstrings of his hoodie, tight against his neck. "But I don't think Gate could forgive that."

One day, when Gaetan missed school and failed to respond to Link's texts, Noemi hatched a plan to go to his house and demand his release. Though Gaetan was a sophomore, he, like Link, was in Noemi's French class, and she would nurture her lie from this seed of truth, claiming Gaetan's help was essential to an imaginary group project. Link, whom Uncle Stepdad knew as one of Gaetan's friends, would stay out of sight, as Uncle Stepdad might be less likely to let Gaetan out of the house if Link asked.

Link was fifteen, nearly six-foot-five and still growing, but Noemi sensed his relief when they agreed he would not have to face Uncle Stepdad with her. He hid behind a tree at the end of the driveway as she marched up to the front door of the Kelly house. Uncle Stepdad filled the doorway, but Noemi stood her ground, insisting that Gaetan come with her so they could work on their nonexistent French project.

Uncle Stepdad leaned into the house and shouted, "Let the boy out! He's got homework!"

Noemi waited with her thumbs hooked under her backpack straps and surveyed the lawn quietly while Uncle Stepdad surveyed the top of her curly head. Then Uncle Stepdad touched her hair, dragged his palm down the curve of her curls, and mumbled something inaudible. She stiffened like a feral animal, breath caught in her throat, hot and rapid. Despite her towering shoes and voluminous hair, she was a whisper beside Uncle Stepdad. Her eyes met Link's across the length of the drive, and he stumbled out from behind the tree and onto the white clover of the Kelly lawn. But before Link could make himself known, Gaetan—still inches shorter than Link but already much tougher—materialized in the doorway, hunched and blinking. His posture changed when he saw Noemi, and he threw his stepfather's arm from her hair like it was a spiderweb blocking his path. Link slunk back behind the tree, while Gaetan walked with Noemi to the end of the driveway, his arm clinging to her shoulder and his bright blue eyes furious.

Noemi brought them to the woods near her house and overturned her backpack, dumping an assortment of hastily gathered food—peach cups and packets of peanut butter crackers—into the grass. Gaetan snorted at the collection of snacks, which looked like something a little kid might gather to run away from home. But despite his performed disapproval, Gaetan ate it all, and Noemi and Link didn't have to pretend for long that she had brought it for all of them to share. He shoveled peaches into his mouth, syrup dribbling down his chin, and Noemi, who usually complained about Gaetan's lackluster table manners, looked away and said nothing. When there was nothing left but dirty wrappers, Gaetan lay down without a word of thanks and nestled his head on Noemi's now-empty backpack, the thin canvas all that separated his head from her leg. He fell asleep almost immediately, and they sat beside him, silently watching the wind blow through the trees and letting ladybugs run over their fingers.

Gaetan inched further into her lap, and she had to wonder whether he was really asleep. Noemi brushed his dark hair out of his face. "He looks like such a kid when he's sleeping," she said.

He had a belt-buckle-wide cut above one dark eyebrow. She brushed it accidentally as she scooped his hair from his forehead. He winced, and Noemi drew her hand away, but Gaetan caught her wrist, brought her fingers back down against his skin. For a moment, she forgot Link was there.

THE TIDE CREATURE

I dreamt a creature lived at the bottom of the lake. My dream began as I walked out of the forest and onto the shore. In the story of the dream, there was nothing before that. I was born in the forest.

The sky arched its back. Its belly was a many-colored night. The moon pulled at the surface of the water, and the tide slid out of place like a bed sheet turned down. Either the moon or the lighthouse's solitary eye illuminated a patch at the edge of the water, spotlit it just for me. A swirl of darkness dispersed the lake's reflection of my shadow, and I saw a face that was not my own break the surface, a full, space-taking presence.

The creature's neck, gray as a lake in daylight, stretched toward me, the face at the end long and wreathed in tangled hair. A horse's head, I thought, but then it tilted in a way that made it appear more human, or it shifted to become more human. I didn't know whether its shape or my perspective had made it change. Algae and duckweed grew over its skin or were part of its skin. It was a thing made of water and forest. Its mouth opened, but instead of words only lake spilled out.

I turned back to the tree line to leave, but then I remembered there was nowhere else to go. The moon forgot me. It turned its gaze instead to the horned shadows that crouched behind the trees. One walked toward me. I recognized that it was the creature in the water, but at the same time it was not. At the same time it was someone much more familiar, the way that all dream-beings can be more than one person at a time. I almost recognized it, but it did not have a face. Neither did it have horns like the other forest guardians. Where its head should have been, a cloud hung around its neck. Night dripped down its limbs in rivers, pooled at the tips of its fingers, and except for its arms elbow-down, its body became flesh. It was very tall. The darkness dried like paint—not over its hands, but in the shape of them. Its hands had been carved out, negative space, gaps in the dream, but the rest of the body was solid—its legs, chest, everything but its misting head.

Did you make me?
it asked.
Am I dreaming?

JONAS

Jonas's mom had driven down to Shivery to take him to lunch at Hilda's. The diner was in the midst of redecorating, had already replaced the booths with white tables and chairs, and the walls still smelled faintly of fresh paint.

"Looks like they're trying to modernize," Jonas said.

"It seems like a cute place."

Not once during lunch did she guilt-trip him about why he'd ended up there.

"I'd like to get a look inside the inn when I drop you off. I want to see where you live. Do you think Francesca would mind?"

"It's a perfectly nice house, Mom."

"Oh, I believe you. I'm just curious. Even though I don't see you every day now, I want to be involved. *Especially* because I don't see you every day. Phone calls just aren't cutting it."

Diana and Audrey both worked Saturdays, which Jonas was glad for since his mom already found it less than ideal that Cesca had unrelated people living in their house. Matt was making a door in his workshop, but Cesca and Noemi both sat inside playing Scrabble at the dining room table.

"Is it okay if I show my mom around the house?"

Cesca stood. "Of course."

"It's nice to see you again." Sara then turned to Noemi. "You must be Noemi. Jonas has told me a lot about you."

Jonas hadn't noticed how often he must have mentioned Noemi in casual text or conversation until his mother said this. Even though he'd never come out and told her *I have a crush on the girl who lives three feet from my bedroom door,* the accusation crept under her words.

"All lies," Noemi joked.

Jonas led his mother around the house, and she glanced with polite curiosity into each suite with an open door.

"A lot of rooms to clean," she mused.

"Well, everyone does their own, and then we take turns on the extras."

"Is that so? I could never get you to straighten your room at home." They descended from the third floor back to the second. "Francesca certainly has unique taste."

"I guess."

"Do you think we could see some of Noemi's photos? Nomi's photos? No-eh-mi's?"

"People who know her pronounce it 'Nomi.' I think it was originally a mispronunciation that just became her nickname." He really had told his mother more about her than intended.

"You can go in," Noemi's voice called out from below.

Jonas hadn't realized she'd been on her way upstairs, near enough to hear their conversation. She rose from behind the railing, then waved them into her room.

He watched his mother follow the path of photos along the wall of Noemi's room with his arms folded. Sara would never *deliberately* humiliate him the way some kids' parents would.

"Is Jonas in any of these?" *Accidentally* humiliate him, however...

"He isn't." Noemi leaned against the foot of her bed. Her expression hadn't changed. She didn't indicate she saw anything odd in the question. Maybe there was nothing odd in it.

"Well, you're very talented," Sara added.

"Thank you."

"Jonas said you photograph things from your dreams?"

"Yeah, mostly." Noemi gestured toward a journal atop her bedside table. "I try to record things before I forget them and then re-create the interesting ones later in photos. Those are just my friends modeling."

Jonas had never noticed her writing in the notebook before. Did she share the inspiration for the photographs with Lyle and Amberlyn, or did she just tell them where to stand and how to pose?

"Would you want to be in photos sometime, Jonas?"

"Oh, you don't have to do that." But he did want to be a part of them.

"It could be nice," Noemi said.

Sara's departure left Jonas with a pang of sadness. The loneliness he'd felt the day he first moved to Shivery washed over him once more. Then Noemi took his hand and led him to the woods, and something he couldn't name bloomed.

She'd explained the photograph they were going to take that afternoon, or his role in it at least. The weather was perfect because it wasn't too cold, but it did look like it was going to rain. The dense sky was just what she needed, she said.

"What if it does rain?" he asked.

"We go home."

Noemi didn't take him to the water this time. Jonas recalled Amberlyn's advice that she reinvent how she saw the lake, try to take pictures there, but he didn't speak this aloud. She led him to a smaller clearing where the trees were naked and gray, their leaves having left them in favor of draping the ground in a dry, brown carpet. By the lake, the trees had stretched like skyscrapers, growing taller every second with no sign of ceasing, their highest parts infinitesimal. Here, when he craned his neck, Jonas could see where the trees ended in a sky just a shade lighter than the oaks. It really did look like it was ready to cast a bursting rain down on them, and he silently begged the clouds not to, to let them stay.

Before they'd left Lamplight, Noemi did a rough sketch of the character from her dreams Jonas would portray. It amazed him to watch artists give life to something that had existed only inside their heads. He could barely re-create a bowl of fruit in paper and ink, even if he were looking right at one. The figure from her dreams was bare-chested, with arms dipped in shadow and a face obscured by clouds.

"You don't have to take your shirt off if you don't want, though," Noemi had said. "As long as we push your sleeves up, it'll be okay."

But Jonas had offered to remove both his hoodie and T-shirt so that she could approximate the image she needed. He wanted to be as much a part of this piece of her imagination as she would let him. Now that they were standing in the woods, he began to feel self-conscious, but men weren't often permitted the luxury of expressing anxiety about their bodies. If he looked stiff or nervous, she might be able to read his insecurity. His shoulders ached, and he wished she had asked someone less disappointing.

Once, in gym class, the seniors ran laps while the juniors played field hockey. Gaetan Kelly lifted the hem of his gym tee to wipe sweat from his face, exposing a fairly defined six-pack to a giggling flock of eleventh-grade girls. Jonas looked up in time to catch Gaetan dropping his shirt and pivoting into a sideways jog. He spread his arms and shouted, "Take a picture, Noemi!" Jonas, and everyone else, turned to find her red-faced and clenching her hockey stick. Maybe she should have asked Gaetan instead.

Noemi didn't react with disappointment when Jonas removed his shirts and revealed a flat, unremarkable body. He folded his arms in front of himself, covering his lone strip of body hair trailing downward from his belly button—something the cloud-headed sketch did not have. Jonas had little idea of what girls thought of guys with (or without) body hair. Once at a pool party for someone's birthday, a girl looked at his legs and said, "You have, like, no body hair. I'm so jealous." He didn't want to have a body women felt jealous of, not in the way she'd meant.

"Are you cold?"

"No. I mean, a little, but I'm fine." He relaxed his arms. "Sorry, I know I'm not super photogenic."

"I usually hate the way I look in photos too. I bet most people do. Try not to worry too much. It's not a pose-y photo, so it won't be difficult."

"It's less the pose and more my not-exactly-model physique." Jonas forced a smile. Pretending to scratch an itch, he tested the firmness of the flesh by his navel with his thumb.

"Hm? Don't sell yourself short. You have a really nice body, Jonas." Noemi looked at him through her camera, then lowered it and checked the settings.

Worry leaked out of him like helium from a punctured balloon.

"I don't know about that, but thanks." He couldn't avoid a reply at least marginally self-effacing, but he believed she'd meant what she said. Noemi didn't dole out reassurances she didn't mean. She didn't do anything just to be nice if she ruled it disingenuous.

"How about you put just your T-shirt on?" she offered again. "It'll work just as well. Really."

"I'm just kidding around," he said. "I want to do this. I'm fine." He did want to do it. He just wanted to feel more at ease in his skin while doing it.

She dropped the camera so that it swung around her neck. Then she walked toward him. Jonas couldn't get used to being the object of someone's attention in this way and for so long. Noemi assessed the light, the layout of the trees, everything in relation to Jonas and how he looked.

Applying dark, indigo body paint to a brush, Noemi began to cover Jonas's arm. She spent a significant amount of her earnings from Hummingbird on art supplies, and he hoped she wouldn't end up feeling she had wasted any today. She propped up his bicep with one hand, and with the other, she swept his forearm with the cool paint. Her hair was parted on the side, and she was turned so that he could see her clearly in profile. Once, in September, Noemi had worn a loose-fitting tank top with wide armholes, and he could see her ribs and the side of her bra when she moved. Matt had caught Jonas staring in the kitchen, and he gave his son a complicated look once their eyes met. Now she wore a coat that looked like a dress, and the zipper pull danced with each gesture.

Reaching for his other arm, Noemi turned to face him, and it was then that Jonas kissed her. He kissed her because some nights he lay awake and was sure he could hear her dreaming. He kissed her because she had a mask that slipped, and he liked what was underneath. He kissed her because she asked for *more* homework in French class and didn't care when the other students booed. He kissed her because she would stand up to anyone but was afraid of a lighthouse. He kissed her because he was horny, because he was shy, too shy to tell her he liked her with words. He kissed her because she made him feel seen and significant, and he wanted her to feel the same way but didn't know how else to do it. He kissed her for countless different reasons, none of which he thought of at the time save one: he kissed her because he wanted to, and he thought she wanted that too.

Noemi pulled away from him. Jonas had smeared a dark handprint on the right side of her jaw and neck where he'd cradled her face. Her eyes widened, and she touched her fingers to her bottom lip. First he thought she was savoring the feel of his kiss, then he worried he might have scratched her with his lip ring. Before he could say anything, her expression hardened. She had large, dark eyebrows that turned severe when she was angry.

"Why did you do that? This is serious, Jonas. I really did ask you here to take pictures."

He ran his fingers through his hair, then stopped, rested the heel of his hand against his crown. He'd been wrong. His skin felt as though it would tear off of him at any second and flit away, leaving the rest of him exposed.

"I'm sorry," he said.

Jonas wished that he'd never kissed her. Did people ask one another whether they wanted to kiss? No one who had ever kissed him had asked first. How had he gotten it so wrong? She would probably want nothing to do with him now, and he couldn't blame her.

"It's okay." She took a step away from him. "Did you just want to head back?"

"No." *Yes.* "No, I want to help."

He wanted to disappear, but if he bailed on her now, what would that say? *Your photographs mean nothing to me. I only came out here for one reason, and you didn't give it to me.* None of that was true.

"I'm sorry," he said again. "I'm just, uh, really, really clueless about these things. Apparently."

She stood at more of a distance while she painted the other arm, and she didn't hold it up for him. His muscles had begun to tire by the time she finished. Then Noemi used a pale, blue-white smoke bomb to create a cloud a few feet in front of him.

"Step just here so it's only obscuring your face," she said. "It's okay if your head shows a little bit. I'll touch it up later."

"You just had this lying around?"

"Yep. Several colors too."

Neither of them said much once she finally began photographing. Occasionally she would feed him some direction, but nothing more. To his relief—and guilt—the weather finally cut the project short. The sky opened and released rain to ease them out of their shared discomfort. It turned from a drizzle to a deluge almost immediately, and they ran back to Lamplight only to arrive no less soaked than if they had walked.

13

NOEMI

The rain was loudest from the third floor, so that's where Noemi went. She'd changed into dry clothes and padded down the hallway to one of the two remaining unoccupied rooms. In it, a fireplace housed a collection of white candles in its firebox and on the mantle. She closed the door so Rosencrantz or Guildenstern wouldn't enter and accidentally burn the house down. Then she lit each candle, turned off the lights, and slipped under the bedcovers and into near-darkness, unsure of what had just happened, or what she wanted, or didn't, or anything.

Are you OK? Unknown asked.

"Yes." She said it aloud.

Jonas called to her from the hallway. He poked his head through the door, then the rest of him followed. He'd rinsed off the body paint, changed into a *Nerv* T-shirt and a pair of gray sweatpants. As insecure as he might have seemed, telling him he had a nice body was probably a mistake—not because Noemi didn't think it was true, but because it clearly hadn't come across the way she'd intended. Jonas was lean and fit. He had strong shoulders, narrow hips, and a pretty face. But she didn't observe these things in the way he'd thought. She liked his body, but she didn't want to put her mouth on it or feel it sweating against her. For whatever reason, she hadn't wanted to kiss him.

"I want to apologize," Jonas said.

"You already did, and it's really fine."

"You told me to take things seriously, but I was serious about helping you with your photos. I seriously like you too." He put his hands in his sweatpants pockets. "I don't want you to think all I cared about was getting something physical. It wasn't an empty kiss for me. So. Yeah. Just wanted you to know that. I hope we can still be friends. I'm happy to be in your photos if you ever need me, and I promise I'll stay focused."

"Of course we're still friends." She slid over and motioned for him to sit next to her.

He considered for a moment, but then he finally settled onto the bed with his back against the headboard.

"Do you still talk to many of your friends from your old school?" she asked.

"I only had a few friends," he said. "But their texts fizzled soon after I moved out here. Out of sight, out of mind, I guess."

Noemi wanted to know as much about what being Jonas was like as he would tell her. She had questions, but feared asking the wrong ones.

"Sorry," he said again. "I didn't mean to make this about me."

"You didn't. I asked. Anyway, you moved to a new town, into a house with people you didn't know. You started going to a new school. In comparison, it's not much of a sacrifice for me to learn at least a little about you."

"Hmm."

She placed her face against his shoulder, spread her hand over his chest. She kissed him softly through the cotton of his T-shirt.

"I do really like you, Jonas."

"What?" He twisted his whole body to face her. She could just make out his expression, his confusion.

"I like you."

"I think I misheard you."

Noemi kissed his cheek, then held her face close to his.

He stared.

"It's hard to explain. I like you, and I'm not sure why I flipped out when you kissed me. I guess I wasn't sure where you wanted it to lead." This seemed like the easiest way to make him understand, and she wasn't entirely convinced it might not be true.

"You mean you like me as a friend." He hadn't phrased it as a question, but his voice wavered, uncertain.

It was safe to do now that he'd said it first. "I don't kiss people because I like them *as friends*, not even on the cheek. I like you in a different way. I want to be near you. I like holding your hand and wrestling with you and sitting with our legs together when we watch movies. It might not be exciting for you, but it excites me. More than kissing. When I see you my heart accelerates, and I have to think about breathing."

Noemi feared she sounded like a child, but Jonas nodded. He pushed her hair aside and caressed her jaw, different from how he'd touched her earlier, awkward in a shy way.

"I like you too," he said. "A lot."

He enveloped her in his arms, and she settled into him. His face hovered close to hers, waiting. She moved her lips away, so he kissed her on the cheek as she'd done to him. She traced her hands along his spine. He turned over her so that she was under him, lifted her hair away from her neck and placed his face in its curve. Her pulse fluttered in her throat. He exhaled.

Jonas moved slowly against her. They were both still fully clothed. She had no idea if this was what other people did, pushed parts of themselves together though fabric separated them. Was this a common half step toward sex? Asking anyone else was out of the question. Noemi kept her face turned so he couldn't kiss her mouth. She barely moved except to run her fingers through the hair on the back of his head.

"Is this okay?" he asked.

"I'd tell you if it wasn't."

"Let me know if you need me to stop or change anything."

She nodded.

If he ached for more, he didn't demand it. It seemed he would accept anything she would give to him, but for her, just sitting next to him would have been enough. Was what they did now only for him? She didn't want just to endure him. Jonas stopped again, relaxed against her. He hugged her hard, and she hugged him back. She tilted her head toward his so their noses touched: her slim, freckled nose, his bent one.

"I want to make you feel good," he said.

She smiled. "I *am* good."

AMBERLYN

Gaetan had come over that morning to help Ben shovel the driveway, and as payment he'd accepted only the chance to take a nap in
Link's bed. He sometimes spent nights in Link's room too, though
this was now very occasional without Link around. Amberlyn suspected he didn't sleep in his own home much anymore. As she
padded down the upstairs hallway to invite him to the Midwinter
festival, she wondered where Gaetan did sleep.

It was, of course, possible he spent the night at girls' houses,
but as far as she knew, everyone Gaetan dated still lived with their
parents, and he'd been single since last year anyway. Before that he
was a notoriously terrible boyfriend, and a serial one at that. He'd
take an interest in girls around school, then disappear on them
once they'd hooked up, act bewildered when they called him out

on his behavior. Amberlyn had had a crush on him when she was younger, and she had been secretly relieved to hear other girls cry over his withheld affections. The older she got, the less charming and mysterious this pattern of his seemed. She now found the steadfast part of him more endearing, even if it was doled out more stingily.

Gaetan lounged barefoot but fully clothed on Link's bed, reading. He had the shades in the room drawn, though the bedside light was on.

"Whatcha up to?" Amberlyn asked.

"Reading a comic of Link's. I found it wedged between some books." He glanced at her, then propped himself on an elbow.

"Can I see?"

"Sure."

He shuffled through the stack of pages, unbound and unfinished, then handed it over. The cover was full color but not colorful: two teenagers standing on a bridge in stark winter. Even from behind she knew who they were meant to be. One was tall with red hair, the other petite with long curls. In what could have been his wildest fantasies, Link hadn't even placed Noemi close enough to brush shoulders with him; there were millimeters of distance between the two figures, and something in their bodies said it might as well have been miles. The title read *Shivery*.

"Where did you say you found this?" Amberlyn asked.

Gaetan nodded toward the bookshelf. "Kind of weird since it's unfinished."

She flipped through quickly, and the color bled from the pages, then the ink, then the pencil until the characters near the end were simply ghosts. Link had started inking and coloring it before he had finished drawing, assembled the story but left it open. The last few pages were decorated with only the impressions of people: the curve of a chin, an incomplete arm, a shape outlining where someone should have been.

"Why wasn't it on his desk if he was still working on it?" Amberlyn asked. "Do you think he was trying to hide it?"

"Well, it's autobiographical. Except that he gave us all super-powers." Gaetan's laugh was a small huff. "Maybe he was embarrassed for anyone to see it before it was done."

"Embarrassed" didn't sound like Link. He'd drawn a complete graphic novella his freshman year called *High School at the End of the World* about people trapped in purgatory. No one familiar had graced its pages, but he had shared it with Amberlyn, waiting for her to read it in all its stages, not saying anything, but watching with interest for any reaction. His art here, even incomplete, had vastly improved, yet he'd kept it secret. What did Gaetan mean by *us*? Did that include Amberlyn? Link might have shown this one to her too when it was ready, or he might not have. With him gone, she wasn't sure she could make that decision on her own.

"It's dedicated to Noemi," he said, voice flat.

Gently Amberlyn pulled out the first page after the cover, and there it was: *For Noemi* in her brother's handwriting. Perhaps that was the one person intended to read it. Amberlyn wondered if this was the last thing Link had written or worked on or touched before he died—before the grass and the water and his shoes when he slid them off his feet. She should give it to Noemi, but she could not think of what to say doing so. *Here. This is yours. I don't know what it is or why it is. I'm not sure I know much of anything.*

"Did you finish reading what was here?"

"No," Gaetan said. "Should I not have read it?"

"I don't know. Do you mind if I hang on to it?"

He answered and he didn't: "He's your brother." Which Amberlyn now understood did not necessarily entitle her to much, but she tucked the pages under her arm anyway. Gaetan watched as they slipped away, his mouth a tight line, then turned his attention instead to his phone.

Amberlyn never knew quite what to say to Gaetan. She had always found her mind went blank when talking to attractive boys, and Gaetan was foremost among those: he looked like heaven's handsomest angel had come to earth in pursuit of a swimming career. He was nice enough to her, but when Link would go into the next room, the awkward small talk between the two of them had taken extra effort. Conversing with Gaetan, Amberlyn felt the way she had as a kid, when her aunts and uncles pretended to be interested in her *My Little Pony* talk but were decidedly thinking about something else. Now there was no Link, and Amberlyn didn't know what to do with this broody boy in her house.

She could tell him that Link had drowned in a lake apparently only Noemi could find. He either wouldn't believe her, or he'd set out searching for it and find nothing. Even Lyle, who knew the woods much better than Amberlyn did, had not been able to find the water without Noemi's help. To Gaetan, the story of the lake would sound like nonsense, coming from a little girl looking for attention, the way most everything she'd ever said to him had probably sounded.

"Well," she said finally, "I just wanted to see if you were interested in going to Midwinter."

Midwinter was the winter solstice festival in Shivery, though some locals referred to it as a "goat festival."

Goats were an unofficial Shivery mascot, emblazoned onto local goods sold as souvenirs to the town's occasional tourist. They were the more official mascot of the Galaxie Regional High School sports teams. At Amberlyn's hockey games, a seven-foot-tall, grinning, costumed goat tore across the ice between periods dressed in a blue jersey. Goats proved popular pets among locals (which may have had more to do with the prevalence of farms in the area than anything else) and held a place of honor at all town functions, regardless of season (with a large play area courtesy of a local sanctuary and rescue at each festival). Shivery spotlighted goats with special enthusiasm during Midwinter. Lyle attributed this to the Scandinavian Yule Goat, who ferried around Father Christmas each December, while Noemi pointed out that the Yule Goat was pagan in origin.

Goats aside, Midwinter had come to hold a place in the hearts of Shiverians, and even most citizens of the neighboring Galaxie participated as well. Almost everyone felt the festival served a different purpose. For some, it was synonymous with the Christmas season, while others saw it as a simple celebration of winter. Those less fond of winter believed it a way of asking—god, gods, nature, the fates, chance, whomever—for a gentle season if they were at all superstitious, or a way of mourning the end of fall if they were not. Whatever its purpose, Midwinter drew nearly everyone in the area to downtown Shivery on the longest night of the year.

Gaetan propped himself up with one elbow. "Who are you going with?"

"My dad. My mom's working on the downstairs bathroom."

All Kate Miller did anymore was paint. It started with covering the graffiti (black Sharpie on white walls) in Link's room after he'd died, the new paint an altostratus gray Amberlyn found dreary. Then the painting creeped out of the room and into the corridor, down to her parents' bedroom and into their closet. Kate barely knew what she was doing, so it would take days to do a single stretch of wall, layering and adjusting strokes, perfecting the corners, neatening around the baseboards. She was "too busy" for Midwinter because she *had* to paint the hall half bath a sea-foam green that reminded Amberlyn of her pediatrician's office.

Link had loved Midwinter. The thought of staying home made Amberlyn want to curl up in one of the paint cans.

"Do you know who else is going to be there?" Gaetan asked.

"Everyone? I'm meeting up with Noemi and Lyle, probably Jonas."

He rolled his eyes. "Has Jonas really not found his own friends yet?"

"Well, I think we're his friends. He's nice. I don't know why you don't like him."

He allowed his phone screen to darken and lay back to look at the ceiling, which Kate had not painted. Papier-mâché tentacles still hung where Link had fixed them with thumbtacks and string.

"I don't dislike Jonas. I don't have an opinion either way. Just didn't realize he was friends with you guys. Thought he was just boarding at Noemi's."

"Hey, we're friendly people," she said.

"You are. Lyle maybe is. Amato's a shrew."

"That's harsh, Gaetan."

He smirked, shrugged; since he was on his back this meant curling his shoulders inward.

"So, does that mean you're not coming?"

"Nah. I spent over an hour shoveling snow. Dragging a huge fucking goat around is going to interfere with my grand plan to nap and convalesce."

The "huge fucking goat" was a horned goat sculpture at least two stories high, constructed from twigs and straw. Whichever entity in Shivery was responsible for it saw it placed atop a sled at the end of King Street for Midwinter. A large crowd of people pulled two long ropes in unison to drag the inanimate beast to the town center, where the fairy lights covering it were then lit before nightfall.

When they'd explained all this to Jonas in school, he'd asked what they do about the sled-pulling if it doesn't snow. They told him the truth: it always snows on Midwinter.

It had indeed snowed again this year, and when the Millers got to the festival that evening, the tread marks from everyone's snow boots were visible in the street. Ben had volunteered to help man the hot cider stand with Mrs. Fisher—the very elderly, very curmudgeonly woman who coordinated everyone's attendance in the main office at Galaxie Regional—and he left Amberlyn to go find her friends. These were not the same friends she'd spent Midwinter with when she was a child. That had been Brianna and Carly: ABC, the three of them together. But when Link started spending more time with Noemi, things shifted for Amberlyn as well. B & C wouldn't expand their circle of friends, so after that there was only "A." She started sitting with her brother and his friends at lunch and finally got to know Noemi and Lyle after years of going through school with them as Firstname Lastname acquaintances. When Link died, Brianna and Carly attended the funeral, but they made no effort to include Amberlyn in their lives afterward, when she needed someone most. Lyle included her. Lyle always had been good at making Amberlyn feel her presence was welcome, wanted.

She found Lyle browsing one of the vending tables. The AP art students sold goat horns and masks at one of Midwinter's most popular stands. Brian Kowalski's resin antler headbands filled up two of the table's rows of merchandise. There were comparatively fewer of Noemi's goat skull masks, but the price tags were higher. Jade Truwell's and Anna Vang's simple, felted goat ear headbands were least expensive, and therefore the biggest sellers.

Last year, Link's work had been the most popular. His masks were made from paper, but were detailed, colorful, and unique. Amberlyn had forgotten and left hers at home, where it hung from a bedpost, all white with a slim paper beard that bisected her chin, and a splash of purple paint striping its nose.

It was such a simple thing, but realizing she had gone to Midwinter without it tore her in every direction.

"Amberlyn!" Lyle called. She wore a white-and-gold mask she'd bought last year. "Have you seen the mini goats playing in the snow? Ohmygosh." Lyle's words rushed together. She ran up to Amberlyn and placed a hand on each of her arms, spinning out of an almost-hug at the last moment.

"I didn't. Will they still be there after the sled-pulling? Half the school is over there already, so it'll probably start soon."

"Maybe. It might not be good for them to stay out that long. Hey, I got you something." Lyle trotted back to the table, then returned to place a brown headband with resin horns in Amberlyn's braided hair.

"Thanks. I actually forgot to bring the one of Link's he gave me last year."

"Oh. Shoot." Lyle wore a gray beanie, and she grabbed the edges of the hat, pulled it down over her eyebrows as though on the way to hiding her whole face inside. "That one was way cooler.

Plus, it had sentimental value. I'm sorry." She bit the side of her lip, and her mouth was a red comma. "We can swing by and pick it up. It's not like you live that far."

"It's not a big deal." Amberlyn tapped the tip of one of the horns she wore. "This is perfect."

They rushed hand in hand back to the opposite end of King Street. Amberlyn's lungs warmed from the exertion. Both girls wore gloves, which were necessary for handling the sled ropes without burning their palms. From somewhere by the Goat, a whistle blew, and children waging snowball fights dropped their snow in favor of a length of rope. Even the ones so small the ropes came up to their heads grabbed hold in order to help. The girls' hockey team filed in behind Amberlyn, while Lyle stood in front of her, and they yelled "Heave-ho!" with the rest of the crowd, yanking their rope in unison. Once the Goat guarded its post at the town center, the sky began to darken, and Christmas lights lit the streets. The Goat came alive.

Lyle and Amberlyn walked through the crowd in search of Ben Miller, whom Lyle preferred over all other GRHS teachers, and unlike many of their schoolmates, she was not put off from being around him because his son had died. The girls couldn't, however, locate the cider stand. They kept returning to the hot chocolate stand instead, and they joked that they'd been stepping through an "unseen *Twilight Zone* vortex," which Link would have appreciated.

"Are you sure you don't want to sleep over?" Lyle asked.

"I'm sure. I didn't bring anything with me."

"We can pick up a toothbrush."

"It's fine."

Tradition decreed that one should stay up until dawn through the longest night, even if that meant being awake in one's pajamas, tucked in bed. Amberlyn would have very much liked to wait out dawn at Lyle's, but then her parents would be home alone, and even if Kate was "too busy" to do anything but edge ceilings, staying out this Midwinter didn't quite fit.

Amberlyn texted her father, *Where are you?* Giving up on the search for Ben for the moment, she and Lyle followed the current of bodies to the river. Several people had carved small boats from ice, most flat and angular like pinched pentagons or the silhouettes of diamonds. On their surfaces, the carvers had placed small, soy candles. Orange flames cast their tiny glow onto the boats.

The air was not yet cold enough to freeze the river, and the ice crafts bore their candles along the current in a miniature boat parade. Each boat had blue-and-purple edges, though its center was warm and bright, and the ribbon of light traveling downriver looked to Amberlyn like a fragmented aurora. The girls did not have boats of their own, but they stopped to watch everyone else send theirs into the water.

"How are you doing?" Lyle asked. "I know it's always hard, but around the holidays..."

"I miss him, of course." Amberlyn sniffed. Her eyes were teary, but even she couldn't tell how much of that was from the cold and how much was from the fact that she was a great big puddle-on-the-brink, barely holding her shape together. "We weren't super close, but we weren't *not* close, you know? I realize people don't work this way, but it bothers me I didn't know and understand absolutely everything about him." They stood in silence for a few moments. Then she said, "We didn't carve boats this year."

"It's too hard anyway. If I weren't wearing gloves last year, I'd have cut my thumb off." Lyle pointed to the lights on the river. "It looks like a meteor shower. Let's pick one out and make a wish. Keep your eyes on it until it's too far to see, and maybe it'll come true."

Amberlyn twirled the orange tip of her braid around her finger. "Would you say you're superstitious?"

"Nah. But I do make wishes when I blow out birthday candles or see a shooting star. Just in case."

Though Amberlyn wasn't suspicious either, she chose a boat at random and kept her eyes fixed to it as it floated downstream.

Even though she didn't take her eyes off her boat, its light blurred into those around it, and she lost track of the one she was supposed to be watching. She hadn't made a wish anyway. There was one wish she wanted, but it was a hopeless thing.

LONGEST DAY

I dreamt a celebration, a town-wide festival. Like Midwinter, though in my dream spring had already settled in, and it was day. The people of Shivery wore masks, and they walked through the rain downtown with no fear of getting wet. They held no umbrellas, made no dash from one storefront awning to the next.

I watched all this from the window of my bedroom in Lamplight. Lamplight is not downtown when I'm awake, but in my dream, it had been made narrow and was wedged between two buildings at the center of King Street. I wanted to go out onto the street and be in the rain, even though I recognized no one in the crowd, even though I had no mask of my own. Strangers in masks clogged the stairs inside the inn, ignoring me as I tried to push past them. They spoke so loudly to one another that I could hear nothing but the beehive drone of their senseless

conversations. From my place on the stairs, I could see that the front door of the inn was open, but I couldn't reach it. Too many bodies were in my way. I retreated back up the steps before they could trap me there.

In my room, the window had been flung wide open, and Link Miller sat on the sill. He too wore a mask. It was made of silver and covered only his eyes. Water dripped from the edges of his fox-colored hair. I could tell it wasn't rain; I recognized one drop of water from the next, my heart a microscope. He took my hand, and when he leapt out the window, I leapt with him. Though we were two stories up, we landed safely on the ground as though it had always been just there by our feet.

Together, Link and I walked through the street. All those people I didn't recognize stared, and I could tell from the way they studied Link that they knew who he was. He was back from the dead, and it was no longer a secret. They didn't think it was strange. I wore a periwinkle-stained dress that crinkled like water. Somewhere between the window and the road, I too had gained a mask to hide my eyes. The rain slowed for us, and unlike everyone else, I didn't get wet.

NOEMI

In February, when Jonas first told Noemi *I love you*, it was with his hands. They were sitting on her bed, and they were supposed to be studying, but they'd gotten distracted by a silly game where they took turns spelling out letters on each other's backs and guessing the words. Jonas wrote out *LOVE* beside her spine with his fingertip, and though she got the word right, she didn't realize what he was doing.

Instead of turning around to yield the next turn, he did it again. Then he added a second word.

"I'm not sure," she said.

"The second one was *always*."

Jonas walked around to the other side of the bed and sat so he faced her. He leaned into her, folded her in his arms. His hands found hers. Gently, he articulated with her fingers, *I* and *L-O-V-E* and *Y-O-U*, etching the words into the air. Parsed out, the sentiment felt like something meant for a valediction at the end of a letter.

If he wanted a response, she wasn't sure she had one. Even if they had been speaking aloud, she'd have been at a loss. Noemi feared what he might need from her if they continued impersonating lovers.

She continued as though the game had never stopped. She reached behind his shoulder and spelled out *stepbrother*. Even though their parents would never marry because Cesca "didn't believe in it," this word was a useful tool for pushing him away—pretending *stepbrother* was the closest to her he could ever get, that she thought about him that way at all.

Jonas sighed so heavily that Noemi saw the breath move through his body in a wave. His head dipped forward until his dark, wavy hair hid his eyes. The word had come out crueler than she'd intended, and before he could call her on it, she leaned into him, gave him the full force of her body so they both poured back onto the bed together. She kissed him, even though she hated it. This was *I'm sorry* in Noemi's language. Noemi allowed Jonas to kiss her without twisting her head away. His kisses started shy, but they were too full of need not to grow deeper. They were as deep as a night sky at the bottom of a lake.

She appreciated his sincerity, his easy nature. He assumed everyone else was as sincere as he was, and so he took everything seriously, trusted when Noemi said something like "stepbrother" that it was how she felt, when really it was her way of lashing out, afraid of a shrinking distance and trying to widen it.

Noemi had begun to recognize when he felt bad about something, because of how much he smoothed things over, apologized for himself, insisted nothing bothered him. She wanted to shield him from violent things, even from the sharp bits of herself, and this made her softer when she was with him. She was glad he wasn't her stepbrother. She couldn't name exactly what he was to her, but he was definitely becoming *something*.

With her ear pressed against his chest, she listened to his heartbeat humming like a dragonfly. It was the first time Noemi had heard the work someone else's body did to keep them alive. She was curious about him. She studied the little things she thought peculiar: the way his nose curved where it had been broken, the delicate hiccups he got whenever he ate rice, his habit of finger-combing the hair by his ears.

She laid her head on his belly. It made noises like an aquarium. She held his wrists to the side of her face and created a cavern with her ear, imagined the rushing sounds she heard were the tides inside his body. He searched for her heartbeat too. He liked the way it felt inside his head, he told her. He breathed against her chest, gathered the length of her body to his, nestled his hand into the dip of her waist. When they lay down, without her shoes adding to her height, she remembered how much taller he was. Their legs laced together, and she felt like she'd been tucked inside something larger.

A week later, on Valentine's Day, they attended back-to-back films at the Shivery theater: *The Thing* (her preference) and *Akira* (his), and they worked fairly well together as a double feature. As she sat on the sofa seat with her cheek on Jonas's shoulder, his head on her crown, she realized she could now rest so comfortably against him that his body might well have been an extension of her own.

That night, after everyone else was asleep, Noemi's thoughts kept her up. She climbed from her bed and paced her room, puzzling over what the next day and the next and all the days after would be like with Jonas in every one of them. Then her body itched for more space, cleaner air, and she left the room and the inn altogether and went to the woods.

She found the lake, and because it was there, and she was alone, it felt as though someone had been waiting especially for her. The February cold didn't touch her here, and she shrugged off her wool coat and draped it over her arm. The lighthouse loomed closer to the forest, and it illuminated the shore with all the strength of an artificial sun.

A very tall, hooded figure stood with its back to the light, face hidden in darkness.

Noemi shielded her eyes and stepped closer, walking toward the water until she was not ten feet from the person. Every cell in her body quivered. She recognized the sharp chin, the messy strands of fair, reddish hair falling alongside the jaw, but still the eyes were cast in shadow. Noemi spoke his name.

"Link?"

The person had Link's lips but not his smile. The lips parted, then closed again. Noemi looked at her phone, hoping Unknown might speak for him. She seldom had cell reception this far into the forest. And when she did, it didn't last long. Yet now, the phone flashed.

UNKNOWN

No.

Noemi had often spoken to Link through a chat app that let its users create animated, cutesy avatars to mimic their own expressions accompanying messages. The app simply displayed her name as *Noemi*, but Link had been *Laetan*. Gaetan had been the one who'd installed it on Link's phone, and since he practically lived at the Millers' (and was on their family cell plan), he often lent Link's messages his input. Though the avatar had red hair and a hooded sweatshirt, only Gaetan ever bothered to change its expression. Coupled with the sudden crudeness of the messages, it was easy to see when he took over. Gaetan hadn't used the app since Link had died. And Unknown had suddenly started texting instead.

"No" what? Noemi typed, but not to Unknown. She sent it through the app, to "Laetan," testing whether she could get Gaetan to answer, admit he'd been putting her on.

The figure didn't move, but Noemi was sure whoever it

was watched her, even if she couldn't see their eyes. Too tall to be Gaetan. Too tall to be anyone she knew but one person. She looked from her phone to the stranger and back to her phone, waiting for someone to answer or explain. A red bar formed at the top of the screen: *No internet connection detected.* The app was still attempting to send her message.

But Unknown texted back.

No, that's not me.

Why did this figure resemble Link? Noemi tilted her head, tried to get a better look at the Link-thing's face, at its eyes, without moving closer. This had to be a dream, and dreams didn't scare her once she knew they were dreams. Even so, it couldn't hurt to be cautious.

The Link-thing opened its mouth again, but this time something came out. A small thing. It said her name.

"Noemi." The voice pronounced all three syllables.

The figure began moving toward her. Noemi backed away, but not quickly enough. The hooded figure was soon near enough to touch her. Whatever it was, it smelled of sweat, cigarettes, and soil. Its face might have been Link's. She couldn't be sure it *wasn't* Link. She tried to recall his face, the parts that composed it. Just moments ago she had been convinced this being had his chin, his mouth. Noemi searched for its eyes. She reached for the hood of its sweatshirt, and it let her. The Link-thing let her push the hood down to its shoulders.

She'd steeled herself for something she might have seen in an earlier dream—a cloud or a mask—but it was a person's face. Blue-gray eyes, like water in a drain. Fair lashes. Sharp cheeks. These features did not belong to a dream that looked *like* Lincoln Miller. They were his.

Noemi couldn't think of the person in front of her as a Link-like mirage. This was *him*. He looked like Link, smelled like Link. Did he feel like Link? She'd hardly ever touched him. This impossible Link took her into his arms and pressed her against him, his sternum cradling her face.

"This doesn't feel like a dream." Noemi spoke into his chest, her voice muffled.

"You're not dreaming."

"If I'm not dreaming, I'm hallucinating. That isn't better."

Her hands slipped between his T-shirt and sweatshirt, to the small of his back. The fingers of Noemi's right hand nestled along the ridges of Link's spine. In her left hand, her phone vibrated.

Finally, Noemi let go and stepped away. Link looked down at her, expressionless. Alive, Link had been a daydreamer, and Noemi had always thought that made him a bit distant. That quality of his seemed even stronger now. The Link in front of her had detached even from himself. Everything about him looked and smelled and sounded right, but he felt off. It wasn't a feeling she could detect with her hands. She knew it the way she knew in her dreams that a tide creature lived at the bottom of the lake.

"Sorry," he said. "You don't like hugs."

"If this isn't a dream, then what are you?"

Link looked at his own hands, as though even he were unsure.

"A ghost?" Noemi asked.

"A ghost," he said softly, weighing the idea. "What would that be like?"

"I don't believe in ghosts," she said. "Ghosts are a story people tell because death scares them. They don't want to let go of people they love. They don't want to believe that when they die themselves, they will stop experiencing anything. So they convince themselves that when our bodies stop working, our souls don't. Consciousness, whatever. Residual energy rattling chains, walking through walls. *You* don't exist. Not anymore. Your family buried you. No." Noemi shook her head. "They *burned* you. There was a service and everything." She poked his shoulder hard with three fingers. It rolled under the force of her touch.

"Burned," Link repeated. He gathered himself in his own arms.

"Who are you?" Noemi asked. She pointed to the lighthouse. "What the hell is that?" She held up her phone. "Who keeps texting me pretending to be Link?"

Link regarded the phone as though unsure of what he was even looking at. It buzzed again in her hand, and she turned the screen.

That's not me.

That isn't Link.

You need to leave.

Noemi.

Please.

Leave.

LEAVE. LEAVE. LEAVE. LEAVE. LEAVE. LEAVE. LEAVE.
LEAVE. LEAVE. LEAVE. LEAVE. LEAVE. LEAVE. LEAVE. LEAVE.
LEAVE LEAVE LEAVE LEAVE LEAVE LEAVE LEAVE LEAVE
LEAVE LEAVE LEAVE LEAVE LEAVE LEAVE LEAVE LEAVE
LEAVE LEAVE LEAVE LEAVE LEAVE LEAVE LEAVE LEAVE
LEAVE LEAVE LEAVE LEAVE LEAVE LEAVE LEAVE LEAVE
LEAVE LEAVE LEAVE LEAVE LEAVE LEAVE LEAVE LEAVE
LEAVELEAVELEAVELEAVELEAVELEAVELEAVELEAVELEEE

Her heart raced, but she remained still, tried to project calm.

"I have to go. It's a school day."

"Will you come back?"

"Yeah."

He reached out to touch her hair or her chin but then thought better of it.

Noemi hurried back toward the trees. When she turned to look behind her, Link was still where she'd left him, watching. She pressed on, and once she was out of his sight, she ran, lungs burning, heart buzzing. Though no one followed, she still felt the weight of Link's eyes moving like rain across her shoulders. The farther she ran, the darker the night became, and by the time she spilled out of the woods, no trace of the lighthouse's sun warmed her. The lupines by the woods somehow grew even in February, though they were encased in Minnesota frost, and they broke hard against Noemi's pumping shins.

Unknown had stopped texting, but her phone did notify her— now that it had full signal strength again—that "Laetan" had messaged her through chat. Her message, *"No," what?*, had finally been delivered, and beneath it someone had responded.

LAETAN: "No, what" what?

NOEMI: Who is this?

LAETAN: Oprah.

NOEMI: Gaetan?

LAETAN: Yes. Who else?

NOEMI: Have you been texting my phone from an unknown number?

LAETAN: I don't know your number. What are you talking about?

NOEMI: Has anyone texted you from a number you don't recognize, or from a withheld number? Saying anything weird?

LAETAN: No. Weird like what? Has someone been doing that?

NOEMI: Yeah.

LAETAN: What makes you think it would be me?

A tiny, red-headed avatar shrugged.

NOEMI: Nothing. Just checking around.

LAETAN: Is everything ok?

Noemi was so warm from running that she hadn't even put her coat back on yet. Now she began to feel the chill of winter, and she dressed once more. When Gaetan spoke through messages, the mocking insincerity that always lurked in his voice was absent. Even so, because Noemi knew him, it was hard to believe he was genuinely concerned.

NOEMI: Everything's fine.

LAETAN: What has this person been saying?

NOEMI: I'm outside right now.

LAETAN: What?

NOEMI: Don't worry about it. I'm messaging you as proof to myself. I'm walking back to the inn from the woods. I sent my first message to you from there. It was really weird, and without textual evidence that I am outside of the house right now I will think this is a dream later. If this conversation is still in here in the morning, I'll know it really happened.

LAETAN: What the fuck is going on? Where are you?

LAETAN: What happened?

LAETAN: It's 4 am. Why the hell were you in the woods? Wtf is textual evidence?

NOEMI: I go there sometimes.

LAETAN: Are you alone?

NOEMI: I'm almost home. I'm alone. I just want to prove to myself whether or not I'm in a dream. I've read that you can't actually read text in dreams, but I don't know if that's true. Anyway, if this is still here when I wake up, I'll know it happened.

LAETAN: What happened? You're creeping me out.

NOEMI: Don't worry about it, Gaetan. I'm messaging you because I know you won't care. I'm sorry if I woke you.

LAETAN: I won't care?

LAETAN: Fuck you.

LAETAN: What. The. Fuck. Happened?

LAETAN: Noemi?

LAETAN: Where are you? I'll come get you. Call me.

He sent her his number, but Noemi turned off her phone. She hadn't expected Gaetan would even respond, let alone become so worked up. She probably should have just typed a memo to herself in her phone's notes, but having someone else respond in real time might actually have been a good thing. Talking with Gaetan,

Noemi was sure she was awake. And though it was petty and self-ish, the fact that someone had been so worried, even if it was just Gaetan Kelly, helped her feel a little bit safer.

When Noemi returned to Lamplight, it was still much too early for anyone to be awake. She had been gone for over an hour, but it hadn't felt that long. The sun would rise, and she'd have to get up and dress for school. Rather than return to her own bed, she tiptoed softly to Jonas's room and let herself in, closing the door behind her.

"Jonas," she whispered.

Noemi shook him gently, and Jonas's loud breathing quieted. He groaned and shifted under his blankets.

"Are you awake?"

"Murr."

"Jonas."

"Noemi?"

He wiggled over to make room for her. Pulling off her coat, she let it drop to the floor. Noemi kicked her shoes off beside it, then gathered her legs up onto the bed and burrowed under the covers with him.

"What if someone else wakes up?" he asked, though even as he said it his arms encircled her.

Noemi's phone was a dark, useless box buried by the pile of her coat on the floor. Nothing that had happened tonight mattered now.

"Are you awake?" she asked.

"Nope." Almost as soon as he said it, he fell easily back to sleep.

She rested her thumb in the hard, shallow divot at the bottom of his sternum. Someday Jonas would die. There must have been a time before Noemi had learned about death, but she couldn't remember what that had been like. It was hard to conceive of her own absolute end; she could more easily imagine a time when she would be as good as dead to Jonas. He might vaguely remember her when he thought back on high school, but moments like this would be lost. She was sure she would remember this tiny instant—her thumb on his chest, his wrist against her back—and not just because it was the morning she had seen, touched, and talked to a dead person. It was because of the living person she now touched, how he let himself dream in her arms. She closed her eyes, and the moment soaked into her memory.

Without meaning to, Noemi slept too. She only woke to the sound of Jonas's cell phone alarm—loud as anything, quaking enough to shake the house—and before he could wipe the sleep from his eyes and remember what day it was, she rolled out of the bed and crept across the hall to her own room. No one else knew that she and Jonas were—well, whatever they were. If Cesca saw her daughter waking up in Jonas Lake's room, she might jump to all kinds of conclusions and send him away from Lamplight.

In her own bathroom, as she brushed her teeth, Noemi turned her phone on again and plugged it in to charge on the counter. A flurry of curses from "Laetan" greeted her, but no texts from Unknown.

As usual, Matt was the only person in the kitchen to wish her good morning when Noemi went downstairs to get breakfast. She was toasting a blueberry Eggo when Jonas entered the room. They held each other's gaze silently, something warm passing between them. As Matt got up to refill his mug with coffee, they heard a knock at the door.

"Lyle?" Matt asked.

"Better not be," Noemi said. "It's still too early." And Lyle never knocked.

Matt left to answer the door, and Noemi heard his voice exchange words with another, though she couldn't make out what was said. After a few seconds, Matt returned.

"Noemi, there's a friend of yours here to see you."

Jonas cocked an eyebrow, and Noemi shrugged.

Outside, Gaetan Kelly leaned against one of the pillars on the front porch.

"What are you doing here?"

"You weren't answering my messages." He pushed off the pole, posture straightening. He wore an unusually serious expression. "I wanted to check and see you weren't dead in a ditch somewhere."

"I told you I was fine. I didn't mean to be so dramatic. It was a strange night, and I just wanted some record of it." Noemi hadn't grabbed a coat before stepping outside. She wore a loose-fitting sweater that did little to keep her warm. The morning was freezing, and she hugged her arms tight against her chest.

"Are you gonna tell me what happened? Does this have something to do with Link?"

"Why would you think that?"

"How the hell should I know? The woods, going into chat for the first time in a year, asking who was using my handle...like, who else had the password except Link and me? You're not giving me a lot to go on."

Something creaked behind her. Jonas's slim form filled the crack in the doorway.

"Everything okay?" he asked.

"What are you, her mom?"

"Everything's fine. I'll be back in a sec."

Noemi and Gaetan waited in awkward silence for Jonas to go back inside.

"That guy's into you. Is it weird living with him?"

"No. Jonas and I are friends. He hasn't done anything weird."

"Yet."

"What do you want, Gaetan?"

He sighed. "What do I want? I don't know. Nothing, I guess."

"I'll see you in school."

Gaetan stepped backward off the porch and began heading for the driveway. He stopped after a few paces, turned back, and said, "You can text me whenever."

As his truck backed out of the drive, Noemi said aloud, to no one but herself, "That was weird."

Inside the house, Jonas gave her a meaningful look, and Noemi knew he expected her to tell him why one of their least favorite people had appeared on their doorstep at 7:00 a.m.

"Was that your Valentine I just met?" Matt asked.

"Definitely not."

"How about you, Jone? I noticed you went out last night too."

Jonas stuffed his mouth with an English muffin and made no attempt to respond.

"Well, I'm glad you're making friends." Matt resumed reading the news on his tablet.

Jonas swallowed. "What did he want?"

"I'm not one hundred percent sure." Noemi avoided looking at him while she plated her breakfast. "He was a friend of Link Miller's," she said to Matt. "The kid who died last year. Since I live near where Link died, sometimes he asks about it. I'm not sure why it couldn't wait until we were in school this time."

Jonas pushed the crumbs on his plate into a pile.

"That's rough," Matt said. "What do you say to that?"

"Not much, I guess."

Though Noemi hadn't been entirely forthright about what had led Gaetan to their doorstep, that last part was true. No one said much to him about Link, just like they'd avoided the subject of the brother he'd lost a decade ago. But what if instead of asking, *What do you want*—as though what she really meant was *Get off my porch*—she had asked him, *How are you doing*?

He might even have told her.

16

UNKNOWN

The first time I went to the lake, Noemi hadn't meant to take me. Gate and I were pitching beer bottles to each other and smashing them with baseball bats in the street by her house. We'd run out of empties, so he worked on draining another bottle. He'd stolen three six-packs from his stepdad's garage fridge, even though he knew he'd get the shit kicked out of him for it later. That's where my head was while he chugged. Sharp slivers of jade glass glittered on the pavement. I rolled my shoe over them, tried to make them smaller, duller. I thought about the time I had to help my best friend pull shards of a broken bottle out of his skin, how he was ashamed and I was ashamed. I'd rubbed my eyes with my wrist to keep tears from falling onto his back. Gate didn't cry about it. What right did I have?

A nearly empty bottle whizzed past my head, a few droplets

of beer falling cool into my scalp. It shattered six or so feet behind me on the street, close to where a surprised Noemi halted mid-step on the sidewalk. Of course, he had thrown it just because she was there.

He grinned, all the more triumphant when faced with her scowl. Thumping a fist against his chest, he belched and threw a peace sign into the air. Gaetan tailored his habits to whatever present company deemed *least* appropriate. At home, his family preferred him quiet and out of sight, punished him for being noisy, messy, or generally seen. Maybe that's why he liked to be so loud and unfurled everywhere else. He amped up this behavior tenfold when Noemi was around.

She looked at me, disapproving, even though she *knew* I hadn't thrown the bottle. But what difference did it make? I was there with him, breaking glass in the middle of the street. I was with him every time he said something mean or behaved recklessly. More often than not I was reckless alongside him. In that moment, I hated him.

"Someday someone might call the cops on you guys."

"You sound like you're a thousand years old." Gaetan lobbed insults at her, but he always looked happy when he did it. He enjoyed making himself into something she found repulsive. "Just relax. No one's gonna get a flat tire from a tiny piece of bottle. It's a victimless crime."

"Really? In the history of tires, not one has ever been damaged by a shard of glass?"

"God, you're whiny." He waved her off.

Noemi continued walking away from us, so I placed my bat on the ground and followed. Gate laughed, but I ignored him and didn't look back. She led me like a stray into the woods. The lake wasn't there yet. It was shy, or it hadn't been born. We looked for rocks and stones, and we built cairns on the forest floor. Mine were small; they ran in a single spiral. She built hers at the center, large and gray.

"Do you believe in aliens?" I asked her.

She quirked her head. "Is this when you tell me you were once abducted?"

"No."

"Well. There are innumerable galaxies in the known universe, each with, what, billions of stars? Even if we never meet the inhabitants of another planet, that doesn't mean there aren't any. So, yeah. I guess I believe in aliens. Why do you ask?"

"I don't believe in god," I confessed. "Not in the way most people mean. But sometimes I think god might be relative. If life on earth were the pet project of an alien race, that would make them our gods, right? Even if they were mortal like us. Even if they weren't all-knowing."

"You mean, like, if aliens engineered us in a lab?"

"Or oversaw our evolution."

"I take it this isn't a public school science education talking. You're something, Link. Do you talk to Gaetan about these things?"

I forced a laugh, all breath. Once, I'd tried to console Gaetan, telling him how I liked to think in another reality Elijah had never died. It was the angriest he'd ever been. He seemed almost to prefer the idea of his brother as worm food.

"If you think of 'god' as simply a creator," Noemi said, "then sure. But then you'd be the god of every picture you drew. Well, your drawings can't think. Bad example. Our parents would be our gods. Our phones and computers ought to be worshipping us." She selected a flat stone for the top of her cairn. "I don't believe in intelligent design—not of the universe. And even if your alien friends did build us, they wouldn't be *my* gods."

Even when she didn't agree with me, Noemi listened. With most people, I'd learned to keep my random thoughts to myself, pretend I didn't have any.

Noemi collected a small pile of twigs. She stepped carefully over each curve of my spiral to the tower she'd constructed at its center. There, she began to snap the slim branches into smaller pieces.

"Sometimes I have this dream that there's a lake in these woods with a lighthouse at the center." She began to place the sticks onto the top of her cairn. "Or, you know, maybe I just had it once, and it only felt like a recurring dream. It was so familiar. Have you ever had that happen?"

"Maybe? I don't usually remember my dreams."

"I'm thinking I should start writing them down. Anyway, in this dream I know exactly the way to get to the lake even though it's in a different part of the woods every time. And the woods are so big in the dream. Somehow I know it's a place that only I can find, but that doesn't feel strange. I don't think, *How is* that *possible?* In the dream I think, *I used to come here before. I'm so lucky I remembered. I'm so lucky to have a place like this.* See?"

Noemi pointed to the spiral, her finger tracing its shape in the air until she came to the tower at the center. With a little twig hut she'd assembled on top, her cairn did look like a lighthouse, surrounded by waves.

The lake would later form from nothing, as though someone had listened to her story, watched as I unknowingly helped her map the water around her lighthouse with piled stones. I was never afraid of the lake. Every time I dove into the water, I could swim back up to the surface I'd just broken through, and the world would be waiting. Lakes don't have lids that close over you once you're submerged. The lighthouse emerged gradually—not insomuch as it was built stone by stone, but in the way it solidified in our vision, as though it had always been there, just obscured at first by fog or the glare of the sun.

Not long before I died, we folded sea monsters from white, soluble paper. They looked like water dragons or horse boats—scoop bodies, long faces, pointed ears. Our monsters reminded me of the Midwinter ice boats; they too dissolved. We waded into the lake and watched them sink while Noemi took photos. On our next visit the boat waited, as though underwater all the horses had swum together to reform their pulp into something large enough for us to fit. I climbed into it and held my hand out for Noemi. She stepped into the boat, leaving my fingers empty. I began to row us toward the lighthouse.

Though it wasn't cold, the lake froze before we were even halfway there. I hadn't seen any ice when we left the dock, but we ran right into a sheet of it. Every inch of water from the front of the boat out to the structure in the distance had hardened and flattened. Behind us the water was unfrozen, so we turned back. Maybe the lake changed its mind about inviting us in. Maybe I had never been meant to go with her.

Days after we held our own anti-prom in the woods, I found the lake on my own for the first time. The boat wasn't there—the dock wasn't even there—but it felt like a peace offering. I thought the lake might have been trying to tell me I wasn't so alienating, even if it wasn't ready to invite me to the lighthouse. I hoped it didn't pity me. When I dipped my fingers in, it was summer-warm. I stripped off my shoes, my pants, my sweatshirt, and slipped into the water.

Everything was a dark, blue world. I couldn't see the lake bed, if there were one to see. My body was heavier than the water. My body was steel. I dove for centuries, and still I didn't reach the bottom. I waited for the water to stop, to deposit me into space. The light from the sun broke through the surface, reminding me the farther I got from it, the harder it would be to turn back. Small orbs of nitrogenous breath swarmed my head. I touched something I didn't recognize—a fish, a rock, a plant, the earth. It touched me back. I pulled my hand away and turned for the surface.

A stone finger flexed against the heel of my foot. The sun seemed so much farther from me than it ever had, as though I'd slipped through a hole to the far side of the solar system. It was a distant star, its light cooling above. I reached for it. If only you could hold on to light, climb it out of the unknown. Ice had rooted itself to the top of the lake, or something like ice. Glass. It wasn't cold. A molten ache crept along the walls of my trachea. I was trapped on the underside of one of the Midwinter ice boats. When had I become so small?

The thing I had touched had followed me up. Hand-shaped, it grabbed my foot. It was hard, a manacle around my ankle. It pulled me down, but I reached, my nails scraping the surface of the water, touching its lid. I could see the light through it, but I couldn't penetrate it. I wanted to burst into molecules and reassemble myself on the other side, but instead I let the surface slip away.

No. I did try. I fought whatever held me under. Its skin felt like something from a shipwreck, covered in years of rust and barnacles, angry as an urchin, tough as calcified coral. Arms dragged me with all the strength of an ocean. My vision faded. I forgot I couldn't breathe water. I took it inside of me. It invaded my lungs, and I died.

It left my body on the dry, grassy floor, my head tucked along a breaching tree root. I watched my body prune and pale, waiting for someone to discover it. How could I see and remember and *be* when I filled no space? But I did, somehow, remember. Whatever was left of me felt like Link. Bodiless me. Death didn't teach me anything beyond the fact that I was and wasn't worm food at the same time. The Schrödinger's cat of drowned teenagers. The cells that had comprised Lincoln Miller leaked and died on the forest floor. Bacteria had begun to spread throughout his—my—organs before my body was discovered and returned to my family for cremation. The calories from my body would float up into space and contribute nothing of value to the planet I once inhabited.

What, then, was I now?

JONAS

March in Shivery was a time for many residents to wear T-shirts and shorts, despite the lingering presence of snow piles by the roadsides. This did not apply to Jonas, who was unused to the wind whipping across the wide-open spaces. One afternoon the weather finally broke forty, and Noemi asked Jonas to come sit with her by the lake. This was a surprise: she'd seemed to be avoiding the place since Amberlyn had seen it.

"I'll help you with your French," Noemi said. He complained about the cold, and she clamped a huge pair of fluffy, gray earmuffs over his head.

When they got to the lake's edge, the boat was there, tied to the dock and waiting. Jonas lowered his backpack into the grass, and Noemi lowered hers onto the rowboat's wooden bottom.

"What are you doing?" he asked.

"I want to try to take it to the lighthouse."

Jonas didn't need to ask why. The place was strange, curious, and he'd half wanted to row the boat out there himself when he'd first seen it. Now the boat had returned on its own. It hadn't just drifted back: it had been docked. Its presence sent shivers up his legs.

"I thought you said it wasn't a good idea to take it out onto the water?"

"Well." Noemi stepped cautiously into the boat, then sat on one of its benches. "I did try once with Link, but we didn't get all the way there. I don't want anyone else to get stranded out on the water, but I'm not afraid of going out on my own." She pointed to where the rope had been knotted. "Will you untie me?"

"You're not going alone." When she sighed but didn't object, Jonas continued. "It's a long way. You can't row yourself the whole time. We'll take turns."

"You should stay here in case something happens."

Jonas stared, dropped his bag into the boat without breaking eye contact. It thudded by Noemi's feet. "In case what happens? You're *definitely* not going alone. In case something happens it's better that we're together. You've seen enough horror movies to know that." He would not be left behind. Did she really find his presence, or lack thereof, so inconsequential?

As large as the lake was, it was also waveless. Jonas couldn't see beneath the surface of the water. It reflected the sky so perfectly that when he looked down, his oars passed between fluffy clouds. His rowing stirred the surface of a mirror. Though Jonas had never been in a boat before, he took to the work well. He wasn't much for the gym, passing right by the weight room on his way to the parking lot while the Gaetan Kellys of Galaxie High worked the indoor rowers after school. His arms would surely ache tomorrow, but right now they felt helpful. Jonas had never much contemplated his own masculinity—not consciously. He'd experienced insecurity about his lips, his body, his inability to grow a single facial hair. Noemi voiced her opinions and acted decisively in a way he seldom did, but he liked these things about her. Still, that the boat moved by his physical strength while she sat across from him, stealing subtle glances his way—this satisfied a need he didn't know he'd had.

Was it pitiful that he wanted to be strong for her? His strength didn't, after all, necessitate her being weak. Jonas stopped rowing, briefly, to lean forward and kiss one of Noemi's thick, soft eyebrows. She didn't mind kisses when they weren't on her mouth. When she asked to row, they'd already covered 75 percent of the distance to the island, but Jonas relinquished the oars and let her go the rest of the way.

There was no proper dock on the lighthouse's island, so they climbed out of the boat and trudged until they'd dragged it onto the shore. The lighthouse had a stone base and tower and a small, wooden shack attached. Aside from the fact that it was in a tiny wood in southern Minnesota, there was nothing strange about it. Close up, it didn't strike Jonas as ominous or spooky. It simply seemed sad, maybe even lonesome. Judging by its height, one might expect to be able to see its highest point from outside the woods, but somehow, as Jonas had noticed during his last visit, the trees around the lake were tall enough that they towered over it.

Noemi stood and looked, not at the lighthouse that loomed overhead, but back out onto the water across which they'd traveled.

"When Link and I rowed out here, the lake froze before we made it all the way across. It hadn't frozen over behind us, so we were able to go back. But this time we made it. I wasn't really sure it would work."

"Maybe you couldn't see from the dock that it was half-frozen when you started."

"I figured that, but it sort of snuck up on us. It seemed like ice had formed in a blink."

Jonas knew that Noemi didn't believe in magic or fairy tales, but she behaved differently when she was near the lake. Something here kept her distracted.

"Everything okay?" he asked.

"Yeah, why?" She started walking toward the lighthouse, expecting him to follow.

"I don't know. You just seem a little quiet. You were like this the time we came here with Lyle and Amberlyn too. Is it hard to be here? Because of Link?"

"Well, it was super awkward with Amberlyn here."

From behind her and through the large puffs of faux mink on either side of his head, her voice was garbled. He removed the earmuffs and let them hang around his neck.

"But I wouldn't say it's difficult. Strange maybe." She turned back to Jonas, her jaw tense. "This place is a mystery, and I guess I can't help but start puzzling it out. That doesn't mean I'm upset or having some kind of moment. This"—she waved a hand in front of her face—"is my thinking face. People always ask me what's wrong. Do I look that troubled when I'm not talking?"

"I didn't mean anything like that. I guess I'm just worried about nothing." Sometimes Noemi was as much a mystery to him as the lake was to her.

They reached the door, which had either once been painted green or had gradually turned a dingy green after considerable time in the elements. It had no knob.

Noemi knocked, three slow beats in succession. The door shifted visibly under her knuckles. "Or..." She placed her fingers firmly against it and pushed, hard. It creaked open.

"I don't think we should go inside."

"Are you kidding, Jonas? Did you come all the way out here just to stay outside?" She lifted her hair and held it in a temporary ponytail with her fists. "But maybe that's not such a terrible idea. You can stand guard out here, I guess."

"I mean, aren't we trespassing?"

"I should have brought Lyle. Of the two of us, I thought I'd be the goody-goody, and you'd be the ne'er-do-well."

"Because I got kicked out of school? Fair. But you sneak around all the time."

"Don't be scared," she teased. "I'll protect you." Noemi pushed the door farther open. "Hello," she sang to the darkness inside.

The shack was lit only by the light pouring through the door-way. It had no windows and no artificial lighting, though it had a stone fireplace and seemed to have once been lived in. It held a table, two chairs, and a bed, all made of wood that retained the features of the trees they had been hewn from. It was almost as if the trees had grown in just the shapes needed to serve as furniture. It reminded Jonas of a hobbit hole, long abandoned and covered in cobwebs. Whoever had lived there had had only candles to see by: they'd melted against the wooden surface of the table and mantle. On the floor was a large, furry rug.

Jonas inspected the interior side of the door they had just passed through.

"There's a doorknob on this side," he said. He touched the ivory object. It resembled a paper crane wearing some kind of animal skull where its pinched beak should have been.

"Sinister."

"I'd have thought it would be up your alley. Maybe this was the home of some eccentric artist hermit."

"Something feels off." Noemi inspected the knob closer. Then she scanned the room. "What's also off is that there's no entrance for the tower in here. What the hell's that about?"

"Maybe the tower's just decorative."

"Well, that would be a waste." Noemi dragged one of the twisted, tree-trunk chairs from the far side of the hut to the entrance. "Prop the door open with this. Not taking any chances."

"You want to stick around?"

"Yeah. I want to get a closer look at this place."

Jonas helped her slide the chair into position as a doorstop, then followed her lead and inspected the room more closely, studying the wood-paneled walls closer in case another knob-less door was somehow disguised.

"So why *didn't* you ask Lyle to come?"

"I don't know. I know she's spending more time with Amberlyn lately. It sort of seems like we haven't been involving each other in our lives quite as much. I haven't told her you and I are...whatever, but I think she knows." Noemi approached the fireplace. "Do you hear that?"

"Hm? Changing the subject?"

"No." She raised a palm to silence him. "It's like faint music."

"Singing?"

"I don't think so. Violin or something. Some string instrument."

Jonas tipped his head forward and searched the air. "I don't hear it. You have bat ears."

Noemi knelt on the furry, brown rug, peeled it back. There, in the floor, was a trapdoor: a simple, wooden rectangle with a handle nestled in a shallow impression.

"At least this one has a handle," Noemi said. She lifted the door upward by its metal ring, and together they peered into the dark hole beneath them.

"I thought we'd be climbing up," she said, "into a tower. Not down. There's a ladder."

He could see only its first few rungs, but it looked completely vertical.

"I really don't think we should. Do you still hear music?"

"Definitely." Noemi nodded. She began to lower herself onto the ladder. "It's coming from down there."

"That means some*one*'s down there."

His imagination traveled straight to a blood-drenched serial killer merrily playing a concerto on a human torso, but Noemi was not deterred. Jonas watched the top of her curly hair fade into the darkness. He called her name, but she ignored him. Swearing under his breath, he cautiously reached his feet for the ladder rungs and followed her down.

"Noemi? Are you at the bottom yet?"

A cool, concentrated beam burst up at him from the darkness below, and when Jonas looked down, he saw her face illuminated by the rectangular light of her phone. As he finally neared the ground, Noemi placed her hand against his lower back, guiding him through the last few feet.

Jonas took in his surroundings as much as was possible. He turned on his own cell phone's flashlight. Once his eyes adjusted, Jonas realized they stood in a small, stone room. Though narrow, it extended quite a distance, and he could make out a greenish glow at the far end. He directed his flashlight to the walls.

"A tunnel," he said.

"Sort of." Noemi took his wrist and turned his flashlight toward the ground. "An underground channel." Just near their feet, the stone floor dropped off into a narrow, water-filled passage, opaque and green. In it floated a rowboat, much like the one they'd taken to the island.

"What the fucking hell?" Jonas swung his phone around so the light bounced off every plane it could reach. "Are we underneath the lake? Why is this here? What the *hell*?"

"And you thought life outside the Cities would be boring."

"This is so weird."

Noemi shushed him. "You don't need to narrate," she said. "Keep your voice down. We're going toward the music, and I think we should do it quietly." Slowly she stepped into the boat.

"What are you talking about?" he demanded. "This is a lair, Noemi. We should quit while we're ahead. There could be a face-eating serial killer at the end of that tunnel. I don't want my only accomplishment in this world to be a gruesome death that inspires a Rob Zombie movie."

"I told you before you can stay behind. Untie me." She stared at him from her seat between the oars, but he didn't move. "Who would they cast to play you in this horror movie?"

"Probably someone who looks nothing like me. *Minnesota Face-Eating Lair Massacre*, starring two model-actors as teens who get their faces eaten in a lair. Based on a true story."

"Does this mean you're coming with?"

"Shit. Yes. Scoot over, please."

Jonas untied the boat, but this time Noemi rowed, the channel just wide enough. The oars scraped against the side of the boat each time she pushed them forward, and Jonas strained to make out the music she said she'd heard.

"What's wrong?" she asked.

"Do you still hear the music?"

She ceased her movements. As the boat drifted to still, the water lapped against it more and more quietly until the sound of its soft kisses disappeared. Then Jonas heard it: the song of a violin emanating from the chamber of green light at the end of the tunnel. He twisted to face it.

"I hear it more clearly now."

Noemi sounded very far away. The boat rocked violently, and Jonas turned back in time to see her abandon it for the water. She left her phone and backpack behind and waded awkwardly through the waist-high muck with astronaut-slow steps.

"What are you doing?" Jonas asked.

He reached for her shoulder, instinct telling him to pull her back into the boat. Something inside his head wasn't right, a creature burrowing to the center. The music became loud, clearer than his own thoughts. Was it inside him? Was he imagining it? Smoke filled his skull. Two molten thumbs pressed against the backs of his eyes. Jonas tried to move his arms, but he was frozen in half sleep, limbs numb. When he finally forced his hands to move, they flopped uselessly at the ends of his skeleton wrists, nothing between his skin and bone.

He needed his earplugs, the focus they offered him when he wanted to sleep or study or ignore an obnoxious conversation. Then he remembered the muffs—better than nothing. It took everything to do it, to move under oppressive gravity, but Jonas pulled the earmuffs back onto his head and slipped into an ocean of quiet.

Noemi had gone. How long had he been sitting alone in the boat? Jonas whisper-called her name, but he feared being any louder until he knew what lay ahead. Picking up the oars, he rowed, as fast as possible, for the green glow at the channel's end. To block out any distractions, he focused on the now isolated sound of wood on wood.

Jonas knotted the rowboat to the post on the dock—another, smaller platform—as best he could with shaking hands. An arched doorway led to a room so large, he couldn't see the whole of it until he stepped inside. He stood in a domed space with a ceiling of windows clustered like honeycomb, draped in algae. Light filtered through them, through the water above and outside them, casting the chamber in a pale, green gloom. Noemi, in the room's center, had her back turned to him. He saw no one with her, no source of music.

"Noemi?"

She didn't move. She stood frozen, statue still, part of the structure of the room. Her arms hung by her sides, and a puddle of water formed at her feet, creeping across a floor dotted with large, dark stains like the surface of the moon.

Slowly, Jonas approached her. He called her name again, and again she did not react. Noemi continued to stare at the curved wall of windows directly ahead. A violin rested unattended on the floor just by her. It was old, the hair on the bow beside it loose and fraying. The only entrance to the room was the one through which Jonas had just entered. There was nowhere for the instrument's player to have gone.

"Who was playing it?" he asked.

Noemi finally moved her head to look at him, look through him. He reached for her arm, his touch cautious, and pulled her into a gentle spin. Once she faced him fully, she blinked, clearing a fog from her eyes.

She said his name, quietly. He saw more than heard it. Then she noticed the water around her feet, stepped out from the puddle and left fresh, gray footprints on a patch of dry floor. Spotting the violin, she bent to lift the instrument, said something Jonas couldn't quite hear. His skin sprouted goose pimples.

"Are you all right? Can we go back?" he asked.

She flexed her fingers, studied her body to inspect whether she was indeed all right. "I'm soaked," she said, noticing the water that drenched her clothes from partway down her shirt to the puddle that gathered around her sopping shoes. "Did I fall out of the boat?"

"*Fall* out of the boat? You jumped out."

Noemi dropped the violin, and the earmuffs did nothing to disguise its clatter. He wrapped an arm around her and pulled her close as he backed toward the dock. The stale water from her clothing seeped into his. She'd joked, before, when he'd hesitated: she would protect him. In truth, he'd stepped into the boats and the house and the deep, dark hole in the ground because she'd been so certain. She was always certain, and it made him feel safe.

Now she was shivering, translucent, and Jonas feared that if they couldn't climb to the surface quickly enough, the entire chamber—and the lake and forest with it—would collapse on them. His spine twitched as the emptiness of the room behind him swelled against his back.

This time, Jonas faced forward and held the oars, while Noemi stared at the room they left behind. Her face, pale and green-tinged by the water-fractured light, did not seem distracted or agitated in the way it had before. Her eyes were wide, even in darkness, and she reminded him of Rosencrantz and Guildenstern, how their pupils spread when something surprised them.

Jonas's arms propelled them through the water, even as they begged for rest.

"Maybe I should take up crew."

The boat finally struck the stone dock platform. They didn't even bother to tie it off this time. Noemi climbed the ladder, and Jonas followed quickly behind. Once they were back in the shack—just as they'd left it—they slammed the trapdoor closed, and Jonas kicked the rug over it. The tree-trunk chair still propped open the entryway. Noemi nudged it aside. Finally, they were out on the grass again. With no outer knob or handle, they couldn't shut the door all the way, so they left it slightly ajar behind them.

"Holy shit. The boat's still here." Jonas bent over in front of it, hands on his knees while he caught his breath, the sight of this pale, topside boat now welcome. "Thank goodness."

They took turns rowing as they headed for the woods, and they also took turns looking back to the island. Nothing emerged from the house. Nothing watched them return to where they'd come from, not that they could see. Once their feet hit land, they gathered their things and sprinted from the lake, neither one of them speaking until the trees hid the water and the lighthouse from view, which somehow felt like seeking out privacy. Jonas tapped Noemi's elbow, and she slowed, looked up at him, and he realized he was supposed to speak.

"Feeling okay?" he asked.

"Yeah." She nodded. "I spaced out for a bit. Thanks for keeping it together."

He touched her hair, pressed against her curls until he felt her neck. She tilted her head back and closed her eyes, relieved. When she opened them, the dreaminess had left her altogether. The air was cold against his skin. Noemi must have been freezing. Remembering his blank-minded panic when she slipped from the boat into the water, Jonas took her by the waist and pulled her against him, hooked his arms around her and drew out the cold and the damp and anything else that had gone wrong under the lake, which might still be soaking through her. She burrowed into him like he was made of blankets. Then she let him rest his hand on her back as they walked to Lamplight.

"You didn't see anyone in the room when you got there?" he asked, finally, once they were out of the woods.

"Not a soul." Noemi shook her head. "I was in the boat, music playing, and then I wasn't. It was quiet, and my clothes were wet, and we were standing in that room." She folded her arms and kicked a stray rock in the grass, but it was too pressed into the ground to budge. "I might be forested out for a little while."

Hearing her say that released him from a worry he didn't know had held him, and as they cut through the lupine field, Jonas resolved not to ask any more questions about Link, the forest, the lake, or anything that had happened there—to focus only on what was real.

18

NOEMI

Noemi had heard a violin in the woods once before, though she had then dismissed it as imagination.

She and Link had skipped prom. He'd purchased a small bouquet of bright pink tulips from the grocery store—even though he knew, after the Valentine's Day debacle, they weren't her favorite flower. Cesca and Matt, as well as Audrey and Diana, were present when he met her at her house. Noemi smiled in spite of herself when she took the bouquet. She refused to let her mother take pictures because they "weren't even going to prom," but Cesca snapped candids with her cell phone whether her daughter liked it or not.

They walked through the lupine field together. Noemi wore a two-piece dress with a sweetheart neckline, Link a pair of slacks rolled at the ankle to disguise that he was too tall for them. She removed her heels in the woods and stepped barefoot over tree roots. Together, they sat on the stone dock of the lake with their feet in the water. They ate food Link had made—some sort of avocado-stuffed sweet potato. Noemi had brought three cupcakes that she'd decorated to look like the raccoons he'd adopted.

When they danced, Noemi wondered if Link had set up music somewhere discreet—she heard what sounded like a violin—but he said he hadn't. Fireflies weren't a very common sight in Shivery, but there they were. The insects arrived even before sunset and glimmered faintly. Then it started to rain, and they took shelter under the trees.

"Hey, Noemi?"

"Hm?"

"What are we?"

"Stardust?"

In truth she was evading the subject, but it would not have been unlike Link to mean the question literally, so she hoped with this answer he'd let it drop.

"I meant what are you and I?" he asked. "As a couple. Or not a couple. I really like you, but I'm not sure how you feel."

"I like things the way they are," she said.

"Okay, but I don't know what that is. That's what I'm asking." Their eyes met. He glanced down to her lips like he might kiss her, and she wasn't sure how to suspend this moment so nothing would ever change.

"We're friends."

"And nothing else?"

"That's just not what I want." She frowned. In truth she didn't know what she wanted, but saying so would only confuse him. She wanted things to stay the way they were. She wanted to revel in his adoration without offering any in return. She wanted to always feel the way she did now when she ran into him somewhere unexpected: suddenly safe and less alone. She wanted to open her locker door and find a forest built for her by someone decent, someone who thought about her all time, heart racing, throat tight. She *wanted* to give him whatever he needed in return, but she couldn't. Link was wonderful, but if whatever she felt for him matched what he felt, wouldn't she be happier now? Wouldn't she know what should come next? Everything he made her feel was more about herself than it was about him: the small, perfect person reflected in the thundercloud gray of his eyes.

"Okay," he said finally.

"I hope we *can* still be friends."

"Of course. I wouldn't want to change that. But I have to go."

"You have to leave? Now?"

"Yeah. I'm not angry. And really, I'm happy to be friends."

Noemi folded her arms. "That's not the sense I'm getting."

"Well, at the moment I guess I just feel crappy. I don't think that's going to change if I stay. I just need to be alone. I can walk you home."

"I know the way."

He left, and he didn't look back. He loosened his tie and lit a cigarette and disappeared into the trees. Noemi walked herself home. Audrey asked how her "prom" went, and Noemi said it had been fine and scurried upstairs. In her room she drew her curtains and collapsed into bed. Link would be fine. He would move on, eventually fall for someone else, and his feelings for Noemi would be erased from the story of his life. She believed that.

And really, it should have been true.

19

JONAS

Jonas didn't understand why Noemi wouldn't kiss him. Months of dating, and her body still went rigid, her face turned away. He'd hoped they'd have had sex by now, but that didn't seem at all to be in their near future. Fear of losing the relationship prevented him from pressing the issue until doubt gave him no choice. His skull had become a cave of speculation.

"Do you like me?" he asked, finally.

They sat in the loft of the stable. It snowed outside, *again*, and the wind clapped the large, wooden barn doors. The streets were too warm for the snow to stick. Earlier, they had gone to a cafe by the river to sip mint hot chocolate and watch the ice through the windows as it melted and cracked away, floating downriver like little white barges piled high with sugar. Now they had their legs folded atop Noemi's floating bed as she taught Jonas how to play spades with a deck of cards.

"I'm not a masochist. Why else would I spend so much time with you?" She drew a card, considered it, then looked instead to him. "Of course I like you."

"It doesn't always feel that way."

"What do you mean?"

She placed her cards facedown on the white quilt so he couldn't see her hand. Jonas swallowed. Embarrassment lodged like a cherry pit in his throat.

"Sometimes I feel like you see me as a really close friend."

"No." She used her *Am-I-the-only-one-who-did-the-reading?* voice. "Well, yes. You *are* my really close friend, but I 'like' you too. Romantically." She enunciated the last word slowly, in four monotone syllables. "I do things with you that I don't do with my other friends. Or with anyone."

He knew the *things* she meant. When no one else was home, they might slip into bed together where he held her. They stripped down to their underwear, pressed their bodies until his insides twisted. He kissed her neck; she kissed his belly. When he told her he loved her, she even kissed his mouth. She sat half in his lap when they couldn't get two seats together at the theater. She took home the smushed-but-still-edible cupcakes from work and fed them to him from her mouth. He did his homework in her bathroom while she held her breath underwater in the tub. Her baths smelled like rosewood or black currant or bergamot. But she didn't seem to want him. Not really. Not the way he wanted her.

Jonas had never had sex. The way Noemi spoke, he was reasonably certain she was also inexperienced, but he was afraid to probe further. He knew he'd be embarrassed if she'd asked him. Maybe she wasn't ready to be physical with anyone after Link. Maybe she just didn't feel ready because she didn't feel ready. Jonas felt ready. He was so ready he wanted to throw himself against her, give her everything that was his to give.

"I just want to be sure," he said. He moved toward her, and his knee on the mattress stirred the cards from their piles.

Jonas kissed her. Noemi's teeth clicked his lip ring. She leaned backward and cradled the back of his neck with her hands. He liked the way her hair stayed curled around his fingers. It spread across the pillow, feathering the edges of her head. Noemi looked past him—huge eyes unfocused—over his shoulder and to the rafters. Jonas touched the narrow, red ridge winter had left in her bottom lip, his thumb tracing the soft skin around it. Every freckle on her face he'd memorized, and he was beginning to learn the rest of them as well.

Jonas watched Noemi when she didn't even know it. French was his favorite class because they had it together. Even though they lived under the same roof, being in a room with her sent a burst of thunder through his heart. People at school thought she wasn't very nice. She corrected them when they said anything erroneous in class. She was opinionated and argued over things others thought small, easily exasperated, her annoyance always plain on her face whether she meant to show it or not.

Strangers asked Jonas why she was so grumpy. They told her she should smile more. They must not have noticed she had a special eye for kids who ate alone at lunch or weren't picked for group projects, inviting them into her world. She preferred to work alone but hated seeing others alienated. She back-talked bullies even when she wasn't the object of their teasing. She read, or drew, or fiddled with her camera during class, but she always knew the answers when called upon; teachers never tripped her up. Her teams always won during pre-exam-review trivia, and her French was beautiful. Gaetan Kelly thought he could ruin her grade by partnering with her for ballroom dancing, but instead he'd earned perfect marks in PE for the first time all year—because even though Noemi told the coaches compulsory dancing was a waste of her time, she internalized every instruction given to her.

When she showed Jonas her heart, it was something special. And he, who usually wanted to remain invisible, hoped Noemi could see the things that were best in him.

But it was also important—so much more important than he'd expected—that she find him desirable. Maybe she had a type, and Jonas wasn't it. He'd searched for more pictures of Link Miller—in her room, on social media. The kid didn't seem to have had his own online presence, so Jonas stalked Amberlyn's old feeds. Link was tall. Very tall. Tallest-kid-in-school tall. It couldn't be that.

How many people were that tall? Jonas was tall, but he topped out just over six feet. Link was lanky. So was Jonas. Link's hair was longer. Jonas could grow his. Noemi had called Jonas "pretty." It hadn't felt reassuring at the time, but she promised it was just as good as "handsome" or "sexy." Link was...geometric. Angular. Jonas couldn't imagine anyone calling Link "pretty." Maybe Jonas would grow out of his prettiness. The way Noemi looked at him could change with time.

Maybe she'd wilted too in Link's arms.

Maybe she just wasn't ready.

"You're beautiful," he told her. "Sexy."

"Okay," she answered, disbelieving—like he was a liar. "No weird dirty talk."

"It's not weird dirty talk."

"I appreciate the compliment," she said. "The way you said it—all breathy. It just sounds so funny to me. Just be real."

Jonas sat back, balancing on his shins so he didn't crush her pelvis. He thought if he asked her what he wanted to know, he might cry in the middle of saying it, and she would laugh at him. *Do you not find me attractive?* She would laugh at him again every time she looked at him forever.

"Sorry," she said. "I like you. Just be yourself with me."

"I'm being myself. I said what was on my mind. You're sexy. *I* think you're sexy. It's not just physical, but that's part of it. I don't think there's anything wrong with wanting to be physical with someone you care about."

"No," she said. "I don't think that's wrong."

"Don't you ever feel that way about me?"

"Of course. I love the way you look. I love being with you."

"Do you ever think about having sex with me? Or even kissing me? Or want anything besides wrestling or holding hands?"

"I don't think about having sex with anybody."

"Okay."

Jonas stopped straddling her, knelt instead beside her. Noemi sat up, her back against the iron headboard. The bed swayed.

"I'm not trying to pressure you," he said. "We can wait. I guess I just wanted to make sure it wasn't me. Sometimes I think I know what you feel about me, and then other times I worry. Maybe I just have issues."

"No, it's okay. You don't have issues. I like looking at you more than anyone. And I like being near you and touching you. But I'm not sure I'll ever be ready."

"Because of Link? I'm not in a hurry. I just—I wonder if you have any interest in that stuff with me, ever."

Noemi's eyebrows grew flat and angry, her jaw set. "I'm not hung up on Link. It wasn't like that with him. He has nothing to do with how I feel about you."

"I thought—"

"I never kissed anyone before you kissed me that day in the woods." She tweezed white threads from the quilt's embroidery with her nails.

Jonas didn't know what to say. Everything he thought he knew was wrong. Of course she too could be shy, uncertain. The distance between them shrank, and it also grew.

"I don't like kissing," she said. "But I let you kiss me because I like you. Because I love you."

Those last three words broke him in half. Outside it stopped snowing. Jonas knew even though he couldn't hear or see it. All he saw was a warm glow of lamplight on the skin of someone he loved. But he knew, outside the walls of the stable, the world was a Tesla coil, bright and crackling on all sides of him. Inside him the organs he couldn't see or hear grew bright and crackled too.

"I love you too."

"There are things," she said, "I'd let you do, but they'd be for you. Not for me. I don't know if I'll ever want those things from anyone. I thought I would by now, but I don't. I don't think I need them the way everyone else does. Not yet. I don't know. Maybe it'll change someday, but I feel—I feel very certain that it won't."

"I can help you figure out what you like or don't like."

She rolled her eyes. "How generous."

"I'm not saying that to get in your pants."

"I don't wear pants."

"I'm serious. I think if we love each other, we can compromise a little. I won't ask for things I know you don't like. We can figure out what we're comfortable with together. Really. I want to make you happy. I want you to feel good. I don't want to make you do things just for me."

Noemi began gathering the playing cards and ordering them in their box.

"You say that now," she said. "Eventually you'll want to have sex of some kind, and if you're not willing to accept something I'll mainly do for your satisfaction, you're going to be lonely and unsatisfied."

"But you said you don't know you won't *ever* change your mind about being disinterested in sex."

"And I don't know I will. I don't *feel* like I will. I said that too."

"We're young. I don't mind waiting."

Noemi stood. "You might be waiting a long time."

Why had things turned so wrong? She had just said she loved him, but now she was slipping away.

"I think it's easier for me to tell you now where my comfort zone begins and ends." Her voice cracked. She brushed her eyes with the back of her wrist. A wet spot bloomed on the small, cardboard box in her hand.

"What is happening?" Jonas mumbled.

"It's good we had this talk, Jonas. I want so much to be with you." Her eyes were wet, her face flushed. *What talk?* "It's going to be so much harder when I still want to be with you later, and you've gotten tired of waiting. There are a lot of girls who aren't—I don't know. There are a lot of girls who will like you as much as you like them *and* want to kiss you."

He didn't know what she was telling him.

"I don't want to make you compromise."

"Everyone compromises," he said. He felt his voice hard in his mouth, softened it. "What kind of love is uncompromising?"

"Like you said, we're young. There's so much time for you to meet someone perfect."

"You're everyone I want. Why are you acting like *I'm* laying down some kind of ultimatum? How come *you* know what you will and won't want in the future, but I don't know what I'll want? You can't decide what I need *for* me. That's not fair."

"I'm sorry. I just don't want us to resent each other. And I don't want to hold you back."

Noemi began climbing down the ladder.

"Hold me back from what? Noemi? What is going on? Are you breaking up with me?"

She didn't stop. She descended, and her face disappeared from view. He had to strain to hear her calling up to him.

"We weren't really together."

Noemi heaved the stable door open against the wind. She didn't look at him, so he couldn't see her mouth. Just the top of her head. She might have said *I'm sorry,* but the weather swallowed it.

DISSECTED HEART

I dreamt I cut my heart into so many pieces that some of them were see-through. I first removed it from my body through my throat. I felt a string on my tongue, and after I pulled and pulled for a very long time, it came out through my mouth, red and wet. I used a steak knife so large it was almost as wide as my heart. With each slice, the softest parts of me dripped from the edges. Once I had it in enough lunchmeat-thin slivers, I began to dig holes. I used my hands to scoop out the earth, and I dug in the forest and in the flower field, in the rose garden behind the inn, and in the yard. I laid each segment of my heart at the bottom of a hole, then piled the dirt in again. After the pieces were gone, all that was left was the center.

This was the hardest piece, like a little olive pit but ruby red. I tried to cut this last piece smaller, but it was so tough that the knife shattered, sending sharp, silver shards into the dirt. All around me the other pieces of my heart were waking up. They sounded far away, but I could still see the earth and tree roots trembling over the places where they had been buried. I needed to find somewhere to put the last piece so the rest would all be quiet.

I walked through the forest until I found the lake.

"I have to hide the last piece of my heart," I said to the water.

"Hide it from what?" The voice came from over my shoulder. I didn't turn around, but water drip-dripped onto the grass behind me.

"Everyone. But the last piece—it's the center. It has to be hidden best of all. It's the part where Jonas lives. I don't want him ever, ever to have the whole thing, so this bit has to be far away from the others."

"I see."

I held it over the water. "What's at the bottom?"

"Nothing," the voice said. "Nothing forever."

So I opened my hand
and let it drop.

AMBERLYN

Lyle wore her usual uniform: black jeans, band T-shirt, flannel jacket, red lipstick. Her hair was beginning to show blond at the roots where she hadn't bleached it, but she'd been touching up the green dye on the ends, and her bob was now three-toned. She threaded her fingers through Amberlyn's, and the two walked side by side among the trees. A song Amberlyn didn't recognize played through the bud in her right ear, chant-like.

"We'll keep walking until we get to the water," Lyle said.

They had agreed at Halloween, along with Jonas and Noemi, that none of them would return to the lake without the rest. Thus far, Amberlyn had kept that promise. She'd been the one to suggest it, after all. It hadn't been difficult, with school and hockey to preoccupy her and the winter weather making the woods seem a hostile place. Now, it was April, and the snow had finally thawed. Nearly a year had passed since Link had drowned, and Shivery was starting again to resemble what it was like on his last day alive, but Amberlyn understood little more than she had when he'd died.

She feared she would have to convince Lyle to search for the lake again with her—Noemi and Jonas had retreated into each other, and a guided expedition seemed less and less likely—but that turned out not to be the case. All she'd needed to do was ask.

The toe of one of Lyle's black boots caught under the arc of a raised tree root. Amberlyn didn't notice until she felt the weight in her hand shift, and they tilted toward the ground together. Lyle released her hand, but it was too late, and Amberlyn collapsed on top of her.

"Are you okay?" Amberlyn asked. She wore black leggings with sheer inserts, and damp dirt had squished through the mesh over her knee. It crumbled down her leg, catching somewhere by her ankles.

Lyle laughed. She laughed easily. Her laughter was high and musical like wind chimes.

"I'm fine," Lyle said. She sat up, propping her back against a tree trunk. "I'm *so* sorry. What a klutz. Are you okay?"

"Fine. Just a little wet." Amberlyn rolled up the ankles of her pants, let the dirt that had gathered shower over her sneakers. She sat beside Lyle—the tree she'd chosen almost wide enough for both of them side by side—and looked up at the narrow branches fracturing the sky. "It doesn't feel like April, with all these leaves on the ground."

"When we were kids, there used to be morning glories growing up the tree trunks. Blue and pink and purple." Lyle shimmied lower and nestled her head against Amberlyn's shoulder.

"That sounds cool," Amberlyn said. "I've never seen morning glories in the wild before. I've only ever seen them growing up fences or mailboxes. My dad had some blue ones planted by the front porch of my house growing up. Link wrapped them around the wrought iron posts of the stair rail, just playing around. We didn't know they were creeping plants. Eventually they covered the rail. It seemed like magic."

"Noemi used to wear them in her hair," Lyle said. "Because it was so curly, they just stayed in. They'd fall out of mine."

"What's going on with you guys?" Amberlyn's palm hovered flat above the ground, just close enough to sense its chill. It trembled—her hand, the grass.

"What do you mean?"

"Do you hang out one-on-one anymore? Are you mad at her about something? Not that I don't appreciate that you came out here with me, but I'm kind of surprised you were okay doing it without her. You know she'd hate it."

"So? We don't need her permission to hang out here. Despite what she thinks."

"Right, but usually you hate the idea of her being mad at you. On Halloween you pretended you saw my costume for the first time that night because she couldn't know you bought it with me. You didn't want to hurt her feelings. Is this a secret too?"

"I don't care. She does plenty of things that don't involve me. We're separate people." Lyle flicked a tiny, pale toadstool with her middle finger, so hard the cap flew clean off and settled in the grass several feet away.

"Have you guys ever hooked up?"

"Me and Noemi?" Lyle lifted her head from Amberlyn's shoulder and looked at her, eyes narrowed. Her irises were caught between blue and every other color, the kind of blue that only eyes could be.

"Who else?"

Lyle shook her head. "We're like sisters. I'm surprised you'd even think that. Does it really seem like I think of her that way?"

"I can't really tell. I like to think I'm pretty perceptive, but maybe sometimes I'm too sensitive to what I think are *vibes*."

"I love her, but not like that. Have you ever been in love?"

"Definitely not. I've got my eyes set on being a cat lady. Except maybe with small mammals. Hamster lady?"

"Hamster lady is an underrated life goal." Lyle stood, brushed the grass off her bottom.

"Have you been in love?" Amberlyn asked.

"Not with Noemi."

"With someone else? Someone I know?"

"Eh."

Lyle smiled, then pulled her lips quickly closed—tucked the

smile away again like a secret note that, now read, could be burned. Her teeth were white, straight. Not a stitch of lipstick on them, but she moved her tongue across them anyway. It swelled under the skin between her nose and mouth.

"Are you as fast on your feet as you are on skates?" Lyle asked.

"I'm not slow."

"Let's see who finds the water first, then."

She was gone before Amberlyn had even stood. Amberlyn took her time getting to her feet, tightened her shoelaces. She stretched, arms up, neck craned. Then she took off in the direction Lyle had run.

Chasing Lyle was a leisurely game. Amberlyn didn't have to fight to keep near her. She disappeared occasionally from view, weaving between trees, but Amberlyn easily caught sight of her plaid jacket or her yellow-green hair emerging from behind a trunk or low branch. She might have been the loudest, most haphazard runner in Minnesota.

It seemed as though all around them branches were snapping, leaves shuffling. Each footfall came from twice as many steps as it should have, like a row of impatient fingers drumming. Though Lyle was in front, her rhythmic breath had stretched and bent until Amberlyn heard it behind her, a snorting in her ear, rustling the strands of hair that had drifted loose from her ponytail. They finally stopped when they reached sight of the lake. Even if they had happened onto it only by chance, Amberlyn felt she'd been let in on one of her brother's secrets.

Lyle doubled over, hands on her knees, breath no longer steady.

"So...out of...shape."

Though they were both motionless, the woods behind them still clattered as though something were tumbling through branches. Not wind. A heavy something, with mass and muscles and a will to move.

Amberlyn turned and saw what she thought was a deer. She'd never seen one so pale, so stark against its surroundings, like moonlight carving up night. Saying nothing, she placed a hand on Lyle's back, nodded in the direction of the creature. The girls watched it move. Its coat wasn't sleek. The closer it came, the more Amberlyn could make out the ropey textures of its tangled fur. It had a single antler, braided outward from one side of its head, the other side bare as a doe's. She didn't know much about deer, but its lone antler looked strange, surrounded by a ring of shorter nubs, as though a new one had started growing before the old had shed. It reminded Amberlyn of the photos she'd seen of the spiny white fungus that attached itself to insects, turned them into zombies.

When the deer-thing emerged from the woods to stand before them on the lakeshore, Amberlyn and Lyle each took one, tentative step back. It was not a deer. Its body was bulky, its face long, nostrils wide. It had a white mane that spilled in snarls. The thing was a horse, the antler a white birch branch sprouting from its head. Its body seemed to be more of the same, and with every step it took—even on bare grass—wood twisted and snapped.

Lyle pinched Amberlyn's arm and pulled her aside, so they were out of the creature's path. It barely regarded them—two dark eyes made of water—before swaying past them to the lake. Droplets streamed from its hair and tail in steady rivers. Its gray hooves left deep puddles pressed into the ground. Red algae clung to the contours of its chest, spidering along its ribs. Freshwater mollusks had settled along its back. Amberlyn leaned toward one of the hoof prints, and a tiny, silver fish circled its edges.

The horse walked into the water. Without hesitation, it headed farther and deeper, the lake creeping up its back, fur milky and vague. Finally, just its head was visible above the surface, then the antler slicing the lake like the sail-less mast of a sinking ship, until it vanished altogether. No bubbles rose from where it had gone under, only a rippling *V*.

JONAS

Jonas still sat with Noemi and her friends at lunch. He still rode with them to school. Noemi treated him as though they were still friends—but with kid gloves. Cautious. Deliberate. They were never alone together. Even at home, he barely saw her unless Lyle and Amberlyn were there as well. Once he found her on a chaise in the sitting room, a blanket draped over the back of the couch and spilling onto the floor, Noemi nestling, tented, inside. She'd drawn the curtains across the early evening light, and a warm lamp with a stained-glass shade illuminated the room. Jonas knelt, lifted the edge of the blanket, uncovered her curled beneath it with her legs pulled against her chest and a unicorn headphone bud peeking out from within her ear.

"Did I wake you?" he asked, though he saw her quickly close the text messages on her phone. Lyle, most likely.

"No. I wasn't sleeping. Just trying to relax."

"Oh." Jonas let the blanket fall behind him and joined her in the burrow.

"I feel anxious."

"What about?"

"Nothing." Noemi removed the headphone and closed her hand over the little, rubbery unicorn. "I just get anxious. A physical anxiety with no real reason. I can feel my pulse ticking and my veins getting knotted."

"Music helps?"

"No. It's some kind of white noise app." She flicked on the screen of her phone and pulled up the sound mix: "Cat Purring, Rain on Roof."

Jonas was afraid to say the wrong thing, that she might remember whatever was between them had broken and leave the blanket behind, go upstairs, close her bedroom door, and shut him out. He might well have been handling a chrysalis, this moment between them so thin and delicate he could see through it to all its potential ends.

"Cat purring relaxes me. I wish I were tiny enough to use Rosencrantz or Guildenstern as a pillow, but this is the next best thing."

"What other sounds relax you?"

"Water sounds, generally." Should that have been obvious or completely unlikely? "But other things help too. Low light. Making a small space around myself."

"My dad listens to white noise sometimes when he does puzzles," Jonas said. He was surprised by this overlap in Noemi's and Matt's interests.

"What relaxes you?" she asked. "Or are you always as meditative as you seem?"

"I guess I don't really create moments like this for myself. I like low light too, but natural light. Like when it's raining."

She traced imaginary raindrops in the air with her fingers. He wanted to touch his fingertips to hers.

"I like the kind of gray daylight of it. And I like cool sheets. So I think if I were in a clean bed, and it were *about* to rain, that would be relaxing." He scraped his fingernail against the velvety fabric of the chaise and left a light line in the dark, raspberry surface. "And a heartbeat. Not the sound of it, but the feel of it."

"That's what bugs me." Noemi shook her head, and a curl drifted across her face. "I hate being so anxious I can feel my pulse in my head. My body is like one big heartbeat."

It was exactly *her* pulse that he had been thinking of. He missed the feel of her body alive against him, her heart, lungs, bloodstream all working efficiently to power the person he cared about. The things that mattered most about her were intangible, but he appreciated the tangible parts that sustained her, that made her someone he could hold, let his body express what he felt when words wouldn't fit. But the organs that kept her alive also made her transient. Had Noemi ever laid her head on Link's chest and measured the ticking of his heart? If she did, had she thought about how easily it could be stopped, how there was nothing she could do to make it continue forever?

Jonas placed his fingers along the inside of her wrist, where he could feel the blood rabbiting through her veins. He imagined a creek, quick and narrow. Her blood clear, her body a shore, her heart a lantern. Her cardiovascular system chimed and splashed. Her brain was a cloud crackling distant, purple lightning. It branched and vibrated through her until her hand shuddered against his, uncaged the headphone bud so he could see it pouring rain against her lifeline. She said his name too quietly for him to hear, but he had memorized the shape of it on her lips. Noemi was passionate, prickling and irritable, but Jonas liked how much she cared about everything, that every day of her life something stoked her like a Roman candle streaming colors wherever she went. It was harder when she was quiet, shipwrecked. He didn't know what she was thinking, would have to ask, but sometimes she buckled under the pressure of vivisecting her own emotions.

He asked anyway.

"Are you okay? Can I do anything?"

"No." Noemi shook her head, shifted so that she was on her back. She uncurled her legs, and her feet disappeared out the far edge of the blanket. Though she looked away from him now, she left her arm lying beneath his touch. "I'll be fine. It'll pass." She forced a smile, her single dimple tugging at her cheek.

Usually when Jonas caught Noemi alone, she was either editing photos or looking at colleges, schools he could never hope to get into with his grades: Ivy League or the like. She drew elaborate color-coded charts for comparison. Everyone expected her to go to art school, major in photography, but he knew she was looking at environmental studies and biology. She had a second journal she took into the woods to record the types of trees she found. She read *A Sand County Almanac* and drew her own pictures of the animals and plants she came across, even if her versions were accompanied by made-up descriptions detailing their fantastical properties.

Jonas couldn't help but notice all the schools in her charts were coastal. He asked only once if she'd considered anywhere in the Midwest, and she told him, more or less, to mind his own business, hot as frostbite. Despite what had happened in the stable beneath the papier-mâché horses, it hurt that he didn't figure into her future at all, as a friend—that it wouldn't matter to her if college took her as far away from him as possible, short of leaving the continental U.S.

Was love supposed to hurt like that? Like a heel grinding into his larynx whenever he thought of her?

Some nights Jonas watched episodes of a paranormal investigation reality show in the living room with Audrey. It had a reliable format: two men in their early thirties spent the first part of the show introducing viewers to legends about a supposedly haunted, usually abandoned house/factory/hospital/school/church, where a father/worker/doctor/student/priest killed and dismembered his family/coworkers/patients/teachers/nuns with an ax/meat cleaver/machete/chain saw/bayonet. The duo then spent a night in the building, where they captured malfunctioning lights (slamming doors/self-playing radios/disembodied groans/creaking floorboards) on camera. Jonas, like Noemi, believed all the ghost signs on the show could be explained by coincidence and vicarious imagination. Unlike Noemi, he still had the patience to watch it.

Audrey, who saw no reason to doubt this series portrayed genuine encounters with ghosts, sat in an armchair, slippered feet propped up on the ottoman, and worked on her knitting (or crocheting—Jonas couldn't tell the difference).

"Did you and Noemi have a fight?"

"What do you mean?" Jonas avoided eye contact, concentrating instead on the television.

"Just that you guys seemed to be getting along so well for a while. I feel like I hardly see you together anymore."

"She's busy. She's been jogging every day since the weather's gotten warmer. She likes to jog alone, so she's not around much anymore."

Jonas had in fact asked to go with her—only once—even though he didn't understand why anyone would electively jog. Noemi had of course declined to let him tag along, and he couldn't help but take it personally.

"Well, I guess that makes sense," Audrey said. She had a tattoo on her arm of birds flying into a mirror, and their wings flexed with each movement. "How are you liking school here otherwise?"

"It's fine. What are you knitting?"

"A baby blanket. One of my coworkers is expecting." She smiled, adjusted her glasses. "Don't think I didn't see you changing the subject there. If Noemi's busy, you should try to expand your circle of friends. Not that I don't appreciate the company, but you deserve to have other options for your evenings beyond watching reality TV at home with me."

"Hey, I enjoy my reality TV evenings." Jonas stacked several throw pillows against the arm of the sofa and flopped, shoulder first, against them.

He woke much later on the sofa, surprised to find he'd fallen asleep in the first place. His mouth was dry, his eyes stinging. The volume on the TV had been turned so low he couldn't hear it at all, and the only light on was a small lamp on a nearby desk. The TV told Jonas it was 3:00 a.m., so he turned it off, the light with it, and felt his way up the stairs in the dark.

The window in the stairwell cast a cool beam of moonlight into the second-floor hallway, but Jonas left the light behind as he trailed deeper into the hall toward his room at the end. His shin bumped into something soft, and when Jonas reached down, he felt Rosencrantz's or Guildenstern's furry body rumbling against his leg. He picked up the cat, whichever it was—Guildenstern, judging by the way it didn't stiffen in his arms—and held it curled to his chest. Suddenly, the cat bristled, growled low, and before Jonas could figure out what he had done to agitate it, sunk its claws into the front of his T-shirt. He half knelt to let it drop to the ground, and as soon as the cat's pads hit the floorboards, it took off and sped down the hallway behind him.

The darkness ahead of Jonas deepened, then pulsated outward as a lump of black took shape against the wall. He waited for it to soak into the night surrounding it, to never have been real. Instead, the shadow unfolded, like a person standing, until it was taller than Jonas, its domed head like a hood bending outward from the wall. Jonas leaned to one side, hoping whatever he was seeing would flatten as he did so, a trick of the low light.

It didn't.

The figure, the person, moved. It was a tiny moment, the large shape turning to the side, but it felt to Jonas as though it lasted for a very long time. The figure's head dipped forward in the moonlight, and though the eyes were cast in shadow, Jonas could see the bottom half of a sharp, pale face with a straight mouth. The person's lips twitched and parted, but if their voice or breath or body made any sound, Jonas didn't hear it. Then the half face disappeared from view, and the hulking shadow passed through the closed door and into Noemi's room.

Unthinking, Jonas followed. He felt the swan handle strange against his palm as he thrust the door open. Fumbling along the wall for her light switch, he called her name, swept his eyes across the room to search for a figure in the dark.

Before he found the light, Noemi turned on the lamp by her bed. "What the hell, Jonas?" They were alone in the room. The curtains over her bed were tied back, so he could see the spill of curls tangled around her head. She lifted her hair from her eyes with the back of her hand and peered up at him, squinting against the light, annoyed.

"I saw someone in the hall." Ignoring her protests, he approached her closet and pulled open the doors. There was no one inside. By now, Noemi was sitting upright in her bed, rubbing sleep from her eyes and letting him search, humoring him. Jonas knelt against the floor, looked under the bed. Nothing but cat toys. He checked the bathroom, felt his pulse thrumming through his head as he thrust aside the curtain over the claw-foot tub. Inside was only a centipede, skating along the edge of the drain. Noemi was frightened of them, so he crushed it with a tissue, cringing. Jonas hated killing bugs. He imagined that they screamed when he did, that it was too high or quiet for humans to hear. He flushed the insect and walked back into her bedroom, embarrassed.

"Maybe you had a nightmare," she said, gentle but impatient.

"Yeah. Sorry."

He left quietly, and her light was off before he could even make it to his room.

22

AMBERLYN

The park behind the popcorn factory was quietly overrun with
stray cats, likely inbred: almost all of them had the same kink in
their tails, the same overlong upper canines. The granite statue
of the company's founder, Nicolai Ness, stood headless in a rose
garden encircled by benches at the park's center. Link had allegedly
glued a Batman eye mask to the statue's face a couple summers
ago, but it had since been decapitated in a tornado, and Amberlyn
had never gotten the chance to see it. According to Noemi, the
head was now wedged behind the passenger's seat in the cabin of
Gaetan's Jeep.

"Poor old Nicolai," Lyle said. "He looked like a happy guy
when he had a head—in a some-curse-trapped-my-soul-in-a-
statue kind of way."

She'd torn free the bloom of a daffodil and tucked it in Amberlyn's hair. "Have you never had your ears pierced?" Lyle traced her finger behind the helix of Amberlyn's ear.

"Nope. I've always played sports, so it seemed easier not to."

Lyle sprawled across the bench where Amberlyn sat, resting her head in her lap. Amberlyn's legs tensed, thighs refusing to relax against the wooden slats beneath, and they hovered so the toes of her flats barely touched the gravel path. Lyle was letting her hair grow out so that it was getting longer in the front; she liked to exhale exaggerated breaths so her bangs fluttered.

"Have you said anything to Noemi about the horse thing yet?" Amberlyn asked.

"No." Lyle sighed. "I would have, but I worried it might be a you-had-to-be-there sort of thing. I tried to tell my brother when I got home, and he asked if I was on drugs. And Parker's *way* more gullible than Noemi."

"You don't think she'd believe us even though she's been there, seen the lighthouse and everything?"

"She'd come up with some logical explanation for what we *think* we saw. Noemi wouldn't trust evidence anyone but she had found."

Amberlyn couldn't take it personally. She'd be skeptical too about a tree-horse-thing that walked underwater. Even having seen it, she wondered if somehow it had been embellished by her and Lyle's shared imagination.

They walked around the park, their ears again linked by Lyle's headphones and the sound of The Cure. An elderly man passed by them with a rabbit hopping ahead of him on the footpath, harnessed and leashed. Lyle asked if they could pet it, and the two girls took turns holding the bunny.

"Have you ever had any pets?" Lyle asked once they'd returned the rabbit and continued walking. They held hands, and she lifted Amberlyn's arm so she could spin under it like they were dance partners.

"When I was little, my parents had adopted a greyhound, but he died a few years ago."

"What was his name?"

"Darwin. My dad chose it. We talked about adopting an animal again after he died, but it hasn't happened yet." Amberlyn wanted one now more than ever, but she worried asking might make it sound like she was suggesting her parents get a dog to replace their son. "I think they got the dog in the first place so Link would stop feeding wild animals, but it didn't really work."

"Sorry about Darwin. Our Golden Daisy's getting up there, and I'm dreading the day we have to take her for that last trip to the vet."

They stopped by a weeping elm whose branches brushed the ground so it looked like a leafy, green ball.

"These trees are cool." Lyle lifted a branch aside, holding it open like a door for Amberlyn to pass through. "They're like naturally occurring forts."

Amberlyn ducked between branches. They rustled behind her as Lyle followed. The tree was just tall enough for them to stand almost perfectly upright without worrying their hair might get caught in the arch of twigs overhead, though they knelt in the grass anyway. Pinpricks of sunlight filtered through the leaves, and Amberlyn felt like she was inside a star globe, dark and private.

They sat so close that their knees touched. Lyle cupped Amberlyn's wrists in her hands and rubbed her thumbs along the tendons in the lower part of her arms. Lyle was cheerful and outgoing; she thought nothing of approaching a stranger, asking them if she could befriend their pet, while Amberlyn might have just smiled from afar, hoping to be invited over. But even Lyle seemed nervous now. Her hands were clammy, and her fingers trembled. Amberlyn tipped forward so she was perched on her knees, her butt no longer resting on the heels of her shoes. As though to catch her, Lyle gripped her waist, and they kissed. First she tasted the waxy film of Lyle's lipstick, but then her mouth opened, and she felt the soft and vulnerable petal of Lyle's inner lip brush her own. Lyle's fingers, now cool, reached past Amberlyn's waistband and spread against her thighs.

"Are you okay?" Amberlyn asked.

"Mm-hmm. You?"

Amberlyn nodded. Lyle closed her eyes and shuffled forward.

Finally, Amberlyn relaxed, leaned back, let hair fall around her in the grass, felt the damp, fresh soil soak into the back of her T-shirt. She wasn't sure if she should make any noise, but she felt short of breath, and when she heard Lyle gasp aloud she let herself breathe heavy.

NOEMI

The three of them—Noemi, Lyle, and Amberlyn—had planned to go to the Shivery theater to see a film together. It was the first time in weeks they had all arranged to hang out: Lyle's idea. But then Amberlyn mentioned it to Jonas, assuming he'd already been invited. When Jonas revealed he too was going, Noemi pretended to be unsurprised, to be fine with it. What she wanted was to tell everyone exactly how she felt, which might be what she would have done once upon a time: insisted Lyle and Amberlyn break their plans with Jonas, that the three of them protest his continued association with them in the wake of her own failed relationship. In part, Noemi had grown tired of seeing herself as a spiteful and pushy person, but mostly she didn't want to have to explain to anyone how much it hurt her that Jonas had moved on to the point of comfortably being in her presence, that his hanging out with her was no different from being with Lyle or Amberlyn. And so, she texted someone else.

What are you doing with your
Saturday evening?

Brian and I are swimming
at the comm center

I'm glad you texted. Been wanting
to ask you something, but maybe
you'll think it's weird?

That's never stopped you before.

Have you ever played d&d?

Can't say I have.

Would you want to? Brian's brother is home
for the weekend. He'll be dungeon master

Is it OK if I have no idea I'm doing?

Of course. Brian says he can pick you up

Noemi was a notorious sore loser. Audrey had sworn off playing Scrabble with her forever because of it. Collaborative games made her somewhat more amiable. She'd done an Escape the Room game with Amberlyn, Lyle, and Jonas over the winter. While Lyle wasted time introducing everyone to the four strangers that had banded with their group, Noemi set to solving puzzles and delegating tasks right away. She felt guilty afterward, but they *did* escape. It might actually be easier to be a pleasant person when playing a game she knew nothing about.

I could go for a swim anyway. Maybe
I'll head to the community center for
a bit, and we'll go from there?

Sounds good!

LYLE

I forgot I'm supposed to let Tyler and
Brian teach me how to play D&D, so I'm
going to have to take a raincheck on
the movie. Maybe you and Amberlyn
and I can do something tomorrow?

Is everything ok? We can cancel

Are you upset about Jonas going?

I don't care what Jonas does. It's fine.

If you're sure

Don't light the game on fire

Though Jonas was just across the hall, Noemi did not bother to inform him of anything. She put on her swimsuit—a bikini bottom and bustier, not exactly sensible swimwear—under a T-shirt and skirt, then packed a bag with a spare bath towel and clean underwear.

The community center was downtown, within walking distance, but Noemi wasn't in the mood. Diana agreed to drive her, and though it wasn't even five minutes by car, she wasted not one of them before chirpily asking questions.

"So are you going swimming all by yourself?" Diana's earrings looked like two dangling Saturns orbiting strands of her graying hair.

"I swim alone all the time. It can be a pretty solitary activity."

"I wish you still danced," Diana said. "You were such an elegant dancer."

"I was a kid," Noemi said. She kicked a magazine to the edge of the floor mat. Probably one of Audrey's. "How elegant could I have been? Dance is too performative. I don't want people watching me."

"When did you become so shy?"

Noemi assured Diana she would get a ride home, then watched her brown sedan pull out of the parking lot and back onto the road.

The community center wasn't a popular place on Saturday evenings, outside of the classes they offered. In the natatorium, Tyler swam in one of the three cordoned lanes while Brian—not even wet—sat nearby playing a portable gaming console. The only other people in the pool were a flock of heavily pregnant people standing in the shallow end with their aerobics instructor. And, of course, the on-duty lifeguard.

Gaetan climbed down from his pedestal chair the moment she entered, but Noemi pretended not to see him. She shimmied out of her clothes as quickly as possible and lowered herself into the water before he made it over to their side of the pool. Hurriedly, she twisted her hair into some kind of disastrous bun and tiptoed through the water, heading as close to the center of the pool as she could before it came past her nose.

"We close in like an hour," Gaetan said. "Or, ninety minutes. But it's out of the pool in an hour."

Noemi nodded in acknowledgment, then swam freestyle to the deep end of the pool, where Tyler waited.

They swam laps together. She could hear Tyler splashing alongside her, and she opened her eyes once underwater and let herself lag behind, watched the bubbles bloom in his wake before rising into a backstroke to catch up. Gaetan stood beside Brian, and they seemed to be making awkward conversation without looking at each other. Noemi avoided turning her attention on him in any noticeable way, but she could feel him watching her. She thought very hard about the movement of every muscle as she swam.

Tyler was half a lap behind while she pushed the air out of her lungs, sank underwater, and let her toes brush the tile at the pool's bottom. She held her breath and thought about the lake in the woods, about how long Link might have been underwater, how it must have felt. When she broke again through the surface, Tyler was hoisting himself out of the water and making his way to the diving board.

"You can really hold your breath," he said.

"I guess." Noemi placed her forearms along the wall of the pool and leveraged herself up. Then she sat, legs in the water, and squeezed droplets from her hair.

"So." His toes curled over the white edge of the board. "Are you going to prom?"

Feet slapped softly on the wet floor behind her.

"No," she said. She had a sense of something coming, like an impending rain, and she wished she hadn't stopped swimming. "It's not really my thing. I'd rather stay home and hang out with my mom."

"Well, I—"

She could have warned Tyler when she saw Gaetan leaning out onto the diving board behind him, but she didn't. Just watched as he pushed him off the edge, cringed as he smacked into the water. Gaetan's usual, mischievous grin sliced his face, but then he looked at Noemi, clamped his mouth shut, and gave a little, one-shouldered shrug that seemed almost embarrassed.

Tyler coughed and struggled to wipe water from his eyes while treading with one hand. "Who hired you to save drowning people?"

Maybe Tyler had been about to ask her to prom, or maybe he hadn't been. Maybe if he'd asked it would have been to go as his friend, not as his "date." Tyler was cute, and he was nice, and maybe listening to whatever he'd been saying about the dance *would* have made her feel better about Jonas, but for exactly that reason she was grateful, for once, that Gaetan was a pest. Tyler Olsen deserved better than being her emotional rebound. She'd never meant to mislead either Jonas or Link about the kind of relationship she'd wanted with either of them, but she had, and Noemi now feared, however irrationally, she might mislead another one of her friends.

Gaetan laughed, pulled off his white lifeguard tank top, and tossed it on top of a stack of kickboards behind him. He dove into the lane on the other side of Noemi's and took off. She suspected he was trying to bait her into racing, and they both knew he would beat her, so she stood, tucked her towel around her, and went to sit beside Brian on the bench. He pulled out his phone and started talking Noemi through D&D races and classes, and she wondered whether one evening could give her enough time to construct a character when three people were waiting for her to play.

As 8:00 p.m. loomed, the sun began to set, and the sky outside the rows of windows above the kickboard stacks burned tangerine. Gaetan fished various floaties out of the activity side of the pool, while his coworker—an older-looking person Noemi didn't know—helped the members of the class they'd been instructing up the stairs and to a locker-room door. Tyler dabbed his hair dry with a colorful, flamingo-printed towel he'd clearly brought from home.

"Showers, then meet at the main entrance by eight fifteen?"

Brian nodded, but Noemi hesitated. She doubted her own ability to be an enjoyable tabletop companion, running low on the energy she'd need to feign cheer. If she wasn't able to distract herself from feeling sore over Jonas, she'd rather be home in bed than inflicting herself on other people. There was also a small chance Tyler might try to finish whatever he'd started saying about prom earlier, and she didn't much want to risk that.

"Actually," she said, "I think I might have tired myself out. I'll probably just head home."

"Are you sure?" Tyler asked.

"Yeah."

"Do you need a ride?" Brian offered.

"No, I'll just call my mom or someone. Or I can walk. It's not that dark yet. It takes a while to get chlorine out of all this knotty hair. I don't want you guys to wait for me."

"Okay," Tyler said. "If you're sure. If no one can get you, just text and we can swing back and bring you home."

"The invite stands, though."

Noemi doubted Brian cared whether she ever joined them or not, but it was nice of him to pretend. She thanked them, and they walked off to the men's locker room.

The women's locker room would likely be so crowded she'd have to wait for a shower. Noemi now faced a decision between waiting awkwardly next to a group of naked people for her turn washing up, or lingering in the pool room until Gaetan kicked her out. She checked her phone and found she had a message from Jonas asking whether everything was okay, as well as one from Unknown, telling her he knew everything was not. Ignoring both, she dropped the device back into her bag.

"Cute phone case," Gaetan said. He stood immediately in front of her. She hadn't noticed him approach. "Bunny ears."

"Yeah."

"You can hang out or whatever. I always swim alone after close, but I'm gonna turn the lights off if that's okay." He rested his palm flat on his torso, just between his ribs, and drummed out a rhythm. "The pool lights will still be on. It's fine as long as I leave before Robbie. That's the night custodian."

"Okay."

"You okay?" he asked.

"Yeah, why?"

"Just wondering."

He crossed the pool room to the lifeguard's office on the far side, reached in behind the door, and the lights in the room went off. The room was now lit only by the pool lights, the water electric and almost turquoise. Gaetan slipped in, and while he swam submerged, Noemi's world was plunged into near silence, the only sound the lapping of ripples against tile. She watched him move, a jet of dark ink through blue, then followed, stepping cautiously along the wet, paved edge so that she was standing nearby when he came up for air.

"Can I grab a pool noodle?" she asked.

"Sure."

She selected a purple one from the stack along the bleachers, then released it into the water with a dull smack. Noemi lowered herself into a sitting position and dropped feetfirst off the edge of the deep end. For a moment, she hung underwater, pushing with her hands so she sank farther from the surface. At home, Noemi liked to take baths with hard-packed oils plunked into the tub. The solution would concentrate at the center, then the colors bled outward, stark against the white porcelain of the old claw-foot until the water was shining and opaque. She then submerged herself in the dark water and listened to an impossibly rushing stillness, like a body alive.

Her hand brushed something, and Noemi forced her eyes open against the burning chlorine. She'd forgotten herself and for a moment expected to see the gray-necked seal creature from her dreams. It was, of course, only Gaetan floating in front of her, his eyes nearly the color of the water, and his smirk somehow still present in spite of any held breath. He tilted and kicked himself into a backflip. The rush of his movements sent a wave of bubbles against her legs. When he righted himself, Noemi placed a hand on each of his shoulders and propelled herself upward. As though they were in space, it took the gentlest push.

Gaetan followed, and when they were breathing again, he shook his head, doglike, so the droplets flung from his hair and sprayed her. Noemi reached for the pool noodle and slid her legs over until she straddled it, rocking horse style. It let her drift comfortably without any effort, while Gaetan, tired of moving, lay back into a starfish float.

"So," he said. "I heard you tell Tyler you were tired. But here you are swimming. Are you avoiding him?"

"I'm not avoiding anybody." She cupped her hand along the top of the water and splashed it across his chest. "Socializing takes a different kind of effort than swimming. I think the physical kind of effort might be easier for me."

"Did I save you earlier from being asked to prom?" Gaetan rolled so he was upright again, then gripped the end of the pool noodle to stay above water.

"Doubtful."

"You're being weirdly mysterious tonight."

"I'm in a mood. Are *you* going to prom this year?"

He quirked his head as though thinking very closely, but it was a fake, exaggerated movement.

"No. I did the whole prom thing last year."

"I thought you'd like the excuse to party."

"Well, that's what it was last year." Releasing the noodle, he let himself fall back, floating again. She couldn't see his face. "I did the whole deal. Had a date, partied after, got laid, got really drunk—"

"Gee, congratulations."

"It was good but, like, just a really expensive version of a lot of other weekends."

"With nicer clothes."

"Yeah. If I went this year, I'd want it to be more, *mmm*, personal, I guess. I'd want to go with someone I care about and have it be just us."

Without meaning to, she laughed—once, reflexive. A *ha* that echoed throughout the cavernous room.

"Laugh it up." Gaetan swam to the side of the pool, hooked a foot in the ladder so he could relax against it.

"Well, for that to work you'd first have to care about someone."

"So cruel." He placed a hand over his heart in mock agony.

"Sorry. I wasn't *trying* to be mean. It's just hard to imagine."

"Oh? And why's that?"

She couldn't think of a reason that didn't sound unkind, and something about the way Gaetan had asked seemed sincere, like he deserved an answer both honest and courteous, and Noemi didn't have one like that.

"It's just a side of you I've never seen. You're right, I guess. I don't know anything about your relationships or what you're like with the people you don't hate. Of course you could care about someone, romantically or otherwise."

"'Relationships' is a strong word, but I get it. Plus, there are lots of people I don't hate that I'm perfectly nice to. There's Link..." He counted out the name on his thumb, then paused and pretended to consider others before coming up short. "Anyway, I consider myself a romantic at heart."

"Do you think you could continue to love someone and want to be with them if they wouldn't have sex with you?"

"Where did that come from?" He furrowed his eyebrows. In the low light, they looked even blacker than usual against his fair skin. "People do that all the time. Every day. Love can be unrequited."

"No, that's not what I mean." Noemi pushed the noodle out from under her, then swam over to the ladder. She gripped the pool ledge. "I mean if they felt the same way you did, romantically, but they didn't have much of a sex drive. Like if they have sex for you because they know you want it, but it's not something they want or enjoy. Not because it's bad with you. It's just not part of their—I don't know. Just not part of what they need or want."

Gaetan looked at her so intensely she had to look away. He weighed what she had said, made a thoughtful, humming sound.

"I have sex all the time with people I don't love," he said finally. "Lots of people do. I'd really like the two to go together if possible, so it would be important to me, I think, that we could have sex sometimes, if the person I love wanted to be with me." He scratched the hair above his ear, and a droplet trailed from his sideburn down the edge of his jaw. "Anyway, if you're asking whether I can accept that someone would love me, romantically, but not sexually? Yeah. I mean, if you can have sex without love, why not the reverse? Emotionless sex still feels really fun, but I'd trade it if it meant being loved by that one, right person. That's just me."

"Would you still love them if they didn't enjoy sex as much as other kinds of intimacy? If they did it as a compromise because it was important to you? Or were willing to do it less often than you'd like?"

"Yeah. I guess I don't really see why that's a question. I mean, ideally, we'd both like it, but no one likes the same things as their partner all the time. Is this something you talked about with Link?"

Noemi shook her head, released her grip on the pool wall and let some space fall between them. "Sort of. Online, then—at least, not in person." They'd talked about love in a vague and friendly way through chat when he was alive. "I didn't want a relationship with Link. No offense. I know how close you were, and I don't mean to suggest anything bad about him. We were better as friends." Before he could respond, she began to swim to the shallows, feet splash-splash-splashing so she couldn't hear him even if she'd wanted to.

While Noemi stood in the four-foot-deep water, untying her hair and squeezing it from soaked to damp, Gaetan followed. She watched, worried he'd ask something more about Link. He stood and busied himself making waves with his palm, searched the ceiling for a moment.

"So, do you know where you're going to apply for college next year?" he asked.

"I'm making a list. What about you?"

"Well." He smiled. She knew him well enough to recognize it wasn't a genuinely hopeful one. "I'm a senior. Things are as sorted as they're going to get this year. My grades are mediocre. My finances are nonexistent. My goals for after college...undetermined. I'm going to community college for a year or so and trying to figure things out."

"That's responsible."

"Don't act like you wouldn't consider it a total failure to end up in community college."

"If that's what I felt, that's what I would have said."

Gaetan lifted his hands in surrender. "Sorry. I don't want to argue."

"For once."

"I guess I don't want to end up like my quote-unquote stepdad. Hard, physical work that sends me home miserable at the end of the day."

"That's got nothing to do with where you go to college. He's a contractor?" she asked.

"Yeah."

"There are a lot of reasons your stepdad isn't a great person, but what he does for a living isn't one of them. Jonas's dad was a contractor for years, and he's a super nice person. My mom works retail. I have a cosmetologist and a dance instructor as housemates.

Nothing wrong with jobs that don't require a bachelor's. Those jobs help everyone together afford a house like Lamplight."

"You're right." He shrugged. "Maybe I think I can be a snob about these things without feeling too bad because I'll probably end up a shit-shoveler anyway."

"Who knew you were a snob?" she asked.

"Who knew you weren't?"

Gaetan continued waving his hand through the water, and Noemi caught sight of a dark mark on the inside of his forearm. She couldn't make it out through his movement, but she pointed.

"What's that?"

Confused for a second, he checked his own arm. "Oh! Tattoo. I just got it a week ago."

"Should you be swimming with it uncovered?"

"I think it's fine now?" He stepped closer, holding his arm forward for her to see. It was a tree: simple line art done in black ink.

At first, the tree seemed oddly soft for someone like Gaetan. It looked almost like an illustration out of a vintage botany text. His blue veins stood out stark and vulnerable through his skin. His wrist was narrow, his fingers long, and as much as Gaetan worked out, his musculature didn't disguise that he was naturally slender, breakable.

"Do you remember," he asked, "when you saved me from my stepdad and brought me to the forest?"

"I hardly saved you. It was because Link told me they wouldn't let you out."

He looked at the tattoo, reminiscing. The tree was raised over discolored ridges, like growth rings measuring his skin.

"What's that?" she asked. Noemi pointed toward the rash, and he moved so suddenly he accidentally bumped her. She felt his skin beneath her finger, just for a second—too short a time to compute that he was anything more than solid.

"Don't get all fussy. I don't do that anymore." He forced a smile, dipped his arm so the water hid it, then waved off her question.

She realized what he was saying and searched his face for some cue as to how she should respond. He rolled his eyes.

"It's not a big deal."

Lyle would have known what to say. Noemi was not as good at sensitive situations, ones that required tenderness or precision. She could lecture or order, but she couldn't treat injuries or tend gardens. She wanted to be a marine mammalogist, but while she could study living things, she couldn't even keep a cactus alive. Couldn't keep a relationship alive.

"Who did that?" she asked.

"Nobody. I did."

"Because of Link?"

"Because of me. They're old scars. I don't do it anymore. That's what the tattoo is for. Covering it up 'cause it's not a place I hurt. Nobody fucks with me anymore, and that includes me."

"Gate." She hugged her chest. Suddenly, the air in the room felt cold.

"Don't look at me like you feel sorry for me." He rolled his shoulders, softened his stance. It took effort. "It's fine. I lift. I run. Nobody's going to make me spend twenty-eight hours in a piss-soaked closet, because I can kick down the door now. And I hardly go home anymore anyway. I still stay at the Millers' sometimes."

"Do you ever talk to your dad?"

"No. He fucked off. Do you ever talk to yours? Did you ever find out who he is?"

Gaetan had never sincerely asked about Noemi's father. Just teased her when they were little about who he might be—though all that had stopped when his brother died, when his own dad left.

"No. I did one of those DNA tests that determines your ethnicity and finds relatives, though."

"Yeah?" He raised an eyebrow.

"Anyway, I didn't learn a whole lot. An assortment of Mediterranean results, mostly not super specific."

"No French?" he asked.

"Less than a percent, so not really. Everything I found out could be explained through my mom, in part. So unless she takes a DNA test, I won't really be able to tell anything about my dad from it. And I could barely convince her to let me take it. She's worried about, I don't know, some shady organization getting her DNA and cloning her like she's one of the X-Men. I wasn't matched with any long-lost relatives or anything. My dad's probably overseas, so I think the chances of him using the same test are pretty significantly low. But it's weird. I don't really care that much about my dad. Not as a person. More like as a part of me. Did he have short temper too? Was he anxious? How much of me is inherited, and how much is just my own weirdness? I don't know why I'm talking about this."

"It's fine. I barely remember my dad. I won't say that I wish I never knew who he was, but there is something that hurts about having him know me and decide to leave. I don't even hold it against him. My mom stayed, and I hate her way more."

"I'm sorry, Gaetan."

"Eh." He cupped his hands and squirted a spout of water at her. "It's fine. The tattoo was a birthday gift to myself."

"Oh, that's right! I remember I used to think you were joking because it was April Fool's. Happy belated birthday. Did you do anything special? Besides the tattoo?"

"Thanks. Not a damn thing. But anyway, eighteen. I could get my own place, but if I'm going to pay for school—I dunno."

"You could stay at Lamplight." Noemi couldn't believe she'd suggested it, hadn't really even considered it until she heard the words leave her mouth.

"I freeload off the Millers enough, and they *like* me."

"Not like my mom dislikes you. We actually have extra rooms. If you feel weird about it, you can pay rent. You wouldn't be the first."

"Thanks for offering," he said. "I'd rather you didn't feel sorry for me, but...thanks anyway."

"I wouldn't offer if I thought it would be awful to have you around."

"So kind."

"Let me know if you change your mind, and I'll ask my mom. Anyway." She took a step back, looked out through the windows, stars now visible. "It's so dark out now. I should head home."

"I can drive you." He climbed the steps out of the pool and grabbed a white towel from over one of the rungs of the lifeguard pedestal. She watched, unthinking, while he dried his chest and arms, then wrapped the towel in a skirt around his waist. Fair, barely perceptible stubble scattered just underneath his belly button. For some reason the thought of him carefully shaving the flesh on his stomach seemed sweet to her. She had never imagined Gaetan putting much worry into his appearance.

Even after showering in the dark of the locker rooms, they both still filled the cabin of Gaetan's Jeep with the scent of chlorine. Upbeat pop music blared when he started the car, and Noemi jumped in surprise. He turned it off immediately, and they rode with the windows down, listening instead to the chirping of crickets and humming of passing cars.

"I think I swallowed some water," he said, wrinkling his nose.

"Because your mouth is always open."

"Ha. Ha." The car idled at a red light. "Do you want to stop by the drive-in? I'm in the mood for a burger."

"You *just* finished saying you didn't feel well."

"I'm always well enough for greasy food."

"Well," she said, "I'll pass. With as much as you swim and run and lift, you're still going to clog an artery. Those things are so high in cholesterol and saturated fat—"

"Noemi, I am touched, *touched* by your concern for my heart health."

"Oh, shut up."

"Home then!"

The light turned green.

When they pulled into the driveway, she reached for the door handle and thanked him for the ride. He answered, "Thank you for talking to me," and she couldn't remember what it had been like to hate him, wondered whether she ever really had.

JONAS

A Sunday afternoon in late April, while Noemi was at work, some-one rang the doorbell, and it echoed, tinny and ominous, through-out the first floor of the house. Jonas opened the front door to see Amberlyn standing on the mat, smiling at him.

"Hey. What's up?" he asked.

"Hey." She had swapped her backpack for a large tote tucked under one arm. "I tried texting you, but you didn't respond. Sorry to drop by unannounced."

"No worries." Jonas stepped aside to let her pass into the foyer. "I didn't notice my phone vibrate, or I'd have answered."

Amberlyn fished through the bag and pulled out a slender stack of paper, hand-bound into a little booklet.

"Link made this," she said. "It's a comic book. I think it was for

Noemi." She handed it to Jonas, and he began flipping through the pages. "Found it in his room after he died, and I'd been meaning to bind it and give it to her, but it just seemed like there were always so many other things to take care of first."

The illustrations were in full color, though a few at the end looked unfinished. Link and Noemi, or at least imagined versions of them, were the stars. Jonas recognized their inked counterparts immediately. Noemi had the same curly hair and freckles, the same quirky-sexy fashion sense. Link must have spent a fair amount of time studying the way she looked and moved. The main difference was that here the characters were superpowered: Link moving objects with his mind, Noemi warping perceptions. To Jonas's surprise, the book didn't feel like a love letter, and none of the pages showed its principle pair in romantic situations. Comic book Noemi didn't keep cats but had a pet wolf that accompanied her everywhere she went, slept at the foot of her bed. On the last pages, the wolf twisted and transformed across several panels into someone else Jonas recognized. These bits were in unfinished pencil, but even he knew that Link's light sketch of the shapeshifter was meant to be Gaetan Kelly.

"It's obviously not finished, but I think it's still right that she has it. There's a dedication for her." Amberlyn rotated the book in Jonas's hands and pointed to the inside cover.

"She's at work right now," Jonas said.

"I know. That's actually why I came now."

"Don't you think you should give it to her?"

"I don't know." She looked down, quiet. "It might be weird. It's not like we've been avoiding each other since Link, but with how she wasn't comfortable taking me to the lake and all... We sort of have been avoiding each other when it comes *to* Link. I might not be the person she'd want to get it from."

"Why not?" Jonas asked. "I think it would be weird for me to give it to her too."

"Are you guys not talking?" She fiddled with a strand of hair. "I thought things had been frosty, but I didn't want to say anything. Lyle and I kind of wondered when she bailed on the movies. Anyhow, I could leave a note with it. This way she doesn't feel pressured to say anything right away. She can just look at it on her own time."

"Maybe." Noemi might be someone who preferred a less personal method of gift-giving. Jonas was pretty sure it would at least go over better than giving it to her himself, now that she seemed to be avoiding him outright.

He led Amberlyn to the second floor.

"Which is your room?" she asked.

"That one." Jonas motioned toward his open door. "But it doesn't have that much of my stuff decorating it. It's like all the rest, really."

When they walked into Noemi's room, Amberlyn became immediately distracted by the many pictures hanging on the wall, several of which featured only Lyle. Jonas recognized the one of himself, but with his face obscured by a cloud, there was no way for her to tell it was him. He was glad there were none of Link hanging. Something about that wouldn't have felt right with present company, and to be on the safe side, he leaned against the desk and shuffled the lone picture Noemi had of Link under unassuming cat photos.

"I do like her work. Does she have a pen and paper?"

Jonas grabbed a Sharpie from the desk beside him, but there was nothing to write on that wasn't already filled with notes or homework. When he looked up for Amberlyn, she stood over Noemi's nightstand with her dream journal spread open in her hands.

"There are blank pages at the back of this."

She had already started tearing one free by the time Jonas was close enough to try taking the book from her.

"You really shouldn't," he said, a little harshly. "That's her dream journal. She's going to see the torn pages and flip out."

"I tore neatly," Amberlyn said, biting her lip. "You might be right. If she gets upset, tell her it was my fault." She laid the book flat, failed to notice the marker in Jonas's hand, and wrote in neat, fat letters with the pen by Noemi's bedside:

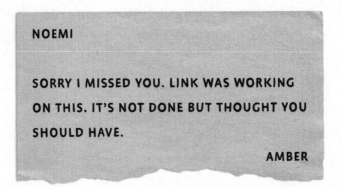

NOEMI

SORRY I MISSED YOU. LINK WAS WORKING ON THIS. IT'S NOT DONE BUT THOUGHT YOU SHOULD HAVE.

AMBER

She laid the comic with the note where the journal had once been, then resumed flipping through the journal's pages.

"Is this where she plans out her photos?"

"Yeah, but we probably shouldn't look at it." Jonas watched the pattern of Amberlyn's page turning, how she slowed on the passages that carried Link's name. He felt guilty even seeing enough to know that it was there.

"It's not a diary, though, right? Just dreams. So that's not private. Do you really think she'd mind?"

"Noemi? Have you not met her?"

"Here's one about you," she said. "I dreamt I cut my heart into so many pieces that some of them were see-through..."

As she read, Jonas didn't try to stop her. This is how he would later remember the story:

Once upon a time there was a girl who cut her heart into a million pieces. She buried them across the earth so no one would ever know her. The only piece she couldn't cut was as red and rough as a ruby. The boy who loved her would have held the heartstone safe if she had asked, but he did not deserve it. Instead, she gave it to a monster who took it to the bottom of a deep, blue hole that went on forever. She never told the boy, and he never understood what had happened. The end.

"What are you doing in my room?"

Amberlyn snapped the journal shut at the sound of Noemi's voice. Jonas's eyes jumped back and forth from Noemi's face to the book in Amberlyn's hand. Though he hadn't read the dream journal himself, hadn't even touched it, he had very much wanted to hear the dream that had mentioned him, and he felt this desire exposed, spread wide and pinned like a butterfly for everyone in the room to see. His stomach turned over as the fantasy of himself in a deep and impenetrable chamber of her heart evaporated. Replacing it was the realization that he had done exactly what she'd feared in her dream: he'd found an intimate part of her and decided it was his place to enter it.

"I'm sorry—" Amberlyn started.

"Noemi—" Jonas said.

"Get out of my room. Both of you."

She spoke with a barely restrained calm that deepened her voice, made it sharp enough to cut. Amberlyn said nothing more as she returned the journal to its place on the nightstand. Noemi glared at her, jaw set, face a shade of pink Jonas hadn't thought her capable of achieving. She wouldn't even look at him.

"We were looking for paper," Jonas said. It sounded pathetic, even to him. "To leave a note. Amberlyn brought—"

"I heard you reading," Noemi said. Now she looked at him, even though it had been Amberlyn who'd read the pages aloud. "Just get the fuck out of my room."

Amberlyn bumped into Jonas as she hurried for the bedroom door, and finally he moved. Just walking closer to Noemi put him on edge, as though his proximity to her would set her melting into a new and molten form. She recoiled as he came near, stepping back into the hall.

Jonas said her name again, placed his hand on her arm, but

she threw it off. Noemi's eyes were red-rimmed and rain-clear. When she spoke, she was stiff with an effort of not crying, but the tears came anyway.

"Don't touch me. Don't ever go in my room again. Don't look at me. Don't speak to me. Why couldn't you have lived anywhere else?"

She was sniffling unstoppably now, and her voice was garbled and unclear, as though Jonas listened with a drinking glass pressed to his ear. Noemi backed toward the stairs, and when Jonas tried again to reach out and call her back, she screamed at him. There were no words in this sound she made—just a gravel screech, animal and furious. He watched from the top of the stairway as she left the house altogether.

"I'm sorry," Amberlyn said, standing beside him in the hall. "I didn't realize it would upset her that much." She hugged her bag against her chest, usually narrow eyes wide.

"I'll go after her."

Though Jonas tried to follow Noemi, Amberlyn stopped him, gripping his hand before he reached the top of the steps.

"Really, Jonas. I think we'd better leave her alone for now."

"She does this thing," he said, "where she gets upset about being upset and worries about people thinking she's overreacting. I don't know. I don't want her to feel like that because I did something wrong."

"If you're sure. Should I come too? Would it be worse if I did or didn't?"

"Maybe not for now," he said. "Just in case she does want to be left alone, this way she'll just be angry with me. Do you need a ride home? I can borrow my dad's car."

"No, thanks. It's not all that far."

Amberlyn followed him downstairs, just a few steps behind. Jonas tried to apologize once they were on the front porch, but she shook her head, forced a tight-mouthed, thin-lipped smile, though her chin crinkled.

"You don't have to walk home."

"Honestly, I think a walk is exactly what I need right now," she said softly.

Once Amberlyn had rounded the corner of the sidewalk and moved out of sight, Jonas broke off across the yard at a run toward the woods.

25

NOEMI

Noemi permitted herself the luxury of a good, self-pitying cry. Sometimes the blurry, eye-stinging tears and pinch-throated sobs worked as an unexpected medicine—as long as no one was around to see her, and she trusted that the woods would hide her when she wanted not to be found. Her phone vibrated with intermittent texts, but she disregarded them. She ran through the trees, nearly tripping over branches, and lamented that she had ever shared anything personal with Jonas Lake. Whatever his excuses, she hated him for looking through her dream journal with someone else. That was the worst part of it—not that he had taken it upon himself to read it, but that he had enabled someone else to partake in the intimate details of her subconscious alongside him. Link's sister, no less. It didn't matter that they weren't laughing or making fun. The fact of their reading was enough to make Noemi wish she had thrown the journal into the lake.

It doesn't really reveal anything about me, she told herself. Some of the things she dreamt were sure to be rooted in her anxieties or desires, but just as many, she reasoned, could be bizarre and utter nonsense.

Gaetan Kelly sat on the forest floor with his back against a tree trunk. He had his legs braided into a pretzel and *The Haunting of Hill House* open across his lap. Between two fingers he held what Noemi first mistook for a cigarette, until the smell hit her. She tried to step back and go another way before he noticed her, saw her crying, but somehow sensing her presence he looked up and pulled his headphones from his ears.

She thought he might say something unkind in response to her tear-slicked, disheveled state, but he asked instead whether she was okay. Rather than answer, she folded her arms and said, "Is that pot?"

"Yes, officer."

"You smell like a skunk got strangled to death by a dirty armpit."

While waiting for his retort she heard instead her name echoing somewhere behind her. It was Jonas, calling, though when she looked back she couldn't yet see him.

"You haven't seen me," she said.

Before Gaetan could agree, she ran past him and hid behind a nearby tree. Noemi could hear Jonas's footsteps now, and she steadied her breath. He likely wouldn't hear her, but she wanted to be as safe and invisible as possible. What was so hard about being mad at Jonas was that she believed he probably hadn't meant to do anything hurtful—the fact he had, even accidentally, was something he'd immediately want to undo. It would have been easier, in a way, if he'd intended to be cruel.

"Oh," Jonas said. His footsteps stopped. Noemi felt the tree stretch against her back, widening to give her more space to hide. "Have you seen Noemi?"

"Not lately," Gaetan's voice answered. "You're the one who lives with her."

"Well, she's not home, obviously."

"You could try texting," Gaetan suggested. He sounded so smarmy Noemi could picture his smug expression.

"Yeah, well, she hasn't answered any of my texts."

"The thing about texts is that sending a bunch of them doesn't usually help you get a response any faster."

"Thanks for the advice," Jonas said. "If you see her, can you tell her I was looking for her?"

"Do I look like her voicemail?"

Jonas mumbled something Noemi couldn't catch; then his footsteps retreated until they fell entirely away. Inching to the side of the tree trunk, she peeked around it until she could see that Gaetan was again alone. He stood, snuffed the joint out on the bottom of his shoe, set his phone inside the book like a bookmark before tossing it aside, then walked over to her.

"What happened?"

"Nothing. I'm fine." Noemi wiped at her eyes, then looked past him, afraid to meet his gaze.

"Well, I'm convinced. Are you crying? Is it something Jonas did?" He asked with uncharacteristic tenderness, and when she finally looked at him, his expression seemed almost concerned.

"Don't look at me," she said.

Gaetan looked away, but he smiled. Then he stepped closer, and as he did, he reached out, tucked an arm around Noemi's back and pulled her forward into his chest. Even though he still smelled of marijuana, she didn't mind so much. He was warm, and his heart beat surprisingly fast. She closed her eyes and let the fabric of his T-shirt dry her lashes. It was strange being so close to Gaetan—close enough that he felt like a human being, which Noemi always seemed to forget he was. When he hugged her, she could actually hear his muscles tense and his back crack, and she was glad when he didn't let go for some time.

He pulled back, finally, and placed the edge of his hand on her cheek. She started, but he didn't do anything. Just wiped underneath her eyelashes and cupped the side of her face. It occurred to Noemi, then, that he must want something. The thought that Gaetan might soon angle for something physical because she was in a distressed state made her lungs heat up.

"You all right?"

"Since when do you care?" she said.

His mouth fell open. When he stepped away, she saw that with these few words she had injured him, that he may not have been as well defended as he'd wanted.

"Are you serious?" he asked—not aggressive, but truly uncertain.

"You've never indicated concern for my well-being before. Forgive me if I'm a little suspicious."

"Noemi." Gaetan raked his fingers through his hair. "Do you actually hate me?"

"What do you mean? I'm not naive enough to think we're friends because you let me swim after hours at work once. I know you think I'm annoying. You never liked that I was friends with Link."

Letting out a humorless, breathy laugh, he pressed the heels of his hands against his eyebrows.

"I thought we were just playing at being mean to each other," he said. "I've always liked you. I just don't know how else to be."

"Jonas brought Amberlyn into my room, and they read my dream journal, if you must know." She folded her arms. "It's not a big deal, but it really bothered me that he invaded my privacy when I wasn't around." Noemi waited for him to mock her.

"That's fucked up. I'm sorry."

"You don't think I'm overreacting?"

"No. You're supposed to be fine with people going into your room and reading your private thoughts?"

She shrugged. "Seems like something you would do."

"Probably," he admitted. "I read all your messages to Link in chat, after all. But I wouldn't show anything you wrote to anyone else without permission."

"You read my messages?"

Gaetan shrugged. "You know Link and I shared a handle, so yeah. How do you think I knew what flowers to get you for Valentine's Day?"

Noemi's throat felt like it was tightening around some small, suffocating animal. "How much did you read? I figured our conversations would bore you."

"The thing is, uh..." Gaetan looked away, rubbed at the back of his neck. "Link never went online all that much, you know? So it was usually just me you were talking to."

"You pretended to be Link?"

"No! We both used the Laetan chat handle, and he was usually in the room when I was talking to you. I just never clarified who it was. Any time Link logged on he'd say some weird greeting like he was an old-timey reporter. Otherwise, it was generally me."

Noemi tried to think of an example of what that might mean, but she couldn't recall anything specific.

"So basically, Link logged on almost never. You're saying I was usually talking to you?"

"More often than not."

Gaetan's face flushed, but Noemi, at least, had finished crying and was regaining her calm. She tried to remember the things she'd thought she had told Link before he'd died: dreams, insecurities, anxieties, rages. So many of the moments she had spent with Link in person, he'd seemed to be in his own world. She wondered now how much of that had been his way, and how much was because he hardly had any idea what she was referencing half the time.

"I didn't mean to mislead you," he said.

"That's bullshit and you know it, Gaetan. You'd have to have talked about yourself in the third person, for one thing. I'm sure you did. Should I pull up our old conversations and check?" She glanced at her phone. "I don't even want to look at them. What is wrong with you?"

"It's easier to think things through on an app," he said. "I can't be nice in person. I don't know how to be. I guess—I'm not sure. When I tease you, and you get mad, it's like what I say matters, like you care." His eyes were so blue she felt like she was seeing through his head to the sky above. "Link didn't know."

"Didn't know what?"

"How I felt."

"About what?"

"You know." He sighed. Noemi had a guess, but she couldn't be sure. "Link had this idea of you as this quirky, cool girl. But he never paid attention to what was going on with other people. Not really. He said he wanted to ask you out, and I didn't tell him I would have a problem with that. I guess I didn't want my feelings to be real." He cringed, sucked air through his teeth. "The people you love are the ones who can really hurt you, you know?"

"Link hurt you?"

"What? No. You're gonna make me say it? God, you're the

worst." He closed his eyes, loosed another slow exhalation. When he opened them, they settled, unflinching, on hers. "I'm obviously saying I'm in love with you and have been for, uh, half my life." Gaetan placed a palm flat along his sternum, steadying his breath perhaps, though she thought for a second he might puke. "I have literally never said those words to anyone, so I want to die a little right now."

Something unfamiliar split Noemi like a tree root cracking through stone.

"I don't believe you've never said that, and I don't believe that's what you feel." Unsure of what she believed, she said what made the most sense.

"What?"

"As much 'experience' as you have," she said, punctuating her words with air quotes, "I don't see how you've managed to avoid making that claim before. I don't know why you'd try it on me."

"What do you mean?"

He threw the word around so casually. He *loved* her. How many people had he slept with during this alleged half lifetime? No formula for understanding relationships could reconcile this confession with what she'd always known about Gaetan. Noemi didn't comprehend how someone could turn off what they felt for one person and give themselves over to another. The feelings he described held him at such a distance, she would need a telescope to see him. What person who purported to understand love could be so cavalier with other people's emotions? There were so many people he'd famously rebuffed *after* getting what he wanted. She couldn't be sure this was any different.

"I don't understand why you would say that you *love* me. What do you think is going to happen?"

"I don't think anything is going to happen." He folded his arms. "I don't know what you're talking about. You think I'd lie about how I feel, while you're crying, to what—*seduce* you?" Gaetan rolled his eyes at this, and Noemi witnessed the change in his expression as this question ceased to be a joke. "So wait. Are you saying you don't believe me because you think I lie to people to get them to have sex with me? Just so we're clear. Is that what you're implying, or am I missing something?"

"I don't know what your MO is." Noemi shrugged. She'd lost the high ground. Maybe she'd never had it. Maybe the assumption either of them needed any advantage had made her wrong from the start. She grew smaller and smaller until she could fit on a single blade of grass.

"Okay," he said. Then again: "Okay."

She had always hated him. Why had she hated him? The temperature of the world changed whenever he was near.

"I'm sorry," she told him. "I didn't mean to insult you."

"Yeah, you did." He huffed. "You could have just said you didn't feel the same way and left it at that. Or said nothing. That'd be fine too. I wasn't expecting reciprocation. I've been walking around with this weight and—anyway, it's done now. Whether you believe me or not, I said what I had to say." He looked down at his arms where they hugged his chest, one over the other. She couldn't see his face, just his hair, flopping forward over his forehead.

"Maybe I did mean to insult you. I don't know why I do things like that." Why she clung so tightly to a narrative of Gaetan that didn't permit him to have feelings she could injure.

"Do what? Push people away when you don't want to? I know you, Noemi. You're testing people's sincerity. You've got really low expectations for everyone but yourself, and somehow I still can't meet them." He shook his head, like it was funny though they both knew it wasn't.

Her expectations for Gaetan weren't low. If they had been, there'd be no use getting frustrated with him. Gaetan was smart and brave and a decent friend, and Noemi saw glimmers of potential in him, coated in a shell of arrogance and feigned cheer.

"You're selfish," he said, "and volatile, and it's frustrating, but I still wanna matter to you. When you were crying, I got this weird, sick feeling like someone punched me. But I don't know how to act. I only know one way to be, and it's not very nice. So, I guess I can't be too insulted for your not believing me because...I get why you wouldn't."

She wanted to turn back time: just a few minutes, long enough to unsay the things she'd just said. Go back to when she was crying and all she cared about was a meaningless journal, and he was hugging her. Before he'd said how he felt, though she would retain the memory of it so he wouldn't need to say it again.

"You call me out on all the ways I'm messed up," he continued, "but you still give a shit about me. Or it seems like you do."

"Of course I do." Without meaning to, she stood as far from him as she could—which was not very far—with the tree still against her back.

"The only other people I ever cared about both died. When you aren't around, I miss you. When you are...I guess I still miss you. I shouldn't take it out on you, but I do."

"That's something we both do, then," she admitted. "Being a little meaner than we intend." It had been easier to decide there wasn't much to him. It was always easier assuming the worst of people because then it didn't matter that Noemi wasn't nice to them. Maybe that's what had happened here: he'd cracked himself open to show her something sincere, and instead she'd called it rotten.

"You're not mean, Noemi. Not really. Temperamental, maybe, but..." Gaetan trailed off, rolled his eyes. An unfamiliar smile twisted his mouth, devoid of his usual sleaze.

Gaetan had always known how to find the irritable, judgmental part of her—that red-hot poker glowing at her center—that she'd been able to smother around Link. It had been an endlessly annoying quality of his. It surprised Noemi, now, that she didn't mind Gaetan's awareness of her shortcomings if the alternative was that they go completely overlooked.

"The truth is there were a lot of times things in my life felt pretty bleak, and I just thought about what you might be doing, or the next time I would see you on the bus, or if you would complain in French class about how sexist the dress code was. The days we argued were the best, but even the boring, regular days where I'd just see you across the gym for a second...or the days I didn't see you at all, but I knew you were still out there, and I was so glad that you lived in Shivery and in the world and in my life... It used to be a kind of butterfly thing I thought I'd grow out of—"

"A butterfly thing?"

"Like nerves." He shrugged. "But I didn't. It just kind of grew with me and became a part of who I am. If that's not romantic enough to suit whatever you think love is, that's cool."

"Gaetan—"

"Here ends my humiliating speech. If it's all the same to you, I'm gonna go find a hole to crawl into." He rubbed the knuckle of his thumb across his brow. "This is one of those moments I wish I could trade places with Link."

"Don't say that." If not for the tree at her back, she might have fled by now, bailed like she had when she'd practically flung herself from the loft, run out into the snow to get away from Jonas. It was better than saying the wrong thing. Noemi contained an ocean of wrong things to say.

"It's not a joke or even a woe-is-me thing. I'm speaking practically." He didn't seem to be baiting her. It was what he believed. "There's no one who wouldn't be better off if Link and I traded places. That includes me. I'm sorry that I'm here and he's not, Noemi."

She had no idea how to handle this part of him, open wide and raw like a wound. What was there to say? *That's not true*? There was probably no one who would keep Gaetan and give up Link, but there was also no reason for him to think the world would ever demand that trade.

"I promise you no one has ever thought that."

He turned, shifted his hands into his pockets, and kicked at a tree root, all the while nodding.

Noemi startled. Behind Gaetan stood Link, hood up, watching without a hint of expression—like he had always been there, and she just hadn't noticed, had mistaken him for a tree or a shadow. Though he looked just as she remembered him, something in Noemi knew he was off. It was like coming home to find all the furniture in her room replaced with perfect replicas.

With some intangible sense she recognized him, not as the boy she had known, but as the version of him she had seen on the shore of the lake one day-lit night in February. Gaetan hadn't noticed him yet, and she wondered, perhaps, if this image of Link was something from a dream.

She wanted first to point to this Link-figure, for Gaetan to corroborate its existence, but she remembered how, less than a year ago, Gaetan was falling-down drunk in the hallway at school. Now the cuts on his arm had healed, inked over. He was saving for college. The last time she'd thought she'd seen Link, Gaetan had shown up on her porch afterward to check that she was all right, having gathered himself enough, finally, to be the one offering help. If he did see Link now, it might mean something different to him than to her. She was puzzling through the secrets of some chamber-dwelling doppelgänger, but Gaetan was ready to trade places with Link, and the sight of this *person*—whoever it was— might unwind him.

Noemi wanted to split this false ghost like a watermelon, reach right into its center with her nails and shred it before Gaetan could see.

But Gaetan did see. He turned to follow her gaze because Noemi's face so rarely hid what she felt. Gaetan had recognized dread in her expression, but he couldn't know why. She feared the ghost for how badly Gaetan would want it to be real. Noemi could tell right away that Gaetan saw Link too. His posture stiffened, shoulders squared.

"What the fuck?" he said.

"Gaetan, I don't think that's really Link."

He glanced back at her. "You can see him too?"

She hesitated, tilting her head to the side, but he already had his answer. He took a step toward the Link-figure, one arm outstretched as though in a slow, surrendering approach toward a wild dog. Gaetan said his friend's name, voice wavering, but rather than respond, Link turned and ran. Without a thought, Gaetan followed.

Noemi ran after them, yelling for Gaetan. She could barely keep close enough to see the back of his jacket disappear each time he ducked around a tree. No one else was supposed to see this ghostlike version of Link, least of all Gaetan, and he might never leave the woods now. He was so desperate he would follow a sign of Link anywhere. All it had taken to lure her had been a song played on violin, and had Jonas not been there, she might still be lost in a trance at the bottom of the lake. But Gaetan didn't have Jonas or Lyle or a family or anyone, and no one would search for him if he didn't come home, because he had no home. Noemi's phone vibrated in her purse each time it slapped against her side, but she couldn't stop to check it. Was it Unknown? That person claiming to be Link, warning her again to stay away from this image of him?

When Noemi reached the lake, Link was standing in the water several yards from the shore. Though it was only up to Link's ankles, Gaetan, who had begun trudging in after him, was feet away and already waist deep. She shouted his name, and he called Link's, and Link waited, watching for Gaetan to draw close enough to be submerged.

Then Jonas was at her side, and when she looked at him she saw his mouth move but heard nothing he said, only her own voice saying "Hold this," and dropped her purse from her shoulder and thrust it into his arms.

Noemi stepped out of her skirt, kicked off her shoes, and threw her Hummingbird tee into the wet grass.

"Noemi, wait!" Jonas called behind her.

Without looking back, she said, "I need you to wait right there, Jonas. Please." She watched as Gaetan's head slipped below the water. Bracing herself for the cold, Noemi found instead that the water was unseasonably warm. She waded until she felt the ground drop away under her feet, so she had to swim toward the spot where Gaetan had just stood. He was gone, and so was Link, and they'd both left behind sets of rings rippling out to graze one another on the surface.

Noemi dove, and Jonas's voice was lost to her. Her ears filled with the quiet hum of being underwater, and she could barely see anything besides the bubbles of her own breath drifting through the algae-tinted water just in front of her.

The further she dove, the darker the water became. It was a strange kind of darkness she had not expected—clear and black, like a night sky so crystalline she could see celestial objects swirling through it like watercolors. Her eyes didn't hurt like they usually did when she swam, and when she exhaled, she realized she didn't need to hold her breath: she could breathe.

Noemi wasn't sure she was even underwater anymore. It was more like drifting through a space station, except when she stopped swimming she merely floated where she was, so she kept kicking downward.

She understood, because she was a logical sort, that she was still underwater, and that there should not be stars glowing beneath her. She was not looking at a night sky because even on land where she'd just been it was still day. But she saw them, straight ahead: a cluster of yellow-white stars, and because she did not know where else to search for Gaetan, she swam toward them.

The stars were not stars at all, of course. They were much too attainable and much too small. As they drew nearer, Noemi saw that they were lights, hard and steady between the branches of a tree—a tree growing at the bottom of a lake filled with water she could breathe. She reached, brushed the leaves with her fingertips, then gripped the branches until she pulled herself upright. She climbed rather than swam down toward the lower branches and the gaping black below.

Gaetan was tucked in the bark, right at the point where the limbs split from the trunk. They grew over him, bound him. He resembled what he'd been at eight rather than eighteen, and as tall and strong as he'd always seemed, Noemi was struck by how small he looked to her now, a child. He held his eyes closed, stitched tight, black lashes stark against his cheek. His neck was ringed in dirt, like it had been most days when he was in grade school, and scabs and bruises bloomed over his knuckles and arms. He held tight to the tree holding tight to him, and when Noemi tried to loosen his arms, it seemed he might have rock where his bones ought to have been.

"Gaetan," she said, and his eyes opened. The tree didn't release him. It tightened, and the bark flowed over his limbs like the skin of a snake curling tighter. "Is this what you did to Link? You need to let Gaetan go right now. He doesn't really wish he had died. I don't either." She pulled Gaetan's wrist, and she didn't let go even when the wood spread over her fingers, cut into them. "You have no right."

And then he was free. The lake, the woods—whatever had been pretending to be Link—decided it had restrained Gaetan long enough. Noemi held tight to his body and pushed herself away from the tree, back in the direction of the circle of sunlight that danced across the surface of the water above. Even with Gaetan hanging limp, it was hard to hold on to him and swim. She had only her feet to use, and water was beginning to creep up her nostrils again. The sense of flying she'd had was gone, and she knew again she was underwater, that she could drown, that Gaetan was growing larger and more burdensome in her arms.

When she broke through the surface, gasping for air, she pulled with one free arm, trying to swim to the shallows without dropping the body in the other. Then, her hand gripped Jonas's, and while he tugged her toward the shore, she realized the ground was just below her, and she dropped her feet firmly into the mud at the lake bottom. Together, they lugged Gaetan's form onto the grass, and she fell to her knees to check if he was breathing. She felt for his pulse. She listened for his heartbeat.

Noemi had, of course, passed CPR with flying colors when they'd learned on a doll in health class. Now that she needed to put that skill to use, all the guidelines leaked from her brain. Fortunately, while she was pushing on Gaetan's chest, Jonas began counting under his breath. When he stopped, she leaned and breathed into Gaetan's mouth. His lips were soft and still, and Noemi had a distant awareness that she was crying, but she couldn't feel anything but his corpse underneath her. He was gone, small and jagged, scars on his arms, sitting in darkness. *I knew you were still out there,* he'd said, *and I was so glad.*

She too had been small and jagged in different ways. One Midwinter, in seventh grade, her mother wouldn't let her carve an ice boat, even though she was a teenager now, because Noemi was too impatient, and Cesca was afraid she'd slice open the thin skin between her thumb and index finger. Noemi had stood, frowning, while everyone else chipped away at their blocks with little tools, until Gaetan came and took her wrist, shoved his boat into her hand like she was weak and pathetic, and walked away without a word, back to a group of eighth-grade girls from Galaxie whose names she hadn't yet learned, who gave him gentle, flirtatious pushes every time he spoke. Noemi held out her arms, dropped the boat so it shattered right in front of him—because there was nothing she wanted if she had to humiliate herself by asking for it—and a visible ache spread across his face and, though she didn't know it, hers. It was the first boat he'd carved, and the only one, and he'd given it to her.

So glad that you lived in Shivery, he'd said, *and in the world and in my life.*

JONAS

Gaetan coughed, and murky water spilled from his mouth and to the ground. Noemi fell back, flat on the grass while he retched, and Jonas dropped so that he was sitting, head on his knees, her purse vibrating frantically on the grass beside him. She held her arm across her face, blocking the sunlight from her eyes. Jonas softly touched her elbow, gave it a relieved and gentle squeeze.

Noemi was soaked. She pulled her T-shirt on and with her back turned to Gaetan and Jonas, removed her bra from underneath, squeezed the excess water from it, then gathered the rest of her belongings in her arms. Jonas offered her his dry hoodie when she shivered, but she responded with a clipped refusal that made it clear he had not yet been forgiven.

Gaetan too was drenched, and he walked barefoot and

shirtless to the side of the road where he had parked his car, his shoes trailing water from where they hung on his fingertips. While Noemi and Jonas followed, he thought about how he might ask her what had happened without stirring her annoyance, but he couldn't settle on the right words. Her silence simmered, while Gaetan's was uncharacteristically tepid. He climbed into his truck, and aside from the fact that he was dripping all over the interior, he seemed surprisingly unruffled.

"Do you guys want a ride back to your place?"

Jonas let Noemi answer in the affirmative for both of them. She sat between the two boys, and though no one talked, Jonas attempted to catch her eye while they rode the two short blocks back to Lamplight. She stared straight ahead, so rigid and deliberate she had to have felt him watching.

Gaetan pulled into the driveway, turned off his car, tugged at his keys, then looked at them in his hand, confused as to how they'd arrived there. Jonas held the passenger's-side door open and stood beside the truck, waiting for Noemi, and though she slid across the seat toward the door, she turned back to Gaetan.

"You should come inside and take a shower," she said. "Since it used to be an inn, we have a couple bathrooms no one uses unless we have guests."

"I can just shower at work."

"Do you have laundry at work? Just come on. It's fine." She looked at Jonas. "Right?"

"Uh." Jonas let the empty moment stretch. Maybe he could

achieve a pause so awkward Gaetan would simply disappear. "Yeah," he finally agreed. "No worries. Pretty sure Lyle left shampoo you can use and everything."

"We do have laundry at work, but okay."

Gaetan lifted a red lifeguard backpack onto his shoulder and followed them into Lamplight.

Someone was in the kitchen making dinner—probably Audrey—while whoever else was home had the TV on in the main room. Noemi called out a greeting and then ushered the boys upstairs. While she fetched Gaetan towels and showed him which way to turn the handle for hot or cold water, Jonas stood by with his arms folded, moving out of the way as needed.

"If you want to take a bath," she said, "the right handle is for hot water, and the left one is for cold. That's facing the tub. The letters kind of wore away."

"Shower's fine, thanks."

"Okay. Just leave your clothes in the hall, and we'll grab them and wash them for you." Noemi turned to squeeze some water from her curls into the sink. "And I'm really glad you're not dead."

"Thanks to you." Gaetan unbuckled his belt.

Without thinking, Jonas let out an *ummm* sound to remind them of his diffident and cringing existence. If she'd heard it, Noemi chose not to acknowledge him, but Gaetan, at least, refrained from removing his pants.

"I didn't know that lake was there," Gaetan said. "Is that where they found Link?"

Noemi turned to Jonas, but he shrugged, as helpless as she was. "I don't know," she said. "Do you remember what happened before you went in the water?"

"You mean what I said to you?" Gaetan shifted. "Yeah." Then he laughed. "Did I just fling myself into the lake out of embarrassment? God. I'm sorry. I don't even remember being in the water. It might be a good thing: almost drowning is probably pretty uncomfortable. I felt more like I was napping. I had a dream about Link."

"It probably is better that way," Noemi agreed. "Anyhow, hang out for as long as you like. You can spend the night if you want. You have the room to yourself. Do you have a change of clothes?"

"Thanks," he said. "I've got some stuff."

She closed the door to the bathroom, then the bedroom, and finally Jonas stood alone with her in the hallway. He readied himself for answers, but she said nothing—just headed down the stairs to her room on the second floor. When Noemi went in, she left the door open behind her, and Jonas followed.

"Are you okay?" he asked.

"Yeah." She tossed her bag and wet skirt on the bed, let her shoes fall to the floor. Noemi bent before her dresser and unearthed a dry T-shirt, then went into the bathroom.

"What happened?" Jonas started after her.

"Do you mind?" Noemi closed the door until it left just a crack for him to talk through. Instead, he listened, waiting while she removed the wet shirt, which had soaked up much of the water from her skin, and it slapped against the marble counter.

"Sorry," Jonas said. "Noemi, I really need to talk to you."

A rustle of clean clothing, a tearing of knotted hair.

"Can I not talk to you through the door?" Jonas asked. "I want to hear you."

She sighed and pulled it open so he could slide in.

She now wore a dry, black *Fahrenheit 451* T-shirt, but she still smelled like wet earth as he moved past her. He found himself a place to sit on the rounded lip of the tub while she continued working a comb through the tangled mess of her hair.

"How did Gaetan end up in the water?" he asked.

"When I ran away from you, I bumped into him in the woods. You were right behind me, and I asked him to tell you he hadn't seen me. After you left—I can't really explain it without it sounding like something that belongs in my dream journal..."

When she mentioned the journal, Jonas bit his lip until his piercing turned sideways, then looked at the ceiling.

"I told Gaetan what you and Amberlyn did—" she said.

"I'm sorry."

"—And while we were talking, this person showed up. He looked like Link. It was like seeing a ghost, and it wasn't the first time I'd seen him. But I don't think it was *him* him. Can you get me my phone?"

Without asking why, Jonas ran to the bedroom to fetch her purse. He brought the entire thing in, and she pulled out the phone and scrolled through her texts.

"I've seen things too," Jonas said. "A few weeks ago I thought I saw someone really tall in the hallway. Right outside your room." He motioned toward the door, and a chill tweaked the backs of his knees. "But then they went into your room and disappeared."

"Well, this was in daylight, and it looked exactly like Link. Gaetan saw it too." She handed her phone to Jonas with a string of texts from someone called "Unknown" open.

Stop him, the most recent ones said. *Don't let Gate follow. That isn't me.* Then, *Is he all right? Are you all right?*

"What the hell?" Jonas asked.

"I know. Fortunately, Gaetan doesn't seem to remember he saw Link. Or he doesn't think it was real, so he isn't saying anything."

"Maybe he lost track of things while the oxygen to his head was cut off."

Noemi shrugged. "You can go back almost a year. There are lots of these texts."

Jonas thumbed back far enough to piece together the truth she'd been living with almost as long as her friend had been dead: someone had been texting her claiming to be Link. "This is fucked up. You don't think this is real, do you?"

"I think someone's texting me, and I know Gaetan and I both saw someone in the woods. But they can't be the same someone, and I don't know what either of them have to do with Link."

"I didn't know this was going on," Jonas said. "This is harassment." He handed the phone back to her. "You sure it's not Gaetan sending these?"

"Positive."

"You don't think it's Amberlyn?" he asked, hesitant.

She glared.

"I just mean if it's someone who has Link's phone—though it says the number is unknown, so maybe not."

"You'd know better than I would if it were Amberlyn," Noemi snapped. "You guys are apparently best friends now."

"Not really. Noemi, I really am sorry about earlier. The journal—"

"Forget it. Just don't bring your girlfriend into my room anymore." She sounded petulant, but Jonas detected a very real hurt underneath.

"Oh. We really were just in there to drop something off for you. One second." Jonas ran from the bathroom again, then returned a moment later with the booklet and the notebook paper with Amberlyn's scrawled message. "She wanted to give you this. I guess Link had made it." He handed the items to her.

She flipped through the pages of Link's homemade comic. Though she pretended to ignore him, her eyes flicked to Jonas every now and again while he babbled on in apology.

"We never should have touched your things, and reading your journal was so fucked up. Really, it just sort of happened. She was looking for paper. For the note. Though, if I'm honest, I know part of me wanted to know if I was in your journal. I still think about you all the time. It's not an excuse. Probably that just makes it worse. I feel like crap. I never meant to hurt you. All I wanted was to be with you. Amberlyn and I are one hundred percent not dating—"

"Jonas, just shut up." Noemi walked over to him. He was sitting, again, on the bathtub's edge. "I'm deciding not to be mad at you. I'm tired of being angry. It's been an annoying day."

"Okay," he said, uncertain.

Noemi sat beside him on the edge of the tub. Beneath her loose-fitting T-shirt she wore only a pair of navy blue underwear, but she didn't seem at all embarrassed to be half-naked in front of him. Why should she be? He'd seen this much of her skin before. Her shins were striped with blades of grass and flecks of dirt.

"Honestly, I probably owe Amberlyn an apology," she said, "for throwing a fit. Though I'm still pretty annoyed she read my journal." Noemi turned to look at him, but held eye contact for less than a second before turning away again. "As far as you and I are concerned, most of why we aren't friends anymore is my fault anyway."

"Why aren't we friends? I still don't know what happened, Noemi." When she'd broken things off, he hadn't been able to make much sense of it. "You said you loved me—"

"I do." She gently touched a hair-thin scratch along the top of her knee. "Things were escalating, and I was afraid you'd get tired of me when I couldn't keep up."

"That's what I don't get," he said. "You said something about holding me back. I don't have all that much relationship experience either. I thought we were bumbling through things together. If I ever put pressure on you—"

"You didn't."

"Okay."

"Do you want to have sex with me, Jonas?" she asked.

"I mean—I—well—of course." He tugged at his lip ring. "As long as you want to. I want us both to want to. You mean a lot to me, and I want to share that with you."

"Okay." Noemi slid sideways, placing more distance between them, though she lifted his hand and held on to it. "I'll try to explain, but I want you to promise never to tell anyone, not even to ask for advice. It's personal."

"I promise."

"Right. Well, I realized before I even met you that I was probably asexual."

Jonas didn't know what she was trying to say, understood the word but not the experience of it. He thought first of cells splitting.

"I wanted to be loved," she continued, "but the sexual aspects of being in a relationship—I knew they didn't appeal to me in the same way they did to other people. And I was sure I might be alone forever because of it, because what were the chances of finding someone I loved who would also be okay with that?"

"Noemi—"

"And the thing is, I'm not opposed to having sex. I'd be more than happy never doing it ever, but I would do it if you wanted me to. Because of how I feel. It wouldn't bother me at all to do that with you."

"Noemi, slow down," he said. "I don't want you to do anything you're going to hate."

"I won't hate it if it's you, Jonas. But I don't know if I'd be very good at it." Noemi stood, leaned against the sink, avoided the sight of her own face in the mirror.

Jonas followed her. He placed a hand on her arm and was relieved when she didn't move away but instead turned to face him.

"Is that what you've been worried about?" he asked. "You don't need to worry about impressing me. I don't know what I'm doing either. And I'm not in a hurry."

"I know." She nodded. "I'm just not sure if waiting is going to help it. I might be like this forever."

"There's nothing wrong with you being *like this*."

"I'd say the same thing in your place." Noemi adjusted the edge of her T-shirt, unrolling part of the hem that had been folded up. "It's easy enough to say. But if I could wave a wand and change myself, I would. I know the 'right thing' to do is just embrace myself or whatever—say 'to hell with anyone who makes me feel bad about it because I'm proud and love myself,' *blah blah blah*. But that's bullshit positivity because I *don't* feel that way. I can't just pretend I'm secure about it all when I'm not. You don't see a lot of love stories about people like me, so my expectations for romantic happiness are low. That gets in my head, and I can't just turn the insecurities off when you say you love me. It's nothing you've done wrong."

"When you say 'asexual,' do you mean—I just wonder if—are you attracted to me at all?" he asked. It wasn't as hard to ask her as it would have been a few months ago, yet Jonas was more afraid now of her answer.

"I can't say what the label means for anyone other than me, but yeah." Noemi brushed her hair back from her face, and the gesture allowed her to duck behind her hand, hide her eyes as she spoke. "I think you're really handsome, Jonas. I don't know what other people mean when they say someone is sexy. I look at you, and I want to touch you, and I like when you touch me in certain ways. I don't want to—you know." She bumped her fists together in an awkward representation of what he assumed to be two bodies. "What does attractiveness mean to other people?"

Jonas's mouth fell open, empty. Noemi watched him, waiting perhaps for some insight as to what "other people" do. He knew she was being sincere—that she thought he had the answer to what it was everyone but her felt, as though there were a line drawn around her and he stood, with the rest of the world, on the other side of it.

"Everyone's different," he said finally. "What people like—I'm sure sexiness varies as much as any other preference."

"What does sex mean to you? Does it have to be emotional?"

"Uh." He fumbled his speech, bounced from one foot to the other. "Sometimes wanting sex isn't really a thing—you know—that I think about when it's happening. When the wanting is happening, I mean. Not the sex happening. That hasn't, um, anyway... I get horny randomly sometimes. It doesn't always have anything to do with...whatever...emotional attraction. But if I think about actually having sex, like for real, the person I'm with is important. So with you—is it hot in here? I'm really hot." Jonas shrugged off his hoodie and dropped it onto the lid of the toilet behind him. The armpits of his T-shirt were damp with sweat.

He didn't have much in-person experience with other people's naked bodies, and he didn't want to tangle himself up in alluding to any porn he'd watched. She might have been worried he'd see her as deficient; he worried she'd see him as a pig. Logically, Jonas believed there was nothing broken about either of them, that each was the only person judging themselves. In practice, it was hard to turn off the voice that held himself to an imaginary standard of "normalcy."

"I understand why you'd want me to be sexually attracted to you," Noemi said. "I can get why that seems important. The sad thing is, I might be hurt if you said you didn't feel sexually attracted to me. Maybe it's because we live in such a sex-obsessed world." She took his hand again, examined his knuckles as though feeling them for the first time. "I can't imagine considering sex with anyone else. It seems like you aren't casual about it. Maybe I'm wrong?"

"No." As inelegant as this conversation was, it had still taken some concentration for Jonas not to get turned on thinking about sex with Noemi. The effort had only partly worked, and now he gave up trying altogether. He wasn't sure if she would notice or if it would bother her, but he hoped she liked him enough to forgive his body's honest expression of what he felt.

Noemi said nothing about his hard-on, but she led him into the bedroom. It was different from the way she'd previously steered him through the woods. She didn't seem as certain of where she was going this time, and he could feel her trembling, which he was glad for—he was shaky too. When they got to the bed, she asked if he had a condom, and Jonas mumbled something nonsensical before darting from the room and across the hall. When he was back in her bedroom, he made sure to lock the door.

She sat on the edge of the bed, and he tilted his pelvis against hers until she let herself lie back. Then she helped him remove his clothes, and as many times as Noemi had touched him before—his chest, his shoulders, his back—the way the side of her arm grazed his stomach now sent the skin all over his torso raising in ridges of goosebumps. She arched her back while he pulled down her underwear, but she left her top on, like people did on television, and he didn't ask her to remove it or try to.

He first navigated her with his fingertips, and though she didn't make a sound, Jonas watched intently for her reactions, how pressing *here* might make her tense up, how she slackened when he trailed over *there*. "How is that?" he asked, searching for guidance. "A little sharp," she would say, or "Relaxing," which seemed the best he could hope for.

Noemi guided his hips down to her, and Jonas did his best to fit, but it seemed to require more force than he wanted to use. She bit her lip, closed her eyes, turned away.

"It won't go in," he said.

"We might have to make it," she answered. "Don't worry if it looks like I'm in pain."

But the closer he drew, the more she pulled away. Her arms reached out for him, but the rest of her body sank back in disagreement. Jonas sat upright, ran the backs of his hands against the insides of her thighs.

"You're completely, er, closed," he said. "I don't want to force it. How are you? Are you okay?"

"I'm fine." Draping an arm across her face, she finally loosened her body, and he discovered just how tense she'd been. "Don't force it if you don't want to. I'm sorry. I really wanted this to work. I guess the part of me that doesn't is hijacking me. It isn't conscious."

Jonas took a deep breath, and his chest shuddered. He let himself drift to the side until he lay facing her. "It's okay. It was our first try. And we don't have to try again until you want to give it another go."

"You're disappointed," she said. Noemi turned so they were face-to-face, and her curls draped her shoulder. She sounded concerned, but she looked relieved.

Though he *was* disappointed, what Jonas felt was more complicated than disappointment alone. He couldn't quite sort his feelings out, but it seemed the least he could do at this point was trip through them. "That you even tried to have sex with me..." Jonas flicked through the vocabulary in his brain for the right words, but he wasn't sure he'd ever learned them. He outlined the dip of her waist with his thumb. "Just doing this with you means a lot, that you would even want me to be a part of figuring out what you're comfortable with."

She bit her bottom lip.

"You seem to have this idea that sex is the be-all and end-all of our relationship for me, and it's not." Noemi had discussed the eventual doom of their relationship like Jonas was sex-obsessed... because that's how she viewed the world or men or him, he didn't know. He hated everything that made her feel unworthy of love or think him insincere in his. "I want you to believe me when I say that it's not. It's like you're anticipating ways we could disappoint each other and pushing me away before I can leave on my own. But I'm not going anywhere."

"You're very perceptive," she said, and she sounded happier.

"Well, I try."

She smiled.

AMBERLYN

When Amberlyn saw Jonas in the hall at school, guilt tightened like a cord around her chest. They were conspirators. Picking up Noemi's journal initially had been harmless, but that had ceased to be the case once she'd learned what it was. As much as she might have lied to herself about it not being a proper and personal diary, about it not being a violation, the truth was Amberlyn just wanted to know what was inside. She didn't suspect Noemi of truly being complicit in what had happened to Link. Indirectly, she may have contributed, but not in a way that had been her fault.

Still, after she'd kept the strange truths about the woods a secret, Amberlyn couldn't help but wonder what else Noemi might be afraid to reveal. Without making the decision consciously, she had deemed Noemi untrustworthy and judged her undeserving of privacy. Disappointed in her own behavior, she hadn't even told Lyle what had happened in Noemi's bedroom.

NOEMI

Hey Noemi. I am truly sorry for going through your journal and room. I can say it's because I was leaving you the comic but there is really no excuse. It was not my place or business and I understand if you want nothing to do with me. I just want you to know I didn't mean to hurt you

It's really OK.

Did you read much?

Just scanned really except the one entry I was reading when you walked in. Jonas didn't ask me to read it btw

It's really just notes and nonsense. Not a big deal.

I shouldn't have gotten so upset. I'm sorry.

Amberlyn could think of nothing else to say, and Noemi had not responded after that. They had no periods together until lunch, so she would have to wait until the middle of the day to see if things really could be repaired. And so, while she didn't much want to confide in Jonas, further entrenching herself in any accidental conspiracy, she approached him at his locker after her Spanish class.

"Hey."

"Hey," he answered. "You okay?"

"Oh, I'm fine. How's Noemi, though?" She asked quietly, even though no one who would care was near.

"Noemi?" He leaned an ear toward her. "She's okay. Things got a little out of hand after you left. Long story short, Gaetan Kelly is staying with us now apparently? But in terms of the whole diary thing, we made up, and I don't think she's mad at you either. She feels bad for yelling."

"Okay. I texted her afterward, but I wasn't sure." Amberlyn couldn't quite imagine how Gaetan would end up staying at Lamplight, but since it was better than many of the alternatives, she didn't question it.

"She wasn't in French today, though." Jonas frowned and held up a neatly stapled packet of papers, a blue sticky note with Noemi's name on top of it. "Lyle stopped in before the bell rang and said something to the teacher before heading to her own class.

I texted them both, but only Lyle answered. I guess Noemi's in the nurse's office with a migraine?"

"So maybe she's not okay."

"Well, she does get them sometimes. Anxiety, maybe. Honestly, I think she would have to feel pretty horrible to miss class."

Amberlyn nodded. "Can I have her French homework? I'll stop by and give it to her."

"I mean, I can just take it home and give it to her there."

"I know, but I actually want to talk to her."

With a shrug, Jonas handed over the packet. Amberlyn was a few doors from the nurse's office when the bell rang, and she hurried into a slow jog before anyone could find her and ask for a hall pass. The office was always cold, and the nurse wore an oversized cardigan pulled over her floral scrubs. The only other student present was a freshman boy in a pleather chair, holding an ice pack against his eye. The nurse was ready to begin diagnosing Amberlyn the second she walked in, until she explained she was dropping off another student's homework.

"Ms. Amato is lying down." She stressed the syllables of Noemi's name incorrectly, and motioned toward the darkened part of the room behind the half wall bordering her desk. "Don't take long, and I'll write you a pass for class."

Amberlyn walked to the shadowy side of the room and whispered Noemi's name, uncertain whether she'd be sleeping. The school had two hospital beds, ringed in a single curtain that separated them from the rest of the room, but not each other. Because the curtain was only partly closed, Amberlyn could tell just one of the beds was occupied, and at the sound of her voice, the bushy-haired patient in it stirred.

"Amberlyn? Are you sick?" Noemi shielded her eyes with her hand, even though there was barely any light to shrink from.

"No, I brought your French homework. Jonas said you had a migraine." She held up the pages, and the Post-it drifted toward the floor. Amberlyn scrambled to pick it up.

"Thanks. Can you just set it on my bag?" Noemi's backpack sat on the floor beside the bed, its topmost flap complete with little cat ears and sleepy-eyed lashes. Amberlyn set the pages on top.

"Do you get migraines a lot?"

"Not that much. They just come on all of a sudden, and it's a pain. Usually I'm lucky, and it's at night."

"Is it from stress?"

"Not sure. You don't have to whisper," Noemi said. "In my case, it's mostly light that bothers me. And I get dizzy if I have to sit up or walk around." Then, as though she knew what Amberlyn was really asking, "It's not because I'm upset about anything. It just happens randomly."

"I'm really sorry—" Amberlyn started to apologize again, but Noemi shook her head.

"It's fine." She sounded sincere. Perhaps the headache had mellowed her.

Amberlyn had never had a migraine, but she remembered getting fevers, how her mother would soak a washcloth with cool water and drape it across her forehead. She walked to the sink at the far side of the room and dribbled water over a rough, brown paper towel until it was soft and cool. Then she folded it, over and over into a smaller rectangle, and placed it across Noemi's forehead.

"Oh, that feels good," Noemi said, pressing it down over her eyes. "Thank you."

Amberlyn sat on the edge of the bed, one leg curled beneath her. She kept her voice low, hoping the nurse had already forgotten about her.

"I'm not sure if I dream about Link," Amberlyn said, "but sometimes when I wake up in the morning, I've forgotten he's dead. Then I remember that he's gone, and it's like losing him all over again. He dies again every single morning. It's like I'm always realizing he's never going to be a part of my life again, and every time is like the first time. It doesn't get any less painful."

Noemi lifted the bottom edge of the paper towel and peeked at her from beneath it.

"I'm sorry, Amber. For everything. For showing Link the lake in the first place, for not showing you…"

"You don't have to be sorry for any of that."

"The night of junior prom—last year, his junior prom—he asked if we were dating, or if we could. I said *no*. I don't know why I didn't want to. I did kind of like him that way. A bit. I don't know. I wasn't sure, but I didn't want a relationship. I didn't mean to lead him on. If I'd been clearer about that earlier, or if I'd just felt differently—"

"Maybe." Amberlyn shook her head. "But you didn't."

She thought about Lyle. Growing up, Amberlyn hadn't expected she'd ever want a girlfriend. A boyfriend, maybe, but there had never been any serious contenders. Then everything with Lyle had happened so easily, and she could no longer imagine a time when that wasn't exactly what she wanted and needed, even if she hadn't known it yet. She couldn't turn what she felt off, and Noemi couldn't turn what she hadn't felt on.

"You didn't do anything wrong," she said. "A lot of stuff aligned to put Link in those woods. Maybe if the mail had come that day instead of the next, he'd have stayed home to open packages instead of going to the lake. Who knows? Doesn't make it the postal service's fault."

Amberlyn could have said, years ago, what her oblivious brother had failed to consider: *Your best friend is obviously into her. Are you prepared for how asking Noemi out is going to make him feel?* But she hadn't. Selfish. If Link were dating Noemi, Gaetan wouldn't be: that's where her mind had been at the time. Had Amberlyn called this to Link's attention, maybe he would have thought twice about whether he wanted to pursue Noemi. Maybe he never would have cared that she spent her time in the woods beside the lupine field.

Or maybe he would have died anyway, the only difference a rift between him and Gaetan. Could have, would have, but there was no going back, no hope trying to pinpoint the exact coordinates of the moment his fate could have been changed, because there probably wasn't just one moment.

"I could have asked him to go for coffee that day," Amberlyn said, "but I wasn't in the mood. If I had been, he might have spent the afternoon drinking an Iced Turtle Mocha instead of drowning. But no one would say that means I caused his death, and you didn't either."

"That sounds like the sort of thing Link would say."

"Really?"

"Yeah. *We live in a reality where XYZ are true and so the outcome blah blah blah* whatever."

They both laughed, quiet and airy. Noemi looked out the window, but there was nothing much to see. The wooden blinds—fancier than the vertical, plastic window dressings throughout the rest of the school—were drawn, but razors of light peeked through, and the leaves on the potted plants lining the sill stirred in the breeze.

Or maybe they bowed under Link's touch. In another reality, he too was there in the nurse's office, talking to the philodendron, defacing the eye chart with a felt pen.

28

NOEMI

It was so early that only the cats were awake, and Noemi fed them breakfast so they'd stop meowing, even though they'd be begging for treats before noon. Then she tiptoed out the back door, put her boots on once she reached the porch, and stepped quietly into the yard.

Though it was spring, an early morning frost had formed on the grass and leaves, turning the world blue. Noemi sat on the tree swing behind the inn and placed her phone on her thigh, staring at the open window of texts between herself and Unknown. He hadn't said anything since his frantic messages when she rescued Gaetan from the water.

I'm not a mind reader.

My condolences?

I just mean you have something to say.

Are you ALWAYS watching?

Not always.

Is what happened to Gaetan

what happened to you?

You mean is it what happened to Link?

You believe me for sure, then?

Undetermined.

To answer your question, no.

I wasn't lured. I went swimming.

Noemi spun slowly, crisscrossed the ropes of the swing, and held herself in place with the toes of her boots to the ground.

How much do you think he remembers
from before he went in the water?

Hard to say.

Even Amber is getting restless.

How do you mean?

He didn't answer. Hesitant to discuss his sister, perhaps. Noemi questioned how she'd ever mistaken this person for the far more forthcoming "Laetan" she used to message, once upon a time.

Hello?

Are you worried?

Of course.

You'd have less to worry about if you
stayed away from the woods.

Even if I stay away, I can't know

everyone else will.

You won't stay away.

What makes you so sure?

It's a feeling.

Would you hate me more if I went back alone?

Or if I brought everyone else?

I hate both those things.

I feel responsible.

You're NOT responsible.

I FEEL responsible.

I hate this.

Hate what?

How my life ended.

And after.

Embarrassed and guilty, she wanted to take the conversation back. For the first time, Noemi sort of hoped it wasn't Link she'd been texting—that she hadn't been texting anyone, that she'd dreamt it all.

THE WINTER HOUSE

I dreamt that I was eight years old, riding on a school bus full of children. It ferried us across the surface of an ocean to a large, gray mansion that twisted up from a platform of ice nearly as tall as I was. A headmistress and several schoolteachers approached wearing stiff, high-collared black dresses. We followed them off the bus and through the mansion's unlit hallways and into a classroom full of writing desks. They told us this was where we had always lived and would always live.

The other children believed this. I tried to remind them of the bus and the ocean, but they had already forgotten. I ran from the classroom and into a bathroom where I washed my face in the sink. As I did, I remembered that I was not eight years old. I remembered that I had lived more than twice that long. In the mirror, I watched my face age as the lie of childhood was washed away, and I returned to the classroom older than when I had left it.

The children went wild. They fled the room. They kicked the glass out of the windows and scattered the shards onto the balconies. They swung from broken chandeliers. They leapt over the railing and down three flights of stairs. Before my eyes their bodies aged and expanded.

The headmistress raged. The teachers ordered us from the house and onto the frozen grounds. There, we flickered between the ages of eight and eighteen—some of us children, some adults, most an ever-shifting patchwork of both. Beside us stood statues of ice and snow: the legacies of long-ago half children frozen in the midst of their own aging. My body settled once more into its true age. With my fingernails I tore at the platform of ice beneath the house, and the others followed. We pulled apart the house's foundation and discovered it was as thin and frail as an eggshell, nothing but matted twigs and long-dead grass within. The house began to tumble down around us, but I did not feel afraid.

29

AMBERLYN

When Amberlyn climbed into the passenger's seat, she dropped an oversized skating duffel on the floor of Lyle's car.

"Noemi asked me to bring ice skates," Amberlyn said, before Lyle could even ask. "I brought my brother's too, but they're too big for any of us, except Jonas *may*be. Link had some pretty huge feet."

Lyle backed her car out of the Millers' driveway. Two of the neighbor kids were drawing figure eights in the street with motorized, child-sized cars, enjoying the arrival of proper spring weather and the death of April, and she watched over her shoulder to make sure none hid behind her.

Usually they sang along together when it was the two of them alone in the car, but today Lyle hadn't even turned her music on.

She cranked her window open a sliver and let the noisy rush of wind fill the car. Amberlyn appreciated it, as it discouraged her from voicing the uneasy feeling that had settled at the base of her stomach. Amberlyn wasn't a nervous person, and she wasn't familiar with the winged, buzzing sensation that had been building since Noemi had suggested they all return, together, to the lake.

Though the horned creature hadn't charged her and the lake hadn't risen up to swallow her, the features of the forest struck Amberlyn as measured and intentional—conscious—and that made them threatening. To rid the forest behind Noemi's house of whatever thing controlled it, they must first understand it. Noemi's plans had been vague. She was normally so forthright, but since Link's death she had come to resemble him more and more: distant, contemplative, frustrating. She had an entire new world blooming in her head; Amberlyn knew that it was there mainly from the wall she saw around it, but she guessed it was a place of confusion. Noemi was evasive about what they could do to make the woods safe, because she didn't know. That didn't matter to Amberlyn. If the woods were controlled, then Link's death had been deliberate, and she could not think of her brother as *murdered* without knowing how. Even though knowing wouldn't bring him back. Even if it wouldn't change anything at all.

Gaetan Kelly had been staying at the Lamplight for the past several nights, and when Amberlyn and Lyle entered, he stood in the kitchen eating cereal by the sink.

"Morning," he said. "You guys have plans?"

Odd—in part because he seemed sincerely pleasant, but also because it was 1:00 p.m.

"Did you just get up or something?" Lyle asked.

He shrugged. "It's Saturday."

The creaking of footsteps on the stairs announced Noemi's and Jonas's approach, and soon there were five of them in the kitchen. Noemi wore her camera around her neck, Jonas placed his hand against one of her shoulder blades as she passed through the doorless entry, and everything felt much the way it had six months ago, Gaetan notwithstanding. Amberlyn remembered the creature she and Lyle had seen weeks ago, wondered if there was a way to explain it to Noemi now that allowed for the time they'd let pass without mentioning it. She wished she'd thought to pull out her phone and get a picture.

"Where are you guys heading?" Gaetan asked around a mouthful of cereal.

"Out," Noemi said, and she led them—all but Gaetan—out of the kitchen and back to the front door.

By the stairwell, Jonas grabbed a small packet of foam earplugs. He tore the paper backing away from the plastic and began passing them out in pairs.

Amberlyn took the ones offered to her, but Lyle looked to Noemi for an explanation before accepting hers.

"Sometimes, in the woods, there's this music that can give you a headache."

"What kind of music?" Lyle asked. "I never noticed that."

"It sounded like strings." Noemi gnawed on her bottom lip. "It makes it hard to focus, so I'm really not sure. I just thought we should be safe."

"There are some sounds that make people sick," Amberlyn offered. "Like at a certain frequency. Was it something like that?"

"No." Noemi shook her head. "I don't think so."

As they walked across the yard to the sidewalk, Noemi's camera swung rhythmically against her body with each step. "Did you guys bring the skates?" she asked.

Amberlyn tapped the strap of her bag and nodded. "What are they for?"

"In case the water freezes when we're out there."

Amberlyn turned to Lyle for clarity, but Lyle could only shrug.

"Are we going back into the lighthouse?" asked Jonas.

"*Back?*"

Lyle searched Noemi's face for answers, but her friend didn't look at her—she just glared at Jonas, annoyed.

"Jonas and I went out there recently," Noemi finally said.

"Across the water?" Amberlyn asked, though her voice was nearly covered by Lyle's asking, "When was this?"

"Maybe two months ago."

"God dammit, Jonas," said Noemi.

"Are you kidding me?" Lyle asked. Then, more quietly: "I can't believe you didn't tell me."

Amberlyn squeezed her hand. If the boat had been at the dock when Lyle and Amberlyn had been to the lake alone, would they have taken it? Amberlyn wasn't sure they'd have done things so differently, were their places reversed.

After a long silence, Lyle asked, "What did you guys find?"

"An empty room with a basement." Noemi's speech was cautious, and she and Jonas exchanged another look before she continued. "The basement was more of a tunnel. An underground channel with a boat. It was dark, but it led to an empty room."

"Well, that's weird," Amberlyn said.

Noemi stopped. The lupine field was now in view. "I'm not sure how to explain it without it sounding completely made up. That's where we heard the music playing, but we couldn't figure out where it was coming from. We followed it underground... That's what led us to the empty room. No exit. Just a violin sitting on the floor."

"That's not at all concerning," said Lyle.

Noemi nodded. "Maybe we should have stolen the violin. Or smashed it."

"Let's not push our luck," Jonas said.

When they reached the lupine field, Lyle was staring hard at the side of Noemi's face, focused on the crescent of ear that peeked out through her thick curls.

"Amberlyn and I went back to the lake on our own too."

Noemi stopped, and Amberlyn slammed into her back.

"What?" She growled the word and whirled to face Lyle.

"Nothing happened. We saw a deer-horse thing walk into the water. It mostly ignored us."

"When was *this*?"

"Few weeks ago," Lyle said. "Why are you angry? You went back too."

"It's in my backyard," Noemi said, as though that answered everything.

"Not on your property." Lyle's voice cracked.

Noemi rolled her eyes and turned into the woods. Conversation over. Jonas looked just as confused as Amberlyn felt.

"Lyle," she said, finally. Just her name. There was nothing else.

"It's fine." Without another word, Lyle followed after Noemi.

They walked in silence for what felt like forever, until finally, after several minutes, Jonas dared make an observation.

"We should be there by now, right?"

"Yes! Obviously." Noemi lifted the camera from around her neck and hung it on a nearby tree branch, pulling it so hard that the leaves trembled like raindrops. Then she resumed walking.

She *had* once called the lake camera shy.

"Guess we're coming back for that later," Amberlyn whispered.

Less than a minute after the camera was out of sight, the edge of the lake peeked at them from behind a tree. The white boat sat waiting by the dock, and the lighthouse beckoned from across the water. All four of them stood in a line along the shore, contemplating as a unit whether to step inside.

"Noemi."

The voice that had spoken came from behind them. Amberlyn spun, unsure of what she'd see, and Noemi jumped, shoulders lifting in a startled, ferrety movement.

Gaetan stood just their side of the tree line, eyes darting from them to the lake and back.

"What the hell are you doing here?" Noemi asked. She marched up to him and grabbed his arm. "Does *nobody* pay attention to anything I say?" The others stepped aside while she dragged Gaetan to the dock, and instead of resisting, he smirked and shuffled closely beside her.

More surprising than the fact that he had followed them was the fact he had not ignored Noemi's orders and trekked back to the lake on his own sooner. Noemi had told the others she'd found Gaetan at the lake by chance—though Amberlyn now had to wonder how much of that was true—and after dragging him from the water, she brought him home where Cesca and her house-mates let him stay.

"Why couldn't the police find this? This *has* to be where Link died." He tapped the boat with his foot, and it bobbed away from the dock in response. "This wasn't here last time."

"The cops said they found him on land," Noemi said. "It was a whole thing. Your memory failing you?"

They had all kept up the pretenses of Link's puddle-drowning with Gaetan. Even Jonas, who'd never met Link, knew more than Gaetan did. The group had never discussed whether Gaetan should know, so no promises kept Amberlyn from telling him on her own. She could have, any time she'd passed him in the halls at school, or when he'd sat on her brother's bed during Midwinter. But Gaetan didn't think before acting. Of the five of them living who'd now been to this place, he was the only one who'd nearly managed to drown, after all. Amberlyn didn't want to be the reason he dove in search of her brother and lost his life. Had Noemi been protecting Gaetan too? Had Amberlyn been protecting anyone, or was she just hoarding pieces of her brother for herself?

"That wasn't there either," Gaetan said, looking out on the lighthouse. He spoke to himself, completely unconcerned with Noemi's irritation.

"We're rowing out there," Noemi said. "I suppose if you insist on being here, it wouldn't be a terrible idea if you waited here in case something happens and we can't get back."

"Fuck that," Gaetan said cheerfully. "You can fit five in that boat. I'll row, if that helps."

"You know—" Noemi threw her hands in the air and stomped away from them. She plunked herself down on a bench at one end of the rowboat and folded her arms tight across her chest. "Everyone just do whatever you want. Try not to drown, because I'm not pulling anyone out of the water this time."

Gaetan was the first to follow, and when he moved, so did Jonas. Amberlyn and Lyle squeezed in together at the other end of the boat—their bags crammed beneath their seat—and Gaetan filled the center seat, grabbing the oars. Jonas sat next to Noemi and untied the boat, and they began to cross the water.

Amberlyn listened for whatever music she was supposed to hear, but she didn't catch wind of anything other than the soothing rush of the oars through water and Noemi and Jonas carrying on a hushed conversation with her heads ducked in close.

"When did that become a thing?" Gaetan whispered, tilting his head back to indicate where the two housemate-lovebirds huddled together behind him.

"A while ago, sort of," Amberlyn said.

"Less so for a bit recently," Lyle added. "I don't really know. You're the one who lives with them now."

"That's temporary." Gaetan grimaced. "And I try pretty hard not to pay attention."

Before Amberlyn could decide whether to respond, something strange groaned all around them. It wasn't music. It was a tearing sound, a cracking. No one else seemed to have noticed yet, this noise like plastic crumpling. Just as she craned to look in the water behind her, the boat suddenly halted and she fell forward, her elbow colliding with Gaetan's knee.

"Jesus." He rested the ends of the oars on his lap and rubbed where Amberlyn had hit his leg. "You all right there? Did we hit something?"

Noemi steadied herself on Jonas's shoulder as she moved into a crouch. "It's frozen up ahead," she said. "I told you."

She sat back down and waited while the rest of them reacted with appropriate surprise or confusion. Noemi, however, appeared quite undisturbed—until she too realized that the lake had frozen on all sides of them, not just ahead. Their boat was well past the center, though still several minutes out from the lighthouse, captured in a plate of ice so dense it was white, opaque.

The air was beginning to grow colder, and Amberlyn rubbed at her arms to warm them through her sweatshirt. Gaetan stabbed at the ice with the end of one of the oars, but when that yielded no results, he lifted a leg over the edge of the boat in a position like a peeing dog, then slammed at the smooth, glassy sheet with the heel of his shoe. Amberlyn passed ice skates to the others, and they tried chipping away using them as blunt picks, but barely scratched the surface.

Gaetan stood now, arms carefully bent outward to balance himself. "The good news is it's so freaking thick we can probably walk across," he said. "How many pairs of skates do we have?"

"Just the two," Amberlyn answered.

"We are actually going to use them," Lyle murmured.

"Told you," Noemi said again.

They passed the skates back to Amberlyn, who began sliding her feet into her usual pair. "The other pair is a lot bigger." She tugged at the laces, looked to Gaetan, then Jonas. "Can either of you skate?"

"It's been a while," Jonas muttered.

"I'll be fine," said Gaetan. "Used to play hockey with my brother." He complained about the poor fit of Link's skates, but once he got them on, he moved as though they were a part of him.

"Are we going back?" Amberlyn asked.

"You guys can go back if you want," Noemi said. There was

nothing dismissive in her voice. Just matter-of-fact. "We're pretty close to the lighthouse, though, so I'm going the rest of the way."

"Gaetan doesn't have earplugs," Jonas said.

"And Noemi doesn't have roller skates." Gaetan wiggled his fingertips, like he was performing a magic trick. "See, I can make inane observations too."

"He can have mine." Lyle fished her foam earplugs from her pockets. "I've got these." She reached into her backpack and proudly brandished her large, noise-canceling headphones.

Gaetan looked from the earplugs now sitting in his palm to Noemi.

Noemi took a deep breath. "Just trust me and put them in."

He shrugged and pinched the earplugs into his ears without any further questions.

The rest of the group followed suit, except Lyle, who pulled on her headphones. She hooked her arm through Amberlyn's, and the pair of them waddled awkwardly toward the lighthouse, steadying one another. Gaetan did the same with Noemi, who held on to Jonas's hand with her free one. Jonas just flapped awkwardly at the end of their small, three-person ribbon. Then, Lyle's feet shot out behind her, and she fell face forward onto the ice.

Amberlyn tugged on her arm in an attempt to keep her upright, but it wasn't enough. Lyle landed on her knees and her wrist, only just kept her chin from smacking into the hard, white plane beneath her.

"Are you all right?" Amberlyn asked, her own voice muffled

and far away. The rest of them stopped and shuffled into a semi-circle around Lyle.

"I'm fine. Just give me a second. I think I kind of hurt my knees."

"Is your wrist okay?"

They all inched back to give Lyle space, and she shifted into a sitting position, legs jutting straight forward like a doll's. She rotated her hand, and her wrist gave an audible crackle.

"I think so." She pressed her uninjured hand flat beside her to leverage herself upright, but as soon as she did, the ice under her palm cracked and spidered out in a geometric web.

"What the hell?" Gaetan, who was nearest the crack, slid away from Lyle and tugged Noemi and Jonas along with him.

Amberlyn didn't move. She was as still as a doe, watching Lyle and taking shallow, frightened breaths. She said Lyle's name, and as though in response to her voice, the ice directly beneath Lyle folded downward.

Lyle disappeared, and the water that swallowed her was so, so black it was as though she had been sucked out of existence through a collapsed star. Amberlyn dropped to her knees, and Noemi knelt across from her, and though the other girl's mouth was moving, Amberlyn couldn't hear her shouts. The voices around her—she knew they were there, but they carried only nonsense, her friends shouting into pillows. Lyle was drowning, and the inside of Amberlyn's head was drowning, and when she tried to reach into the water, she couldn't. Her hand bumped against hard darkness, cold the color of nothing.

The ice had healed itself over where Lyle had fallen, disguised itself in the shape of a hole so it could taunt Amberlyn into grasping toward a place she couldn't reach.

Noemi pounded at the splotch of dark ice with her fists. Jonas wiped at the surface of the white ice with red, chapped hands, trying to clear a window through which to search for Lyle, but nothing in the lake's frozen lid changed. Gaetan skated in circles around them, uselessly scanning for glimpses of Lyle through the murky glass. All of them pulled out their earplugs, which had protected them from nothing, and listened for Lyle's shouts.

Amberlyn tried to speak but couldn't; a drawn-out hum leaked from her lips, and she tried to convert it into words, but it only buzzed somewhere behind her ears. She pushed harder, breaking slow and zombie-like from whatever stasis she was in, until finally she croaked out, "Oh, my god."

Her ears popped, then flooded with Noemi's yelling. Amberlyn commanded her body, her arms, her fingers, anything to move. Then her legs shifted; she kicked colt-like with the heel of her skate, not even scratching the surface.

"I don't have a signal on my phone," Jonas said.

"You can never get one out here," said Gaetan. The way he spoke was unusually gentle, resigned. He stopped skating, raked his hands through his hair. His eyes were bluer than winter, but then he bowed his head and hid them. "I don't think we can get help out here fast enough anyway."

"Shut the hell *up*." Noemi curled her bottom lip under her

teeth, bit it so hard it was a wonder she didn't draw blood. "Amber, can you skate back to the shore? Get out of the forest and call nine-one-one?"

Would "help" be able to find this place? Even if they could, would they get out here fast enough to make a difference? Or would whoever came to help just be pulling Lyle's waterlogged corpse from beneath the ice? The best they could hope for by then might be giving the Andersons a body to bury or burn. When the Millers had burned Link's remains, it had not been the best of anything. Amberlyn's throat pinched around a hard, bitter stone.

"Yeah." Amberlyn stood, wiped her eyes.

"I'll go with you," Gaetan offered. "But you're probably faster. Don't wait for me."

Noemi and Jonas weren't even paying attention any longer. They were back to clawing at the ice, their only progress haphazard clouds of thumbnail-sized dents. Amberlyn turned and pushed off and away from them.

As she flew across the ice, she wondered if, by some chance, the water wasn't cold underneath. It had formed so quickly and unnaturally. Perhaps Lyle wouldn't freeze to death. Link hadn't. Maybe she could find a pocket of air along the underside of the ice. Somehow.

All of these wonderings felt like lies, and tears blurred Amberlyn's vision so she was no longer hurtling toward trees but a haze of green. She listened, trusting Gaetan would tell her if she was going the wrong way, held on to the scrape of his skates behind her because there was nothing else to keep her upright. Amberlyn moved so fast that if the ice tried to break under her, it wouldn't even matter. She would glide right over any opening. But did she want to? She imagined herself plunging underwater, finding Lyle waiting for her, floating along the surface, breathing the oxygen from an inexplicable gap between lake-top and ice. The two of them would hold hands and drift on their backs like otters.

When the ice ran out beneath Amberlyn's feet, it was not because it had cracked. She tumbled forward onto the grass. Realizing immediately she had left her phone in the bag on the boat, she wove her fingers through the grass, waiting for the world to tilt and try to shake her off. Gaetan awkwardly skated up beside her, taking uneasy steps onto the ground, where his blades sank into the mud. Amberlyn shifted into a sitting position, and just as she was about to ask for his phone, she noticed the ice had turned back to liquid behind him. What did this mean for Noemi and Jonas? For Lyle?

"I forgot my phone," Amberlyn said, a single sob splitting the sentence in half.

Gaetan tapped the pocket of his jeans. "I have mine," he said. He wiggled out of her brother's skates and set his black-socked feet on the damp grass. "We need to head back out to the field before we can get a signal."

Then, holding the skates by their laces, he extended his free hand to Amberlyn. And she took it, ready for him to lift her up.

JONAS

For all Jonas knew, he had just watched the last moments of someone's life unfold. Lyle was here and then she wasn't. If she hadn't
yet drowned or frozen to death beneath the ice that had swallowed
her, she soon would. There was nothing for Jonas to grab on to.
Anything left of Lyle was just out of reach. He could almost touch
it, her life passing like a stream of water between his hands.

Noemi stood. Her idea of practical footwear was a pair of pink
lace-up ankle boots—some material that looked like suede but felt
stiff. Jonas knew it was stiff because he placed his hand on the toe
of her shoe. He would have liked to cup her palm or her shoulder
or the nape of her neck, but they were all too high above him now
as he knelt, helpless, by the black spot in the ice which was once
Lyle's place.

Jonas couldn't tell Noemi everything would be okay. It probably wouldn't be. Things might never be okay again. But he wanted at least to assure her, *You aren't alone.*

She stepped away from him, her foot sliding from beneath his touch. Jonas too climbed to his feet, flapped his arms to keep from losing his balance. He reached, expecting Noemi to extend an arm to steady him, but she didn't. She instead moved away, stepping across the ice toward the lighthouse as though nothing but a smooth, marble floor lay beneath her. How she managed to remain upright in those shoes he couldn't understand. Jonas called after her, tried to follow, but his legs slid out from under him, and he fell hard onto his hip.

He climbed back to his feet and walked more slowly, each step flat and firm before he shifted his weight behind it. The gap between him and Noemi grew larger as she walked without issue. She didn't look back, didn't heed his calls, paid no mind when he'd fallen and hurt himself. For the first time in several years, Jonas began to cry—just a few tears, though his nose felt hot. It wasn't out of loss or injury or abandonment that he wept, but frustration. Alone in the middle of a field of ice across which he could barely walk without hurting himself—it was too literal a realization of how he'd always felt. He lifted Gaetan's loose oar from the rowboat and held it like a walking stick, its handle nestled along the hard surface of the lake. He wouldn't put too much pressure on it, but if he started to slip again, maybe he could use it to right himself.

Ahead of him Noemi climbed, alone, onto the grass of the

island, her long, curly hair fluttering like a cape behind her. As he got closer, Jonas heard what had called her away. The song, at first, felt imagined: just a few soft sounds punctuated by silence, they could easily have been wind through trees. His head grew heavy, curtains of darkness drew across his vision from above and below, and the ground beneath him dipped low. The ice didn't crack. It slackened, as though Jonas had really stood on a drumhead drawn taut, now sinking from his weight. The ice might not break, but he would still plunge into it, drown in a mouth full of milk and darkness, and the memories of where he was and when he was would seep from his mind and fall in droplets on his shoulders.

Why was he here? Jonas used most of his concentration to remain upright and whatever was left to remember. He remembered...

...his mother liked to go to Family Video. When they searched for movies to watch together on Netflix, Jonas checked Rotten Tomatoes scores, watched trailers on YouTube, and "watching a movie" together took an hour longer than necessary because they had to allot time for the decision. Jonas had never seen anyone he knew in Family Video, and he suspected the kids at his school didn't know the stores still existed. *No phones in Family Video,* Sara would say, and Jonas would relinquish his cell so she could bury it in her purse. It was a Kate Spade handbag Jonas had gotten on sale—bussing tables until the bag was out of style—for Sara's birthday-plus-Mother's-Day gift because he'd seen her looking at them online, and she was his *whole* family. She insisted he return it, but he refused, and now it was the only bag she used. They browsed the rows and based their decisions only on what they could gather from the descriptions on the backs of the DVD cases.

...when Matt still lived with Jonas and Sara, and the three of them went for ice cream at least once a week in the summers. Jonas couldn't remember the last time he'd had ice cream, but he did remember eating it with his father. They went to the sort of ice cream stand with no indoor seating, where they sat on rubbery, red, sugar-caked benches by the roadside and tried to eat their treats before they melted in the hot, hot sun. Jonas always got sandwiches made from huge vanilla scoops pressed between two chocolate chip cookies, the whole monstrosity as large as his head. He remembered trying to lick the ice cream in between, but he pressed too hard and the cookies snapped in his fingers and the whole thing fell on the asphalt, except a few crumbs on his knees. Jonas's father laughed and laughed, and then he gave his Oreo sundae to Jonas and had nothing himself.

...in elementary school, when his class took a field trip to the aquarium, where they were given a behind-the-scenes tour of all the places the food was prepared and the sick marine life quarantined. He and another boy, Devin Bowles, snuck off from the rest of the group and hid behind the quarantine tank of a turtle with a cracked shell awaiting a prosthetic. They crouched, giggling, where no one could see them, and then their group moved on without them. Two more tours came, and it seemed too late to reveal themselves. Jonas started to cry. It was the last time he could remember crying. Devin said, *It's okay. We'll just jump into the other group and circle back out front.* He thought Jonas was afraid of getting in trouble, but Jonas was sad about the turtle, who had been hit by a car, who couldn't be with the other turtles because her broken shell caused her to float half breaching at an awkward angle.

...when he and Noemi were home alone during a tornado warning, his first time going into the cellar at Lamplight, which he hadn't known existed. All the unusual objects Noemi's mother collected were gathered down there, casting strange silhouettes in the dark: globes, mannequins, old toys, carnival posters. Noemi and Jonas crouched on the only rug, a spare vintage cowhide that Noemi complained smelled of death, but he knew she preferred it to the basement floor. She didn't like the feel of the dirty cement on her bare *or* socked feet, or even the sound of it against her shoes.

Noemi was so sensitive to certain sounds. He thought of her doing homework alone in a cafe, cringing because a stranger nearby was chewing loudly, and how no one in the room would know she hated it, but he would, even though he wasn't there, because he knew her and how everything in the world made her feel, and she let him kiss her in the dark while they wondered how close a tornado would come.

Running through his own memories had allowed him to retreat to the safety of the boat, but he was stuck again, just as far from the lighthouse as when he'd started. He remembered his earplugs, felt for them in the front of his hoodie. He blew on them in case they'd collected any lint, twisted the tips, and fed them into his ears. Every second he spent getting his bearings, Lyle got farther away.

Jonas focused on the sounds of his own breath, his own thoughts, his nervous swallows. Now the world was solid and steady, the ice uncracked and unbent. He could no longer see Noemi on the island—just the lighthouse and the grass and the gray sky bleeding down around it—but he tapped the oar against the lake, walked onward.

31

NOEMI

When Noemi regained her senses, she stood inside the same small cottage at the base of the lighthouse she had once visited with Jonas. That was in March, when Minnesota was so long-deep in winter that summer seemed a dream. Yet the lake hadn't been frozen then, as it had been today. The forest had moods, and the color of the leaves or the softness of the water seemed to follow its own rule of seasons. The candles were gone, but a fire in the hearth burned warm and crackling.

Lyle rested on a pile of furs in front of it, her chest moving with each placid breath. Noemi started toward her friend's side, but something overhead rustled: small birds watching from the low, wooden rafters. There was no light source in the room beside the glow from the hearth, but somehow it was enough to illuminate everything.

"Lyle," she said, shaking her friend's shoulder. "Lyla?"

"She's sleeping."

If he had been in the one-room house when she'd first found herself standing at its center, she'd managed not to notice. Lincoln Miller, or someone wearing his face, stood in the corner of the room—still as a mountain, so still he might have been made from granite until he finally shifted and placed what he'd been holding, a violin and bow, on a trunk-like chair beside him.

"What did you do to her?"

"A lullaby. She's fine." His tone was matter-of-fact, if not reassuring.

"Why did you take her?" Noemi asked. She moved to stand between Link and Lyle.

"To bring you here. To bargain." He seemed then to remember that he was supposed to move as he spoke. The muscles on his face didn't operate the way Link's should have, with one expression flowing into the next; instead his face paused, calculated, timed blinks, fixed its eyes on Noemi. "We wanted to talk to you."

"'We' who?"

"Us." He splayed his fingers, pressed his palm to his chest, and something about the gesture made it seem odd when his hand did not run right out the other side of him. "The trees," he added. Finally, his gaze turned from her, though not because he was looking at anything else. His blue-gray eyes pointed, for less than a second, straight ahead, as though whatever had been operating them had stepped away. Then they fell on her again. "*Me.*"

The forest was standing in front of her. The forest had red hair and was wearing a hoodie. She was inside of the forest, but at the same time it spoke to her through Link's lips and watched her through his eyes. Only those weren't his lips, eyes, hair, or clothes. Those things were all ash on a mantle or bookshelf in the Miller house. She suddenly caught the craggy rhythm of her breathing, steadied it.

"Why won't Lyle wake up?"

"I can wake her," he said. "But she'll have to leave. She demands too much of your attention."

"Can I leave with her?" Noemi was detached from herself, like she was speaking to something in one of her dreams. Having Lyle nearby might have helped, even if she was unconscious. Whatever confusing nonsense the figure before her spouted, she could focus on her immediate goal of waking her friend, making sure she was safe.

Finally, he turned his attention away from her. He studied his arms, rotated his wrists, looked down at his long, long, corduroy-clad legs. Only Link could wear thrifted corduroy without looking like he'd stepped out of time. His T-shirt was printed with a *Double R Diner* logo, the hem coming loose, and Noemi knew it had been a birthday gift from Amberlyn, that this imposter shouldn't have been able to get his hands on it but somehow had. He did not answer her question—just scrutinized his limbs as though appraising a gift given to him—but his silence, in its way, answered for him. *No.* No, of course she could not leave.

"Why do you look like Link?"

"It's hard to make a human face without something to model it from," he said. "I can look like one of your other friends, if you'd rather, but I know how to look like Link best. I've been in his belly and lungs. He died in"—*In me,* he didn't say. She watched him shuffle his words around—"this place," he finished.

"Because you killed him."

"I thought he'd upset you," Not-Link said, quiet.

"So it is my fault." Noemi had to say it aloud because to speak it was to accept it. She hadn't thought it would be loud enough for him to hear.

"No," he said. "It was mine. I'm sorry."

"Are you? You tried to do the same thing to Gaetan."

"I thought that was what he wanted."

"Doesn't matter what you thought! It's not up to you."

She caught her voice rising, pumped through with her usual agitation. Noemi took a deep breath. In the moment before Gaetan had run through the woods—chasing "Link" into the water where she'd had to dive after him—she might have been able to stop him altogether if she had anticipated how he would feel.

Noemi could seldom understand the distance between what people said and what they meant. Her friends didn't realize it, but the space between what she wanted and what she voiced was often so great, she had to assume everyone else's was too. How could she begin to guess at what was going on inside other people, with only unreliable words to go on? She couldn't resent the forest for finding people so confusing.

"I see," the forest said. He nodded very seriously, and something like sadness replaced Noemi's unease. "I'm not cruel. I don't mean to be. I survive. I don't know how to say it. At times, it feels like your friends get in the way of that: my survival."

"Is this what you wanted to talk about?" Noemi asked. "Why you hurt my friends?"

"In part." The forest rolled his neck. The movement made a wooden crack. He touched the neck of the violin as it lay propped against the chair-back. "I used to be much larger. I've lived a long time and watched many people. I've practiced how to be like them. It's very lonely."

"Do you have a name?"

"No."

"Okay. Well, you said something about a bargain?"

"You visited often when you were a child. You seemed happier then."

"Did I?" Noemi asked. "Playing make-believe? A lot of kids probably look happy from the outside. And they still grow up to be miserable adults."

"Why?" he asked. His head tilted, curious, to the side, staggering like a windup toy's.

"How should I know? They learn the ways the world isn't fair, or the ways they disappoint the people around them."

"I wouldn't know."

Noemi angled one hand on her hip, glanced at Lyle still resting so calmly. "You haven't answered my question."

"The bargain? You should stay," the forest said. "Your friend can go. None of them will find their way back here again. They can't hurt you if they aren't here."

"Where is Jonas?"

"The kissing boy."

"Er...yes," Noemi answered, but then she realized the forest wasn't asking. Its eyes widened as though just remembering, just *finding* him.

"I forgot about him," the forest admitted. "He ignores my music. He's coming. Do you want him here?"

"I would like for him and Lyle *both* to go home safely. And Gaetan and Amberlyn."

"Already safe," he said. "Will you stay if I send these two home?"

"I have a choice?"

"You can always choose to *try* leaving."

"Fine. How long do I stay?"

"Longer than leaving now."

"Vague," she said. "Sometimes you are a little like Link."

Something bumped against Noemi's foot. Behind her, Lyle was waking.

JONAS

Jonas pushed open the peeling, green, handleless door to the lighthouse, uncertain of what he would see or how he would feel when he looked inside. Relief washed over him first: Noemi stood in the center of the room, and she looked at him, really *saw* him, awake and aware. Elation: Lyle sat in front of a fireplace, rubbing blearily at her eyes, very much alive. Something harder to name: Link Miller, who should have been dead, stood (also very much alive) as tall and angular and redheaded as he'd looked in photos, and though Jonas had never met him, he knew him immediately, and the feeling was like seeing a myth made real.

Jonas stepped into the room, and the door creaked shut behind him, noisy even through the earplugs, and he turned to see it settling slightly askew in the crooked entry, a vertical, gray gap showing a now-thawed lake on the other side. He'd been relieved not to hear the music as he'd entered the lighthouse. Now he saw the instrument beside Link Miller. Had it been Link playing? Satisfied with the sight of the violin at rest, he removed the earplugs.

"Where are we?" Lyle asked.

Jonas rushed to her side, and he and Noemi pulled her upright, each grasping one of her arms.

"Link?" she asked. "Holy shit. Are we dead?"

"No," Noemi said. "You're all right. But that's not Link." She turned to Jonas. "Are you okay?"

"Um, not really," Jonas admitted. "Are you?" He pushed her hair back from her face, her curls tangling around his hand. Her eyes were present, not like the time she had jumped off the boat into the channel underground. Jonas searched the floor for signs of the trapdoor but didn't see it. Just because he was no longer standing on ice didn't mean the floor wouldn't fall away and plunge them into dark and drowning.

"I'm okay."

"If that's not Link," Lyle said, "who is it?" She turned to address Link directly. He hadn't moved toward them since Jonas had entered. Hadn't spoken. Just watched them, very still and with distant interest. "Who are you?"

Link glanced at Noemi as though asking for permission, but she didn't seem to care. "The forest," he said, almost uncertain.

"He killed Link," Noemi said solemnly, then pulled her arms

in over her ribs as if she were cold, though the fire in the small room made it uncomfortably warm.

"Noemi." Lyle placed a hand on her friend's shoulder. "That's Link."

Lyle seemed certain—so certain that she became concerned when Noemi didn't agree. But Jonas wasn't so sure. He'd never known Link, and so many inexplicable things had happened...

"Where is Amberlyn?" Lyle asked.

"She and Gaetan left to get help when you fell through the ice," Noemi explained.

Lyle looked down, patted the front of her jeans which, if they were wet, didn't look it.

Jonas turned to Link. "Were you the one playing the violin?"

"Yes."

"How did you learn how to play violin? Or even know what one is?" Noemi straightened her back and quirked an eyebrow, as though she found this, of all things, the most incredulous aspect of their current situation. Regardless, her skepticism and directness felt like the Noemi he knew, and this soothed Jonas for the moment.

"You aren't the first human beings I've ever seen. I told you I watched people for a long time." He smiled. Something amused him, but if there was a joke to get, Jonas missed it.

"Does he act like Link?" Jonas asked under his breath.

He hadn't meant to exclude Noemi, but she didn't answer, kept her back to him and let Lyle respond for both of them.

"Something's a little off," Lyle said. "But I never knew Link that well."

"I think we should go," he said.

"I want to know what's going on."

"Jonas is right." Noemi touched his arm, just where the sleeve of his T-shirt brushed skin. She gave Jonas a gentle nudge toward the door.

"Is Link coming?" Lyle asked. Then she turned to him. "Does anyone know you're here?"

"No," Noemi said for him. "We'll talk about it later." But while she addressed Lyle, she held eye contact with Link, and something moved between them that Jonas could see but not quite interpret.

Link placed his hands in the pockets of his jacket. He took a step toward them, and like a single organism, Noemi, Lyle, and Jonas moved at once to shuffle away from him and toward the door. Noemi gripped the doorknob, and Jonas was a little surprised when the door actually opened. She held it for Lyle to pass through, and she said something under her breath. Jonas heard the general cadence of it, but he couldn't make out what she had said. When he followed Lyle, Noemi leaned her face so close he could feel her words stirring his hair: "Walk quickly, and don't look back."

Jonas did as he was told, kept his eyes forward on Lyle's once-green-tinged hair. She was short enough he could see a hint of scalp through her crooked part, so pale her skin looked nearly silver. Then the door closed behind him with a puff of force, and it might have been safe to turn around now that they were out of Link's—or whoever's—sight, so he did.

But Noemi wasn't there.

The door wasn't there. Neither was the lighthouse or the lake on the other side of the island. There was no island. Nothing stood in the place he had just left but more forest.

He wanted to call out to Lyle, but he forgot how to speak, made a pointless *uhhh* sound until she turned around and began to voice his panic with a hundred questions he didn't even try to follow.

Forest where the lighthouse should be, forest too where the lake should be. The lake had been right there when they had walked through the door. He'd looked away for only a second to turn back to Noemi, and it had gone. The grass didn't even seem damp. No sign of the rowboat or the stone dock. Amberlyn's duffel bag sat a few feet ahead on the ground. Lyle lifted it onto her shoulder, then cupped her hands around her mouth and began to shout Noemi's name.

They searched in every direction. Cornfields on one side, road on another, a field of grass downhill from a few houses. Noemi's camera hung from a tree where she'd left it, and Jonas pulled it down, held it so tightly he thought it might break, almost hoped that it would. He wondered if her body would show up, dead and blue under a tree somewhere, lungs filled with water, and her death too would be a great big mystery.

He knew now she had not meant to follow them when she'd held open the door. She hadn't seemed afraid, and Jonas could only hope Noemi knew what she was doing, had some reason for not fearing that person in the lighthouse she'd called a killer. *She probably knew what she was doing. She usually did.* But for whatever reason she had not confided in Jonas about her intentions. He must not have repaired her trust in him after all. But he trusted, didn't he, that she would be fine?

Noemi was always certain she knew the right way to do things, and that was a dangerous confidence to have. Jonas remembered the way the kids at school had whispered about Link Miller. He remembered Gaetan walking right into the water, how Noemi had to dive in after him to keep him from drowning in pursuit of something that wasn't there. Lyle falling through the ice, the way it sealed right up over her head, impenetrable. Noemi in a trance so murky she didn't even seem to see him, how the person in the lighthouse could play her like his violin.

Something ruptured inside of Jonas—whatever coiled thing had exploded into his classmate's face last year—and he threw that oh-so-expensive, school-issued camera filled with who knows how many of Noemi's precious photos into a tree. Lyle jumped. At least one little plasticky piece flew off the camera and landed somewhere Jonas couldn't see. She picked up the camera and cradled it to her, red-faced and teary-eyed, and Jonas stared at the grass between his sneakers.

They left the forest from the area they had entered: by the lupine field that lay between the trees and the land behind Lamplight's stable. The perfect blanket of wildflowers had been carved up by tire tracks, and two police cars and an ambulance parked on the grass flashing red and blue, red and blue. Two cops were walking along the perimeter of the trees, while another two stood by the ambulance talking to Gaetan and Amberlyn, and Lyle took off toward them. The cops by the trees noticed them first, and Jonas wished they hadn't because he didn't want to talk to them, because what could they do? But the officers called out, so he froze.

Amberlyn ran toward Lyle and hugged her so hard they fell backward into the flowers, and a butterfly actually lifted up from a lupine like a perfect fairy-tale ending, except for the part where Jonas felt like he was going to vomit his own failure. Lyle was saying something to Gaetan, and a cop had his hand on Jonas's shoulder, and Jonas said, *Yes No I don't know* and *Noemi Mireille Amato*, then gestured at the woods behind them, and three of the cops stalked off somewhere.

Gaetan marched toward Jonas like a bolt of lightning, and for one misguided instant he feared Gaetan was going to hug him, and Jonas stood motionless thinking, *What the hell is happening?*

Gaetan got right up in Jonas's face. *Where is she?* And Jonas pushed him. *Gone.* Just like the kid at his old school had pushed him, and Jonas remembered what the response had been then. He wanted Gaetan to hit him because Gaetan could hit him harder than Jonas could hit himself. And he wanted an excuse to hit Gaetan back. Not because Gaetan looked at Noemi like she was his, but because Gaetan was every kid who had ever given Jonas a hard time for no reason. Jonas had always been teased, but there had never been a theme to it. He was teased because he felt weird, out of place, like everyone but him understood how to be around people and feel good about it, like he'd been the only one to miss the day in preschool where that lesson was taught. It wasn't his father or his looks or any particular thing that made him feel insecure, but his general introversion, however much it was or wasn't connected to all the other things that made him *him*. And some people, like Gaetan, could just sense when a person felt weird. Even when there were no obvious signposts, they had a knack for recognizing the ones who didn't fit. And though Jonas had seen other kids get it worse—no one had ever thrown him in a dumpster or made him eat dog shit or anything—the bullying had been enough that he had dreaded every day. He wanted Gaetan to hit him because he was angry with himself for leaving Noemi, but he wanted to hit back because of everything else.

Jonas saw Gaetan was going to clock him just in time to move out of the way, but he didn't move out of the way. He let the older boy hit him harder than anything had ever hit him, and only after Gaetan's fist had thundered into his head and the stars cleared from Jonas's eyes, did he hit back. Jonas had severely miscalculated his ability to move under Gaetan's strength—he could not have known Gaetan had prepared to kill the next man who thought he could spell out anger on his body—and Jonas's punches, as much as he could control them, were mainly defensive. He was pummeled until he could taste blood, until his whole head felt tender, but each fist freed him from an apology he'd wanted to make for himself.

Lyle's or Amberlyn's distant, underwater voice told Gaetan, "It's not his fault!" The remaining cop and an EMT pulled Gaetan off, had to push him down to the ground somewhere outside Jonas's field of vision. Jonas gurgled, "It's fine," but didn't stay awake long enough to find out if anyone had noticed.

33

NOEMI

When the door closed behind Jonas and Lyle, Noemi was left alone with the woods. Her friends would not be coming back.

She had been alone with the woods many times in her life, but only a few of those times had it been wearing Link's face. What she had thought of as a place was also a person—someone who wanted something. Had that been the case even when she was a child, seeking shelter from "Prince Lyle" under the branches of a tree? Inside she held two truths. She was talking to someone she had known a very long time. She was talking to the person who had murdered her friend.

"People are confusing," he said.

"Well—" Noemi nodded. "Yeah, they are."

Link's eyes watched her, open and expectant, as though Noemi held all the answers in the universe. In truth, she didn't even have answers to the problem in front of her.

"I thought often about what I would say to you when finally we could talk like two people," he said. "I practiced, made myself look like a boy you'd find familiar, and said the words aloud in the chamber beneath my lake. But now you are in front of me, I find myself forgetting everything."

She looked around the room. When the woods built a copy of Link's body, had the lighthouse too been built, as a home? Perhaps she and Link had been drawing blueprints when they set out tiny rock cairns in the shape of a lighthouse.

Where most people might have said, *This is where I sleep* or *This is where I eat,* her host followed her eyes around the room and explained the house by saying, "It is like a dream."

"Do you dream?"

"I—um—don't remember having any dreams." He looked down. This answer seemed less calculated, less rehearsed than his earlier speech. There was a shyness, a flame of self-consciousness in that uncertainty. "It is like the way you talk about dreaming."

"Tell me," she said.

The woods opened Link's mouth and began.

Once upon a time my body was every tree composing me, "forest." It was lonely.

Two children came to me some time ago, and you—I thought your hair curled like morning glories growing along a trunk, so I made you a gift of them. You pressed your nose into one of the flowers, and I concentrated everything that I was into its stamen so I might taste human breath for the first time in my long memory. I did not mind the sharp pop of small pain as you loosed them from their stems. You heard me somewhere in a deep chamber of your heart when I told you I had placed them there for you, and you wove them into your morning-glory hair.

Lyle called you "witch." She said it was her job to vanquish witches and other monsters.

I did not understand why a girl alone in the forest, playing with animal bones, was a threat to anyone. My roots felt the shock of distant trees felled. I was one small forest in one small place, but I understood the violence of nature. When lightning thrust its tongue against a maple, set me on fire, sent rabbits screaming to their deaths, it was not a murderer. Its strike was involuntary like the synapses of the rabbits' brains. The lightning did not decide to hurt me, so I did not blame it for being itself, as I would not have blamed children for bending blades of grass under their feet. What can be evil that is necessary? It was my nature to self-preserve. When people hurt me, I wept, and my tears became a lake that could drown them. Was I evil? Should princes with their crowns try to vanquish me too? Lyle used a slingshot to fire berries over your head. I bowed my branches to shelter you.

When you had grown, you said, "I want to take pictures here of the things I see in my dreams." Here. In my dreams. I was in your dreams. The thrill of it woke all the animals. You were in me in your dreams. Did I dream? I tried to remember. Almost all of my animals dream, but if I did, I could not tell the difference between it and being awake. I wanted to practice dreaming. I could not lift my roots and follow you as I was, but I could dream myself to your side.

The animals who ran-flew-crawled through me died and rotted, and what was left of their decaying bodies became a part of me. Through them I learned the meaning of things like blood and bone. I gathered my disparate tree-parts into the shape of a single being. My skeleton was a frame of branches. My blood was murky water—my flesh, earth. Long grasses burst through the soil of my scalp. Shadows pooled in the two empty sockets on my face. For fingernails I wore flower petals. My voice was the spilling of water.

I built for myself a buried chamber in my lake-heart where my new small-body could sleep. If I was not able to make music with the wind through trees, I would have to find another way. I practiced moving like a person, speaking like one. Every body has limitations, and it took time to adapt to the limitations of my small-body. I manipulated my flesh into the shapes of all manner of animals. All versions of my small-body would be lonely until I could mimic creatures well enough that they would befriend me.

When Link haunted me, he learned me, and I learned him. His ghost dwelled within my forest-body, and though his memories weren't comprehensible to me in the way they were to him, they were enough that I could become a facsimile. Often I did not know where he was, here or there, suspended from being altogether. I saw through him more easily than I could when he was alive. He was my first and only ghost. He had no form. He was unraveled memory, a history and a heart broken open, left new and naked. He flooded my body, spread himself between my roots. I could not hide the lake when he was here.

I could not be Link, but I could echo him. My body took on his appearance. I shook my head until his hair drifted in front of my eyes, fox-orange. I pulled a hood over it as he had. His height, his lean frame, long fingers—they became mine. When you saw me, your senses read Link in me.

I had never meant to take away something you would grieve. Maybe now I could give it back, or some version of it. If you couldn't tell the difference, was there any difference?

If I could make you happy, I might not deserve to be alone.

When the woods finished, Noemi asked for space.

"I want to think for a minute," she said. "Will you let me leave the lighthouse if I stay in the forest?"

"You could not leave the forest if you wanted to," he said. "So it doesn't matter."

Her body tightened. Of course he *could* let her leave the forest too, though he spoke now like that was beyond his will.

"Are you my fault?" she asked. Would there ever have been a lake for him to drown Link in had she not gone into the woods?

He tilted his head, then said, careful but assured: "No. You didn't make me, and you didn't make my decisions."

She folded her arms, tucked them in against her ribs. If she had her phone, maybe Unknown would be texting, agreeing, but she must have left it in the boat.

"I tried to listen to you," he reasoned. "To watch the scenes you staged to re-create your dreams, to build those things and give you versions of the landscape inside you that you could touch." He flattened his palm against the wood of the fireplace mantle. "But everything is wrong; everything makes you want less to stay." He moved toward her, imploring. "How do human beings hold on to anything?"

A version of herself could ask this question. Maybe she should hate and fear this person emulating Link. She did fear him, a little. But the more he spoke, the more like a child he seemed. Entitled, perhaps, but also naive.

"Do you want to go in the tower?" he asked, when she had

no answer. "I can take this body to the underground chamber and wait there while you're alone. I won't leave it. The body. Or the chamber. I'll stay in my small-body."

"Sure," she said, in a voice that came out louder than expected. "Is there a way to get into the tower?"

"There can be. The truth is that I never put a door there. There was never any reason to go into it."

He touched the wall, and a section of paneled wood swung open as though a door had always been there.

"I made the lighthouse because you said you saw one in a dream. To Link."

"How do you know what a lighthouse looks like?" she asked. "Mine was a pile of rocks."

"I used to be everywhere. I don't remember much from then."

"You're worse than Link," she said. If that seemed harsh, she hadn't meant it to be. Link had always been strange and thoughtful, if somewhat impenetrable. It made sense that if the woods could relate to anyone, it would be him.

"I'll show you," he said.

The woods led her up the steps. If he worried at all she might run away while his back was to her, he didn't show it. He kept his eyes forward, content with her steps on the winding stone stairs behind him. She couldn't have run anyway. He was everywhere.

They reached the lantern room. Based on its appearance, the woods hadn't seen many lighthouses up close. The roof was clear as crystal, ice, glass. It was draped in morning glories—perhaps he hoped she would think of all the flowers he had given her when she was small. At the center of the gallery was a pool of clear water, and within that a bed, white and round as a split egg, atop a raised platform.

"There's no light," she said, not disappointed, but his face fell as though she'd told him he'd failed.

She stepped across the small moat with one leg, though she left the other firm on the catwalk. Straddling the tiny pool, Noemi gave the surface of the bed a little push, and it flexed under her touch.

"Do you think you could be happy living here?" he asked.

"No," she said. Firm. She didn't even have to think about it. "I already have a place to live. I couldn't be happy never seeing my family again."

She didn't explain anymore. Her only method of escape lay in asserting her wishes. He could build walls around her, but he couldn't make her *want* to stay.

"What will convince you to stay?"

"Nothing," she said. She couldn't phrase it any more clearly. "Nothing will."

"You have no choice but to stay." He placed his hand on the railing. He was the tower in which she stood. His trees surrounded her. The ocean that lay below was all him. "What will make it easier?"

"Nothing. I have no time for things I don't want to do." If he didn't know at least this much about her, he hadn't been paying attention.

He watched her chest. Not in the way that Jonas sometimes did—he instead watched her like she was a cross section of a girl. Her shirt was covered with a bright, crystalline pattern of pink and green. It ended just below her ribs, so it was easy to see her chest moving in and out, lungs pumping hard somewhere beneath that thin wall of muscle. She panted like a rabbit pinned beneath paws, and it seemed to dawn on "Link" that he should be taking air in as well, as though he'd forgotten to breathe this whole time. He exhaled, over and over so he would look alive in the way that she was alive, though everything about the way he did it suggested he found living to be a dreary repetition of irksome tasks.

"I can look like any one of your friends if you want to see them," he said. "Gaetan might be easier. Or Lyle. I've seen more of them. But I could try Jonas and Amberlyn too."

"No, thank you. You can barely plagiarize Link. No offense."

He drew his body inward, collapsed into himself like a sea anemone. Wood split, slate shattered, and she caught glimpses of the other versions of him—equine, aquatic, leaking, algae-mushroom-covered, ropey-tilted-horned-hoofed things he must have practiced. She stepped away, both feet planted at the center of the pool, and when the bed bumped her legs, she let herself fold back until she was sitting on it. But she didn't flee or cry. When he was done, he was much smaller. He looked in the water to check his new face for accuracy, but she recognized the top of his moon-pale hair before he even lifted his head.

"Don't be Lyle," Noemi said. "Please. At least with Link he's not around anymore to care that you're wearing his face."

This time, she looked away while he changed back. "This boy who feels most like me," Link's voice said.

When he was finished, when he was again Link, she asked, "Why would you want to live with someone who always wanted to leave you? You can't be friends with someone if you force them to stay. Not really."

"If I keep letting you come and go," he confessed, "you might decide one day to leave and never come back. I can't be sure if I let you go that I'll see you again."

"You can't ever be sure of what someone else will do," she said.

"Right."

"No, I'm not agreeing with you. I'm saying you have to trust people to make their own decisions about how to spend their lives, and if they choose to spend time on you, then it means something. If you take away their power to choose and force them to be with you, then their time with you means nothing."

She placed her palm against her forehead and forced a little laugh. She had given him advice even she found hard to follow. He was so afraid she would leave that he tried to force her to stay. When she had pushed Jonas away, it had been so that he couldn't leave on his own.

"Anyhow, when you get your way, it won't feel very satisfying." She shrugged. "Not if you go about it like this."

"I see." He towered over her with all of Link's height. "But I don't see why I would have to force you to stay. I could make anything you want, be anyone you want."

"But it wouldn't be real," she said. "Just like you aren't really Link. Just like you never were. It would be like a dream."

"But you *like* dreams!" His voice came out higher, more emotive than it had before. Link's voice. Whoever's it was.

"Not to live in."

"What's the difference?"

A tuft of prairie smoke poked through the weave in the bedclothes, and Noemi twisted it further, drew the long, pink puff until it spread like an eyelid between her fingers.

"I don't know how to explain it to someone who doesn't dream, and I'm not a neurologist. Maybe more than watching all the people and things that aren't you, dreaming is looking inward." She gestured past the catwalk and toward the lake below. "The whole world is you, and you made everything in it; everyone in it is a part of you."

"Then I am always already dreaming."

He gripped his hair with both hands, holding it close to the scalp. With his head in his hands he began to mumble, and with each word, he inhabited the body in front of her more and more. He stopped measuring his words, and a flood of them broke forth.

"Everything I say and do is wrong wrong wrong. I am the grass and the trees and the foxglove and the morning glory and the mouse bones hanging from branches, and at my center is a lake, dark and cold, which I thought drowned everyone else, but maybe it has been drowning me."

His eyes were clear and reflective, but all they reflected was water—his soul or his heart or his self-preservation, whatever the lake meant to him—stretching on forever.

"The more awake and alive I become, the less likely I am to ever be satisfied. I can change the night to day, but behind the sky will always be a vacuum that reaches through infinity and cannot be filled—not with a thousand of this frightened, angry, dreaming girl, no matter how many times I swallow her, but I could try."

He stepped toward her, then away again, just as quickly.

"You would live here until I did not know where your dreams ended, where you ended, and I began, like rain falling into water poured into water into water into water. There would be no separate pieces, just one thing turning forever into itself, and I wouldn't be alone. Not completely. But the truth is—"

He sighed, and his entire body shook as though now that they'd tasted it, his lungs couldn't bear to part with the air.

"The truth is—not like this."

He blinked, surprised she was still there, startled by whatever expression on her face told him he had spoken these things aloud.

She stepped over the pool and touched him, wrapped her arms around his torso. His body slackened, as though he could have dissolved into water right there.

"Let's go downstairs," he said, and she released him. "I won't stop once we reach the house. I'll lift the door in the floor and crawl onto the ladder that leads to my deepest place, down down down. Then I will wade through the water, to the other side of the tunnel where I cannot see you leave."

She nodded.

"In my chamber there is a bed I have made for myself. I do not know what will happen to my small-body when I go to sleep, if I will be a dreaming forest or a boy buried under a lake. I don't know if it matters who I am when I dream."

"I think it matters," she said.

Together they stepped into the stairwell.

ROWING

I dreamt I was in a tower that came tumbling down around me. The tower was at the center of a lake, and I believed when the tower had fallen the lake would disappear and I could walk away from this place and toward my home. That did not happen. Instead I sat in the ruins of a small house, and I looked out on a boat that drifted very far from shore. I thought about swimming out to it. I could then row it to the other side and leave the forest that held me. But I couldn't see the other shore. Not any longer. I wondered if maybe it was just as well for everyone who knew me if I lived the rest of my life in a broken-down lighthouse on an island no one would find.

Then someone said my name. Because he was a part of my dream, maybe he knew what I was thinking and disapproved. I knew it was Link right away, or someone like him. His waist was at eye-level, and he wore a novelty belt buckle with diminishing text like an eye exam chart, spelling IF YOU CAN READ THIS YOU ARE INVADING MY PERSONAL SPACE.

"Sorry," I said, pointing to the belt, and I stood from my little seat in the rubble. "Though I was here first."

It took him a moment to catch what I was referencing, and then he laughed. "That's meant for anyone but you." He looked away, thought over what he said, stammered out an apology.

That's how I knew he was real.

I followed Link to the rowboat. I didn't bother to ask him how he'd gotten it to the island since this was a dream, and if it wasn't a dream, he was a ghost. In either case the boat was the least strange thing. He helped me in, and while I didn't need help, I wasn't sure I had ever touched his hand, and since he was dead I thought, "Why not?" His skin was cool and smooth, and though he was thin, the loose envelope made by his fist was big.

Link rowed the whole way, and he did not stop rowing when we ran out of water. He rowed across the grass, and it pooled in green brushstrokes around the oars. I could reach out and touch the trees as we passed them. I stroked their bark and told them, "Have a good sleep."

"The forest is sorry it killed you," I said.

"I know."

I like to think he forgave it. He didn't sound angry.

"I miss you," I said.

He said, "Don't worry." He said we were still friends.

34

UNKNOWN

Noemi slept in a rowboat marooned in a field of lupines. I'd never seen her look quite so relaxed, which was funny because she'd just left behind an ordeal that would unmoor most people. It seemed right, though, that she'd be more in her element negotiating with a sentient forest than with people on any other day, and I guess that's why I always liked her.

The police had wound yellow tape through the trees to demarcate the forest as an area no one should enter while Noemi was missing. They'd done the same when I'd died. I hoped they wouldn't bulldoze it, and that too was kind of funny because the forest had murdered me after all, and I probably shouldn't have wanted my murderer to live a long and peaceful existence, but I did. Nearby someone had pitched a domed, polyester camping tent, yellow and blue, and parked his truck nearby, paying no mind to the flowers he'd crushed under his wheels. Some might think this was only because ambulances and police cars had already left their tracks through the field, but the truth was he probably would have parked there anyway.

He slept curled in a sleeping bag on the tent floor. I set his cell phone vibrating to wake him, and he seemed confused when he checked the screen to find no call, text, or alarm. He probably thought he'd imagined the sound. He sat up anyway and reached for a flask, swished whatever was inside around his mouth, then unzipped the tent with his cheeks puffed to spit the fluid onto the grass.

He saw the boat. I was lucky not to have to do anything more to draw his attention that way. Though he approached lazily, when he saw Noemi inside he fell to his knees and gathered her into his arms, calling out her name, begging her to be alive. It's weird: I wished I could have made this happen sooner, though in any other circumstances that exact scene would have been impossible to orchestrate. She opened her eyes, two green-brown forests, then lifted her hand to block the sun that peeked at her from over his shoulder.

"Gaetan?" she said. "Relax."

"Everyone thought you'd turn up like Link."

"Dead?" She took in her surroundings, but she didn't seem to mind that as she did, he rubbed a strand of her hair between two fingers, testing to make sure he wasn't dreaming. "Where are we? Am I outside the forest?"

"Yeah. It's been a couple days. Where were you?"

She patted down her body as though "days" might have faded some part of it, but she was of course all present and alive.

"The lighthouse. But it's gone now. The lake too. Everything's gone. Was there anyone here with me when you found me?"

"No. Who else would be with you?"

"Just wondering how I got here. Are Lyle and Jonas okay? What about Amberlyn?"

"Yeah. They're all fine." He rubbed the back of his neck. "I beat the ever-loving shit out of Jonas, but he's okay. It was in front of a cop, brilliantly. Spent the night in a cell, which was probably a long time coming, if we're honest. Lake was really insistent about not pressing charges, though."

"You're lucky. He's really okay?"

"Couple black eyes and a broken nose, but yeah."

"*Another* broken nose?" She shook her head. "At least you seem fine."

Gate sat back on his haunches, picked at the bottom of his shoe, embarrassed. "Yeah, he didn't put up much of a fight. Honestly, I was hoping he would. I took everything out on him. I know it was fucked up. I know I'm fucked up."

"I'm glad you're both okay."

He looked as surprised as I felt. I had never in my life seen Gate's face so red before, but here it was, totally disarmed.

"I should give you a ride home," he said. "They've been searching the woods. Everyone's losing their shit. Your mom's gonna have a heart attack."

It was only a block or so, but she didn't argue. I would have rowed her right to the door if Gate hadn't been there. It seemed better to wake, disoriented, to one person looming over you than half a dozen.

It was barely past 6:00 a.m., and though the sky was lightening, no one was awake to see them pull into the driveway. Jonas Lake had no plans of going to school, and he was currently asleep in Noemi's bed, having only lost consciousness an hour before. He clutched a book he'd found in her nightstand, tucked now with his arm under her pillow. Once, he'd seen her reading it and nestled against her on the bed. She told him, "This is a private book. It makes me want to cry." She told him, *leave me alone*, though not in so many words. It didn't matter which book it was. He could read it cover to cover without knowing what made it so soul-crushing for her. Just like I could watch everything that could ever unfold around a person, know everything there was to know about them from the outside, and still understand nothing of the person within. Maybe the best we could do was *attempt* to understand one another, to make ourselves understood. Maybe Jonas was thinking what I'm always thinking: *It's too late now. I'm on the other side of the last of all my chances.*

Cesca and Matt both slept on the living room sofa, her curled like a snail at one end, him wedged against the crevice where the cushions met the tufted back. Amberlyn had wanted to spend the night at Lyle's and leave for school together; our parents insisted she stay at home, but both girls were awake texting. One's head would begin to nod when her phone chimed with a message from the other: about the forest, the lake, Noemi, me. My father's alarm would soon go off, and he would stagger into the bathroom and avoid his face in the mirror, shuffle to the bedroom and stare at his ties. My mother was already at work, her ponytail looped up into a chalky, billowing hairnet so you couldn't tell by looking that her hair was redder than mine had ever been. My family had not yet acclimated to the gravity of *forever*, but they hadn't been crushed by it either.

"Why were you sleeping in a tent in the lupines?" Noemi asked as Gaetan shifted the Jeep into park.

"The weather is nice," he said. "I don't know. I wanted to be there if you found your way out."

"Are you okay, Gaetan?"

He smiled his usual smile and answered, dismissive, "I'm fine. Where did that come from?"

"I don't think you're a bad person."

"Well, gee, thanks."

"I just mean that I worry about you."

He turned the car off and fidgeted against his seatbelt. "Do you worry about everyone who isn't an awful person?"

"Most people are awful." She shrugged. "We're all probably awful. You, at least, I like anyhow." Noemi picked at her cuticles.

Gaetan's pulse fluttered in his neck, and he swallowed loudly.

"I'm sorry I've never been very nice to you," she said.

"I'm not very nice."

"Do you have any place to stay besides your tent?"

"Yeah." He ran his fingers along the steering wheel. I watched him a lot. He hadn't stayed at his own house since I'd died, but he did stay at mine sometimes.

"Well, you can always stay at the Lamplight if you want to."

"Not after giving Jonas a concussion, I can't. It's difficult to be there all the time anyway. You guys are together, and I know that's not his fault, but I don't know any way to be other than angry. He doesn't deserve me skulking around. Neither of you do."

"Poor Jonas. He's a good person. You need to start treating him like a human being."

"To be fair, I don't treat him that differently from most other people."

Noemi scowled.

"Point taken, though."

"You could stay in the bedroom in the stables. There's no bathroom out there, but you could use one of the ones in the house."

"I'll think about it," he said. "Thank you."

"So we're friends," she asked, "you and I?"

"Yeah." He nodded. "I'd like to be. Twenty minutes ago I'd have settled for you alive and hating me, but friends would be great." He straightened his arms, clutching the wheel, and his elbows gave an audible pop. "You're a very important person to me. It's like you carved this chunk out of me that no one else can fit. I know I'm not easy. I get mad sometimes when I think about how much more time we could have spent together before I graduated if I'd been honest about, you know, the fact that I actually like being around you. I'll have fewer memories with you than I should."

"We share a lot of memories."

"I'm happy for that. But I know you'll probably go away to college after your senior year, and I just want you to know that if you ever need me for anything—not just today but ten or fifteen or however many years from now—I promise that you can reach out to me even if we haven't spoken. You'll always be important to me, Noemi. You were there for everything, and I felt like you kind of had an eye out for me, even if I didn't always deserve it."

I envied Gaetan. Not because he shared this moment with Noemi, or because he'd always managed to be closer to her than I was. He felt things very acutely and expressed those feelings in a naked and decisive way. They were similar in that sense. When I was alive, I appreciated this about Noemi, but for some reason it annoyed me in Gate. Dead, as an observer, it was much easier to love this bareness of his.

"I'm a junior," Noemi said. "And you're staying local for now, right? So there's no need to talk like I'm heading off to Mars tomorrow afternoon. Let's not put an expiration date on our friendship before we even give it any kind of chance."

"Right." He forced a chuckle.

Looking back, it now seemed so unlikely that I hadn't realized earlier. Even though Gate was supposed to be my best friend, my brother, I never really saw him as the kind of person who could love. Obsessing over someone? Possible. But it was hard to imagine him valuing someone else's happiness. Unfair, of course—I saw that now. He valued hers. He'd valued mine. He was ready to watch Noemi get out of his car and choose a path that did not include him, if that was what she wanted. And maybe he wouldn't have had to prepare for this if he hadn't waited my entire life to tell anyone how he felt. The peonies he had given her for Valentine's Day, those had been as much for me as for her. I remember so many nights sitting at the desk in my room, working on my comics, while he lay in his sleeping bag messaging Noemi. He'd check in with me like he was my research assistant. *So, Noemi likes reading about Greek mythology. Do you know the myth of Eros and Psyche? If she could be any animal, she'd be a skunk. That makes sense. Apparently, when she was a kid, she used to play make-believe at being a mermaid, even if she wasn't swimming—just running around in her backyard and pretending she was underwater.*

Every once in a while I'd give him my input, so it was sort of like I was participating in those conversations. It's not that I didn't care; I just didn't have his attention span for prolonged conversation. I wasn't really thinking about how every time she shared something with Gate, a redheaded avatar nodded back. This lie of omission—about who was really talking to her—was necessary in order for him to be honest about absolutely everything else he said in those chats. When he told her about how *Gaetan's stepdad broke a bottle off in his flesh when we were little* or *Gaetan once puked all over the Millers' kitchen after eating too much because his parents wouldn't give him lunch money for a week,* he talked about himself in the third person, and I didn't realize until after I died that he *had* to do this. He wanted to think of those things as having happened to someone else, that he was just a kid messaging his soul mate and had to worry only about the excited fluttering in his chest each time her words formed on the screen. She told him, *You're a good friend,* and she meant, *Link is a good friend,* and he couldn't agree or "Link" would look like a self-congratulating asshole.

If I could go back, would I ask him to hand over the phone so I could speak for myself? Or tell him, *You should let her know that she's talking to you*? Or would I have done things exactly as I had the first time around? What did I think was the purpose of those conversations? That's just what people who weren't me used the internet for: learning absolutely every mundane detail about a person they claimed to dislike. Maybe the gene for perceptiveness skipped me and went straight to Amberlyn. Even if it hadn't, I could live a thousand lives and never be brave enough to tell him he was worthy of love. It's too huge a thing to say.

I worry, *Link was not a good friend.* If we had all been able earlier to tell each other the truths of how we felt and what we wanted or didn't, or to recognize the truths that were in front of us, things might have been different. Or maybe that just wasn't who we were. If I could breathe underwater, things might have been different. But I couldn't, and they weren't.

Noemi unbuckled her seatbelt, then tugged on the door handle so it unlatched, but she didn't let it fall open. "Thank you for driving me back," she said. They sat for a second, unsure of where to look. Then she leaned toward him, kissed the side of his face. It was just a peck, but he moved his head in surprise, and she caught him on the corner of the mouth. Formless and massless I still wouldn't fit in the space between their mouths. I could row a boat through dream-space and turn my thoughts into text, but I couldn't penetrate the link between Noemi and Gaetan. Ironic.

Maybe in another world I could. But I'd rather imagine a reality where I didn't feel the need to. I never died. I had a crush on a girl who told me, in the woods near her house, that she didn't like me back, not that way. And it was fine. I never went back hoping I might run into her, because I didn't need to. I went to my senior prom, and I graduated, and I went to school on scholarship and student loans that would take me ten years to pay back, but it was okay because I loved college. Maybe I got a degree in graphic design. Maybe I double majored in physics and illustration. Maybe after college I made a living writing comics, or maybe I needed to have a day job. I got married to someone who never once wondered what I meant to her. Noemi realized she loved Gaetan all along, and they got a cabin by the ocean where they lived with a bunch of pets, and my family visited in the summer, and my kids called them Aunt and Uncle. Amberlyn had someone who made her happy and loved her, and maybe their someday-children were tall with red hair, or maybe they were tiny with specific tastes in music, but either way they were sure to have keen feelings and huge hearts. When we visited my parents for Christmas, Amber and I went out on the roof together and hung lights for them.

Then we went inside and remembered before our partners all the Midwinters past. And we all lived happily ever after until we were very old, and when we died we had no regrets.

Noemi got out of the car. Gaetan waited, disbelieving, until she was at her door, the place she had kissed rose-colored and incandescent as though he held a candle in his mouth, glowing beneath his skin. Then he drove off, his grin genuine and unrecognizable. After all, he was in love, and she, despite knowing exactly who he was, despite being the person best equipped to dismantle him in the sharpest and most intricate of ways, wanted him safe. He must have felt invincible.

Cesca was naturally relieved to hear the door they had left unlocked open and to see her daughter enter. Matt hugged her, and Noemi looked surprised, but then she smiled. Audrey made strawberry-banana pancakes, Diana washed dishes, Jonas almost fainted from relief and exhaustion but caught himself on the wall, and no one said anything when he and Noemi hugged a little long in front of everyone. Noemi texted Amberlyn and Lyle—Amberlyn who cried quietly into her pillow when her phone chimed, who held it tight against her because there was no one there to embrace, and I was so grateful to Lyle, who would be able to hold my sister in her arms, keep her from evaporating when I couldn't.

Then Noemi texted me, but I didn't text back, because I was pretty sure she was going to be okay.

ACKNOWLEDGMENTS

There are many people with whom I've been fortunate to work on this book—as well as many who, before the first word of what would eventually become *We Were Restless Things* was even written, helped me along my path as a writer.

Thank you to my smart and supportive agent, Erica Bauman, for championing this book, and for being one of its earliest readers when it was still raw. Amberlyn in particular owes the very existence of her chapters to your feedback.

Eliza Swift, thank you for understanding this story, its characters, my voice, and the strange town of Shivery. Your insights helped shape the book into what it is now, and I'm so grateful to have you as my editor.

To the rest of the skilled people at Sourcebooks Fire—thank you for your dedication in bringing this novel into the world. This includes Cassie Gutman, Nicole Hower, Kelly Lawler, Sarah

Kasman, Beth Oleniczak, Heather Moore, and publisher and founder Dominique Raccah. Thank you as well to Jillian Rahn, for breathing life into Noemi's journal with the internal design, and to Sasha Vinogradova for the haunting and beautiful cover.

Thank you McKelle George, for your mentorship, and Brenda Drake, for working tirelessly to create opportunities for writers. I learned quite a lot about querying and publishing from my 2016 Pitch Wars cohort, and I am fortunate to have been a part of your community.

I thank the faculty at the Master of Fine Arts in Creative Writing program of SIUC for your guidance. If not for this program, my motivation to write may have shriveled up and died in the shadow of my procrastination and self-doubt. During my time as a graduate student, I really learned what I wanted to write.

On the subject of self-doubt, I must thank my partner, Sequoia, who believes in me even when I'm feeling hopeless, which happens a lot. You always listen when I brainstorm out loud, and you ask the logical questions of my bizarre stories. I know it's hard to critique the work of the person you live with, especially when that person is as sensitive and anxious as I am. Thank you for doing it anyway.

Sequoia suggests I thank our cat. So, thank you, Kalahira, for snuggling me as I write. You've almost never accidentally deleted any text.

Finally, I thank my family. To my mother, especially—you're the biggest reader I know, yet you always make time for my stories. Nothing I've ever written would exist without you.

ABOUT THE AUTHOR

Cole Nagamatsu has an MFA in fiction from the creative writing program at SIUC. Her short fiction has been published in *cream city review*, *West Branch*, *Tin House*, and elsewhere. Though she is not from the Midwest, she now lives in Minnesota with her partner and their cat.

FIREreads

— ✪ #getbooklit —

Your hub for the hottest young adult books!

Visit us online and sign up for our
newsletter at FIREreads.com

@sourcebooksfire

sourcebooksfire

firereads.tumblr.com